Nameless Queen

NAMELESS QUEEN

REBECCA McLAUGHLIN

CROWN ♛ NEW YORK

Text copyright © 2020 by Rebecca McLaughlin
Jacket art copyright © 2020 by Sammy Yuen

All rights reserved. Published in the United States by Crown Books for Young Readers, an imprint of Random House Children's Books, a division of Penguin Random House LLC, New York.

Crown and the colophon are registered trademarks of Penguin Random House LLC.

Visit us on the Web! GetUnderlined.com

Educators and librarians, for a variety of teaching tools, visit us at RHTeachersLibrarians.com

Library of Congress Cataloging-in-Publication Data
Names: McLaughlin, Rebecca, author.
Title: Nameless queen / Rebecca McLaughlin.
Description: First edition. | New York: Crown, [2020] | Summary: In the city of Seriden, the thief called Coin is Nameless—she has no family, no legal rights, and no standing in society—but she inherits the throne and the power and danger that come with it.
Identifiers: LCCN 2019004432 (print) | LCCN 2019009397 (ebook) |
ISBN 978-1-5247-0027-0 (ebook) | ISBN 978-1-5247-0026-3 (hardcover) |
ISBN 978-1-5247-0078-2 (glb)
Subjects: | CYAC: Kings, queens, rulers, etc.—Fiction. | Robbers and outlaws—Fiction. | Names, Personal—Fiction.
Classification: LCC PZ7.1.M4624 (ebook) | LCC PZ7.1.M4624 Nam 2020 (print) |
DDC [Fic]—dc23

Printed in the United States of America
10 9 8 7 6 5 4 3 2 1
First Edition

For the feeling of "I hope I can"
In defiance of "I don't belong"
And in honor of who I've become

NAMELESS
QUEEN

CHAPTER 1

I wake up the same way I fell asleep: knife in hand, boots for a pillow, and Nameless.

When I push away the heavy wood pallet, a shiver runs up my arms. My shoulder aches from sleeping on my side, but the best way to stay warm is a small space and a good coat. I pull on my boots, wiggling the numbness from my toes.

Curling my fingers into my threadbare sleeves, I leave behind the pungent puddles and uneven alley brickwork for the smoother cobblestone street bearing the morning foot traffic. Passersby shrug off yawns as vendors shout their prices. Two iron rings for a jar of dried apples, three copper coins for a cut of a morning pastry.

The city of Seriden is waking up.

Hat waits for me at the corner. Usually she's leaning against the dark bricks and staring out at the morning crowds, her shoulders even and strong, a small smile on her lips that she doesn't notice. She'll trade our stolen coins for a breakfast of stale cornbread or day-old fish and oats while I pick out bump-grab marks. The easiest are pudgy-faced Legals with leather purses flaunted at their waists or flashy gems dangling past their stiff, starched collars.

Today she's fidgeting: shoulders pinched, fingers twitching. Never a good sign.

"Bad news?" I ask. Fresh air, sharp with ocean salt, chases away the last of my morning lethargy.

She grabs my hand and pulls me back down the alley. So much for fresh air.

"Bad, then." I wrinkle my nose, but she doesn't seem to notice the smell. She's surprisingly resilient for being twelve or thirteen years old. "Did the bread caravan break down again? Last time that happened, the markets were a mess. Legals can't survive without their sugar rolls, can they?" I laugh, but Hat shakes her head.

Her bright red hair frizzes in an energetic halo around her face, and a rare frown curls her features. Somehow Hat easily manages what I can only strive for: optimism. On days when we see a little kid starving in an alley, my stomach twists. Hat always hands over her breakfast with a smile. If Hat's frowning, it's serious.

"Two more Nameless kids went missing last night," she says. "It was Judge and Spinner. And you know Anchor, that kid who disappeared two weeks ago? He turned up this morning. Dead. It was . . . I don't like it, Coin."

I give her a soft pat on the arm. "It'll be okay, Hat. You just have to come straight here in the mornings from now on, okay? And keep your knife handy."

Hat scans the edges of the rooftops, distracted.

"What else is wrong?" I ask.

"I didn't see Devil this morning," she says.

Devil is a Nameless girl a bit older than me who always has the latest gossip. Want to know which guards are good for bribing? Looking to hire a thief? Ask Devil. She's posted in the same place every morning, and she'll trade news for food or trinkets. That's how she makes her living as a Nameless. Instead of thriving on thefts and cons, she thrives with information. That and a smuggler's business.

Hat visits Devil early in the mornings, staying in her good favor by sharing any gossip. If Devil's not around, she knows something we don't, something bad. Or . . .

I ask the question I don't want to ask. "Do you think she's gone, like the others?"

Hat's frown deepens. "She's older than most of the ones who've gone missing."

"Devil's strong, though. Smart. A fighter. She once robbed a Legal's house of all its doors and windows for cheating her out of a deal." I try to keep the mood light. "She's probably off sweet-talking the new Royal Guard recruits."

"I doubt that." She struggles to keep the frown.

I rub my sore shoulder. "I can see that from the excellent unibrow you're working on."

She breaks into a grin. "Is this better?" She furrows her brow even more, and a few strands of hair come loose from behind her ear.

"Almost perfect." I place a finger on each eyebrow and scrunch inward, completing the bridge.

She laughs, her forehead smoothing back to normal. Her small shoulders descend from a pinch into their sloping, natural curves.

"Okay," Hat says. "We'll grab breakfast and look for Devil."

✦

As we near West Market, the bustle of morning vendors grows louder. The crowds are starting to gather on the streets. The air is layered with cardamom and cinnamon, vanilla and rose perfumes, and the subtler scents of ash, dirt, and salt. As Legals arrange their wares and unpack shipping crates, Hat and I linger between a stall selling early spring harvests from local farms and a shop selling imported and strenuously taxed goods from inland cities.

Hat says, "It's pretty scary, right? These Nameless going missing, I mean."

She doesn't sound scared. She sounds as if she wants something. I groan, already knowing what it is.

"It's not safe for you or me to be walking out here alone all the time," she says. "You should let me live with you." I trudge a bit faster as if to escape the conversation, but she keeps pace nimbly.

"We've talked about this," I say. "I can't look after you all the time. It's better that you stay with Marcher. I move around a lot. I get into a lot of trouble. I *create* a lot of trouble."

"Do you really believe that?" Hat says. "You think I'm better off in Marcher's crew? You should know that's not true. You

4

used to be one of us. You left when you were my age. The way Marcher tells it, you were the best grifter he ever trained. And yeah, I'll miss the kids and having my own spot to sleep—not to mention I have all my keepsakes—but I want to be on my own with you. I'm sick of going back there. Giving him everything I steal. I'm sick of *him*. Isn't that why you left?"

I roll my shoulders uncomfortably. I hate this conversation every time we have it.

"Marcher may be a spetzing bastard," I say, "but he knows how to keep you safe. Most of you, anyway."

Hat frowns at me, confused.

"You're getting good," I say, redirecting the conversation. "Really good. Won't be long before you can strike out on your own. Just like I did." I try for a reassuring smile, and she offers a half-hearted shrug in response, but I know better than she does how hard it can be to leave Marcher's crew and how difficult it can be to go it alone. I can't spend every night and morning with the weight of her life in my hands.

I spy a heavily guarded shipment of jewelry from the mountainous city of Tuvo, but most Legals can't afford pricey gems like that, not as they're losing their jobs every time the paper mill cuts its workforce. There's been a rising tension in the air, and I've been getting more dirty looks than usual—it's not my fault that being a thief and grifter is steady work. They're jealous, I'm sure.

Most of the foot traffic is Legals, who linger between stalls, with a few Royals mixed in, identifiable by their bright, colorful coats of blue, gold, and violet. Legals wear softer, pale colors, mostly grays and pastels. The Legals are the loudest, shouting discounts and goods for sale, while the Royals strut calmly among the stalls with the silence of those who don't need to haggle over prices. The Nameless are on the outskirts, dressed in castaway clothing scavenged from the trash.

That's the easiest way to find the Nameless. We live on the streets, and we look it.

"Got your eye on a mark yet?" Hat asks, casting her light brown eyes around the stalls.

On a typical day, it's my job to pick the mark and decide whether we'll con them or pickpocket them. It's all about finding people with enough coins and rings to make the grab worthwhile, but not someone so rich that they'll have us executed immediately if we're caught.

I send her after a Legal who is browsing a jewelry stall. The man is debating between a brooch with a quartz frame and one with gold, so I know he—unlike most Legals—has decent money in his pockets. As Hat moves through the crowd, a dark cap hiding her bright hair, my instincts prickle. I scan farther down the street, and that's when I see him. Marcher. Black hair hangs past his chin, gray stubble shadows his face, and pale skin crinkles around his emotionless green eyes.

He's the worst of the street runners, with a crew of Nameless orphans trained to pickpocket Legals and pull small-time cons. He knows *how* to keep them safe, but when a big-enough score comes along, he doesn't care if they get caught or killed. Like Hat said, I used to be one of them. And, technically, Hat still works for him. I tell her to only volunteer for small jobs.

Nothing dangerous. But if he sees her pulling a grab, he'll come after her for the rings and coins she gets. If he knows she's doing it with me, he might go so far as to get her caught.

In a fluid motion, I rip off my dark maroon coat and start a quick pace out into the crowd. I snatch a beige coat from a Legal stall. As I move, I bump into a distracted Nameless man, causing him to topple a large bag of red beans.

"Nameless cur!" the vendor shouts at him, bending to recover the beans. "Look what you've done, alley trash! Gather them up before I call a Royal guard."

No one notices as I pull on the Legal coat.

I move swiftly as I fasten the top few buttons—enough to cover my dirty green shirt. I roll my shoulders and straighten my posture, pulling my long dark brown hair behind my shoulders to hide the uneven, frayed edges.

Snatching a few segments of cinnamon bark from a spice stall, I take a few running steps to catch up. I cut in front of Hat, just in time to bump into a well-dressed Royal.

I plaster an apology on my face and speak in a fake sweet voice. "Oh, pardon me!"

The Royal stumbles and meets my eye as I hold his elbow to keep him from falling. He's mostly bald, and the wispy hair clinging to the sides of his head is pulled back with an elastic band.

I force an even exhale. Wearing Legal clothes is enough to get me thrown in prison, or if the patrolling Royal guards are in a bad mood, I'll get a quick trip to the gallows. Times like this, I'm glad for the hungry hollow of my cheeks and the strong tilt of my jaw. No food or parents to speak of, but they give me the appearance he would expect of a Legal girl.

"Quite all right," the Royal says.

I brush invisible dirt off his bright violet waistcoat. With deft fingers, I probe the lining but don't find his purse. I give him a second glance. This Royal smiled. Blushed, even. His gaze lingered. Time for a different tactic.

I steer him to a spices stall, where the vendor is off arguing with a neighboring seller.

"Please," I say, gesturing at the array of fragrant flower petals, sliced herb roots, and pouches filled with ground spices. "Take anything you want. A token of my apology." I angle myself around the corner so he can't see the patched holes in my pants.

The Royal skims over the spices as I sort the cinnamon. When his gaze lands on me, a bit too far south from my face, I grab a spice pouch and offer it to him.

"Here." I fix a guilty expression on my face. "A collection of our most expensive spices."

He gives a coy smile, his head burning red. "I couldn't possibly." He reaches into his coat and fetches a soft blue velvet purse from a deep pocket. No wonder I couldn't reach it. He pours out a few gold rings and silver coins, and before he can count them, I lean forward.

"I heard there's bad news floating around today," I say. His blush and curiosity feel like a real heat coming off him, and I take a moment to focus.

His fingers hover above the coins. His coy smile turns

mischievous, as if he's letting me in on a secret. "I suppose Legal whispers don't travel as quickly as those of the Royals. My dear, our beloved King Fallow passed away last night. Dreadfully sad, I know."

He is absolutely not sad. His face is alight with the drama of it all. He grins and adds, "The next heir could be anyone, whoever has the crown tattoo!" He winks at me, as if I could be that lucky Legal, and he leans close to savor my surprise.

Don't scowl. Don't scowl. I place the spice pouch over the gold coins, slipping all three from his hand. Despite the sweat glistening at his temples, his hand is cold like a shock, and suddenly, instead of staring out at the market and the bustling Legals, I'm staring down a long corridor with a narrow band of red carpet stretching out beneath my feet. I'm standing on my toes, peering into a room as a Royal guard shoos me away. I almost catch a glimpse of the dying king inside, but I bustle off down the corridor in disappointment. I run a dry hand through the white hair on the side of my head as my sharp black shoes pad quietly on the carpet.

I let go of the Royal's hand, and my vision snaps to the market. The sounds of arguing vendors and customers return to my ears, and the Royal before me looks dazed.

"I saw him, you know," the Royal says. "Caught a glimpse of him on his deathbed just last night. Quite tragic, in its own way." The man shakes his head to clear his thoughts.

I regain my composure and realize I'm still holding the gold coins. I palm them and cross my arms in concern, dropping them into my pocket.

I struggle for words, trying—for the sake of the con—to ignore what just happened. "When do you think the heir will step forward?"

He shrugs and idly slides his coin purse into his jacket. He runs a sweaty thumb over the spice pouch. "We'll have to wait and see."

I give a gracious curtsy and thank him again. He rejoins the crowd as I duck out of the stall. Hat still stands where I cut her off, arms raised in a sustained shrug. As I approach her, she pulls the black hat from her head and replaces it with a blue one.

"Why did you cut me off? I thought my approach was solid," Hat grumbles as we move to the edge of the crowd.

I show her the three coins, scratched and worn but still shining. Then I point over her shoulder at Marcher. When she sees him, her face pales and she moves closer to me.

"You know he'll still try to take it," Hat says. Marcher stands on the corner, glaring at us.

"Run along, Hat," I say. "I've got an argument to get to."

She scampers behind me, moving closer to the alley, but she doesn't quite leave. Marcher storms up to me.

"That's *my* grab," Marcher says.

I pinch the gold coins between my fingers, fuming. "No. She was going to pick the pocket of a sprightly Legal, and I decided to pickpocket a Royal. This is mine. You know it is. She couldn't have grabbed anything from a Royal."

"You did when you were her age," Marcher says slyly. "You always had a gift for improvisation."

"That makes you stupid *and* a bastard," I say. Even though I'm taller than him now, he's still looking down on me.

"Even so," he says, and he leans forward and snatches the coins from me. As he strolls away, a brazen tilt in his steps, heat rises in my chest. The heavy presence of the market crowd flattens into the background.

I stomp after him, and I know I shouldn't make a scene.

I kick the back of his knee, sending him down. I *definitely* shouldn't make a scene.

I pretend to reach down to help him up, but I push him hard onto the ground instead. A flare of dark satisfaction burns through my chest, but it freezes when I see the coiling smirk still on his lips. I slam my knuckles against his left eye. So much for subtle.

The market has created a bubble of space around us, with most people passing by and ignoring what they think is a Legal beating on a Nameless, and a few of them idling with mild interest. If it gets too far, they'll start placing bets. If it goes even further, they'll call the Royal guards.

Hat catches up to us, and she pulls me by the hand as if she's leading a child, guiding me down the nearest alley. Marcher knows better than to bring any more attention to us, but he throws a withering glare from his good eye. At least he's not smiling anymore.

"I know, I know," I mutter. "Not good." Hat hands me my dark, ratty coat, which she rescued from the barrel I left it on, and I pull it on over the beige coat. I don't want to ditch something nice just because wearing it could get me killed.

Hat tries and fails to hide an approving grin. "You guys were getting along so well, too."

Marcher and I have a solid history of mutual hatred. I throw his dock stash in the harbor; he raids my winter stocks. He foils my long con with a wealthy Legal; I send a couple of Royal guards to his latest hideout. He sees me as a competitor. He always has, even when I was a child. I see him—as I always have—as a spetzing bastard.

I can handle the Legals and Royals, their condescending snarls and the pitiless angle of their chins. I can suffer their ignorance, their disrespect, and their blatant disgust. It's normal from them. But I won't take it from the Nameless. I can't. Especially not from Marcher.

"So, the Royal shared an interesting rumor," I say, and Hat's frown makes a spectacular recovery. "King Fallow died, and none of the Royals have the tattoo."

"No one's stepped forward? What Legal wouldn't want to be king?" She leans close enough for me to see the uneven, patchy weave of the hat on her head. "Seriden hasn't had an empty throne before. Not in our lifetime, anyway. You know how people get when there's no one to tell them no. They always want something or someone to be angry at." She gestures between the two of us.

She's right. Most Royals and Legals hate us. Not only are we thieves and grifters, but we hate them right back. With gusto. It isn't illegal to kill us, but it also isn't illegal for *us* to commit crimes. Except that if we're caught, it's a toss-up whether we're imprisoned or executed. There is no petitioning of the judiciary for us.

"That's just what we need." A pang of something like fear tightens in my stomach. "But here's the thing. That Royal I talked to. I think he did something to me—I think *he* has the crown tattoo, maybe? Because when he touched my hand, he showed me his memory. I think."

"Do you want to track him down and find out?"

I shake my head. I want to be as far away from Royalty as possible right now.

"We still have time before the morning rush ends," Hat says. "Let's go to East Market."

"East Market," I mumble unhappily. "It always smells like fish." I take a deep sniff of the cinnamon and pepper clinging to the Legal coat.

"Well, fish happens when you make a scene." She laughs and playfully nudges my left shoulder.

Pain shoots from my shoulder to my arm, down to the pads of my fingers, and I cry out, grimacing and curling over.

"Are you all right?" Hat immediately retreats, as if she's accidentally kicked a puppy.

"Yeah." I pull down the two layers of coats and my long-sleeved green shirt. It feels like a wasp sting, but it's too early in the season for that. "Slept wrong last night. Must've bruised my shoulder. I did just sort of get in a fight, too."

Hat laughs. "Better you than me. I'm not old enough to kick him down like that yet. But give it time." She's about to say something else, when her eyes widen. From her face, I think it must be a nasty bruise. I twist to get a good look, but there's no bruise. Instead, a black ink tattoo surrounds my upper arm like jewelry.

We both know what it is, but neither of us can speak. The bustle of the market rises to fill the silence, and I'm suddenly very aware of the throngs of people not too far away.

But it's unmistakable: the sloping angles of the design, the crisp edges, the sharp points.

It's a crown.

Impossible. The king couldn't speak my name, because it doesn't exist. I am not a Legal. I am not a Royal. I am Nameless. Yet the crown on my arm means that King Fallow named me his heir. It is impossible, yet somehow true.

I am Nameless.

I am queen.

CHAPTER 2

I laugh, thinking it's a joke. I pull my thumb over the ink, expecting it to rub off, but pain flares from my arm to my chest. It takes a second to catch my breath as the pain eases.

"What? How?" Hat scrutinizes the black design, almost metallic.

It doesn't make sense. It's beautiful. Hat pokes my arm, sending another jolt of pain to my fingertips and across my chest. I skip away, glaring at her.

"Seriously?" I say. "You see a big magic tattoo on my arm, and you poke it."

"I'm testing a theory." She taps her chin.

"What's the theory? That you're a jerk?" But I'm not really mad. I'm too stunned and confused.

Hat squints at my arm. "That it's not a regular tattoo. That someone didn't give it to you while you were asleep."

"Yeah, because I wouldn't notice *that*. I've never been that drunk." I slept right through the night, but if someone *did* give me a fake tattoo, they would have had to drug me, and I don't feel hungover or hazy. I went to sleep in the alley under the wooden pallet, and that's where I woke up. The tattoo is definitely sensitive to the touch, except that the pain resonates deep in my bones.

Hat pushes her hair behind her ears and inspects my arm. I hope she'll find a clasp, and the tattoo will come off like a stolen bracelet. But she lowers my arm with a quizzical frown.

Hat stares out at the flurry of bright colors beyond the alley. "How could the king speak your name if you're Nameless?"

Her frown is filled with suspicion and accusation.

I take a shaky breath. "The tattoo probably isn't real."

"If it's not real, then you're lying and got a fake tattoo—which could get you *killed* if anyone sees it. If you didn't get it, then it's real. You're queen, which means you can't be Nameless."

The alley walls press against me, my heartbeat overwhelming the steady thrum of voices in the market.

"I am *Nameless!*" I shout. "I can't be queen, Hat. The king couldn't say my name, because I don't *have* one. You think I would be sleeping on the streets if I had a name? You think I'd be running bump-grabs in the markets, risking execution every single day? You think I wouldn't be in a house, with a pet cat, and a bath, and a basement full of food, and . . . and you and me bartering and getting jobs . . ." I lean against the alley wall and slide down into a crouch.

Silently, Hat leans against the wall and sits beside me. She waits. She breathes.

She smiles.

I don't know how she does it. She sees a feast where I see stale, crumbling bread. She sees friends among the Nameless where I see competition. Everything in me wants to see what she sees. But I can't. I don't know how.

Hat speaks earnestly. "You know, Coin, you *could* have a name. You don't know what it is, but someone out there might! If someone, *anyone,* in Seriden knows it, then you aren't really Nameless. The king must have known it in order to give you the tattoo, which proves it exists!"

I shake my head. "The tattoo is real. That's all I know for sure. That's why I saw into that Royal's head in the market. I was . . . experiencing his memories, I think."

"Will it work on me?" she asks excitedly, sticking out her hand for me to touch.

It won't, but I take her hand anyway. "The sovereign's magic doesn't work on the Nameless. I think that's why they've always hated us."

Hat pulls her hand back. "Forget it. It was a silly idea." Her small spark of hope burns a little less brightly.

I take a deep breath and try to push it all down. Push everything—the black crown, what it means, the terrible pain of almost wanting something—down into the pit opening inside me. I am unsettled and shaky, trying and failing to bury the fear of impossible things.

Every time I imagine my future—on those endless nights when I tell myself I'll survive long enough to see it—I always see a house. It's small, and dust filters from the ceiling with each ocean breeze. Maybe it's abandoned. Abandoned and mine.

I don't want anything special. I don't want anything grand. I just want to survive. That's all I've ever wanted. I've never tried to want more.

"We shouldn't stay out on the streets today," I say, breaking the silence and changing the subject.

Hat jumps to her feet and gives a flourishing bow.

I tilt my head. "Really?"

"Consider yourself lucky." She remains awkwardly bent, speaking to the ground. "This is probably the only time I'll bow before Royalty." She straightens up and extends her hand.

It's strange to accept her help when she's younger than me and I'm the one who's supposed to be teaching her. I sigh, put aside my pride, and let her haul me to my feet, wiping brick dust from my arms.

She adds, "I bet you're a princess. How else would King Fallow have known your name?"

I frown at her. We both know Royalty isn't passed through bloodlines anymore, not since the peace treaties were signed over two hundred years ago, when the territory borders were set and fourteen crowned sovereigns took ownership of their cities. That was long, long before either of us was born into this life.

I adjust the two layers of coats on my shoulders. "Let's go somewhere safe."

Hat's eyes are bright. She's still excited about this spetzing crown. She doesn't realize she's daydreaming of a future where, yes, I might be safe and protected by the Legal status of having a name or the Royal status of this crown . . . but that is a world she can't live in. Hell, it's a world *I* can't live in. Royalty has become a game of names instead of blood. A game someone like me isn't supposed to win. A game I *can't* win. Even if this tattoo is real, I would be killed the moment I set foot near the throne.

I can't be queen. I can't.

"Let's just go straight to Devil's. She wasn't at West Market, so she must be lying low, which is what we should be doing. She can give us a safe place to stay." I pull Hat down the alley, but she shakes free of my grip.

"I can't go straight to Devil's!" she says, almost mocking. "My things are at the crispy house."

That's what she calls the burned, hollowed-out shack in the South Residences where Marcher houses his crew of child thieves. When I was part of his crew, we lived in a maintenance tunnel near the northern sewers.

"Your things? You don't need *things*. You need *safety*." I've never understood what she calls her "keepsakes." From what I gather, they're a blanket and a few trinkets that she keeps in a box.

"Well, maybe if you let me live with you, I'd have my things with me and this wouldn't be a problem! I won't apologize for having things I care about!" Before I can stop her, she spins on her heel and runs down the alley. "I'll meet you at Devil's!" Then she's gone.

I growl in frustration, kick the brick wall, and stalk off in the opposite direction.

Devil is one of the only Nameless who have something that would qualify as a home.

She's everything a clever Nameless can accomplish. Six barrels of bricks, two broken-down carts, and the dark wood of a sloop in disrepair, and Devil walled off an entire alley between a millinery and a bakery.

I approach her home from the alley network as opposed to the street. I've only visited Devil a handful of times, but she has never let me inside. There's a rule. There's a string through the bricks on the alley-facing wall of her home. You pull the string, and Devil somehow knows someone wants to speak with her. Then she sort of appears behind you in the next ten minutes. But I don't have time for patience. Seconds after I pull the string and feel a faint sense of clicking on the other side, I'm shouting over the wall. It's not long until a rope ladder is thrown over the top and swings at my ankles.

When I make it to the top, I sit on the edge of the wall to catch my breath before swinging my legs inward. At this height, I can see across the rooftops of the nearest businesses. A couple have smoke easing from their chimneys, and between the rooftops of the millinery and the glass shop, I glimpse the towers of the Royal Court. The five towers are pressed together like organ pipes. But they're not musical—they're an ornament, a crown for the city of Seriden, piercing the sky, no doubt visible by ships coming along the coast.

I ease myself down onto a high platform. As my eyes adjust to the shadows, I see that the platform is really the top level of stairs that lead down into the alley. The stairs are dark, with the faint scent of brine. They end a couple of feet off the ground.

At the base stands Devil, pointing a rifle directly at me.

"Welcome to my home," Devil says with a sly grin. Her brown eyes are a few shades darker than her tanned skin, and her hands are steady, never for a moment lowering the rifle. Where in the world she got one of the new rifles instead of the older muskets, I have no idea. Not even all the Royal guards have gotten the newer weapons yet.

"What do you want?" Devil asks. Her voice is smooth and low, like a strong whisper.

"Sanctuary," I say.

A smirk plays on Devil's lips. "From what?"

I measure my next action carefully. I pull down the shoulder of my coats and shirt, showing her the black-ink tattoo.

"Real or forgery?" she asks, not missing a beat.

"Real," I say. "Somehow."

Devil's gaze never leaves my tattoo. "I bet they'd offer me a pretty gold necklace if I turned you in to the guards."

"You wouldn't turn me in," I say. "If you do that, no one will come to you again. Plus, who's to say I won't have you arrested? This tattoo means I'm the sovereign, after all." Heat floods my face. Did I just threaten Devil?

Devil chews her lip, slightly amused, before dropping the barrel. "True enough." Her shoulders slump, and she plops down into a chair and throws her black-booted feet up onto the table. If my threat bothers her, it doesn't show. She reaches over and pulls on a rope, hauling the ladder up and over the wall.

The extent of Devil's home is impressive. It's long and narrow, and a strange furniture collection sits below us, with everything from a sawn-in-half sofa to a set of mismatched dining chairs to a mattress with gold-colored sheets. A decorated Royal headboard serves as a table, with unlit candles cluttering the surface, perched on stray playing cards. The rest of the alley walls are covered in shelves stacked with oddities: coral from the ocean, a cat's skull, a variety of walking sticks, and an impressive number of different-sized leather shoes.

"So. For sanctuary. What are you offering?" Devil picks up the small cat skull, idly petting it with a slender finger.

I have twenty iron rings and two gold coins.

"Fifteen iron rings." I cross my arms.

Devil's eyes rise slowly from the cat skull. "Do you swear by everything Nameless?" The rifle leans against her chair.

Swearing by everything Nameless is the strongest promise we can make, invoking the essence of what we are. It's our only sense of unity: what keeps us apart keeps us together.

"All you have for a single night of refuge," Devil says, and her gaze pauses on me, eyes twinkling.

"Twenty and two," I admit.

She returns the cat skull to its shelf, reaches under the collar of her leather jacket, and pulls out a necklace of twine threaded with silver and copper rings. She takes it off and tosses it to me.

"Just the rings, please."

I string the twenty iron rings onto the twine, tie it off, and toss it over. She beckons me down, slinging the necklace over her head.

As I descend, the scent of oak, leather, and bone dust settles around me.

"This is it," Devil says, spreading her arms out and pacing farther down her alley. "If you want refuge, you can stay here. I'll have to send May to put a hold on the shipments of blood-wood and . . ." She trails off, turning toward me. "Yes, well. I'm a gossip and a smuggler. Anyway. Find a place to sleep. Not my bed. Well . . ." She casts a sidelong glance at me that makes me blush. "Don't touch the shelves. Everything is arranged just so."

The half couch rests against the brick wall, a stack of books propping up the end with no legs, but it's sturdy enough as I sit down on it.

"One more thing," I say. "Hat will be joining me soon. Do you want the coins for that?" I hold them out to her. She gives me a look as if to say, *That's not the type of coin I want.* I insist, not lowering my hand.

Devil sighs in disappointment as she moves past me and sits at her table. She pinches one of the candle flames into a wisp of smoke and bends over an iron ring, filing at the edge with a small, rough stone. I slip the coins back into my pocket.

"I'll keep watch for Hat," Devil says. She lights up after a moment, and she leans on the table in my direction. "Or I can get you out of the city tonight, if you'd like to repurpose your payment. But you'd have to move fast. We'd have to leave now, if you're prepared to go. There's a ship leaving in . . ." She pulls an old leather case from her pocket, flips it open, checks the watch inside, and flips it closed again. "Twenty minutes. If you hurry."

I hesitate. I imagine the cool ocean breeze against my skin and the constant rush of water against the wooden body of the ship. I can almost taste the salt of the open air and the freedom from Seriden's walls.

Then I picture Hat showing up tonight or tomorrow here at Devil's, bouncing and excited to join me on an adventure outside the city. I imagine the moment her face falls when she realizes I'm already gone, without her.

I shake my head. "I have to wait for Hat. I don't think I could leave without . . . I'll wait."

"I've met a lot of people who have left their cities and abandoned the place they were born," Devil says. "Maybe they've committed a crime, they've offended the wrong guard, they're curious to see the world, or they're not attached enough to the life they're leaving behind."

I raise an eyebrow as if to ask, *Which one am I?*

"You're none of those, Your Highness," Devil says with an amused grin. "You're the kind who needs to leave but won't. With that tattoo on your arm, either you're dead as soon as they find you, or they'll force you to name a new ruler and *then* they'll kill you. Either way, that tattoo is a death sentence for you."

It's a death sentence for anyone like me. The Nameless

don't win this game. The Nameless are killed. That's the fate waiting for me.

"But sure, you can stay," Devil says cheerily, leaning into her chair and continuing to file at the edges of the ring. "You can be loyal and wait for your little friend."

"She's not my—" I start, but I cut myself off before I finish. If she's not my friend, then what am I still doing here?

I curl deeper into the couch and try to force myself to consider my options.

I wonder if I would leave Seriden if I had a place like this to sleep every night or if I was one of those Nameless with a family. Would I leave if Hat was with me right now?

I try to understand why Hat's possessions are so important to her, but I can't. Maybe they are tokens of a former life. Maybe Hat was part of a Nameless family once. Maybe there's something that ties her to that blanket and those trinkets in a way I never *could* understand.

Hours pass, and I fall asleep thinking of Hat, of black ink tattoos, and of an impossible life outside these city walls.

—✦—

When I wake, I immediately search for Hat, but she's not here. It takes me a minute to recognize where I am. There are shelves filled with weapons and pieces of glass and other organized oddities that glint in the morning sunlight. I'm in Devil's alley.

"She never came," Devil says.

I sit up, alarmed. "Are you sure?"

She glares at me from her station at the table as if she didn't move all night. Of course she's sure.

What's Marcher up to? Or what if she's gone missing like the other Nameless?

"Oh, gaiza, if she's been . . ." I put my head in my hands.

Devil gauges me. "If you want to leave the city, I can still get you out. There's a ship heading north for Devra this afternoon. I can get you on board before the crew settles in."

"Now?" I try to consider it, but I'm already shaking my head. "I can't. I can't go without Hat. She's . . ." I don't finish.

"I thought you might say that," Devil says. "Which is why I also got a report from a street runner that Marcher is at East Market this morning. Funny that East Market leads right to the harbor. You may not make the ship heading north, but that's where you'll find your friend."

CHAPTER 3

I hate fish.

I hate the ocean.

I hate all the slippery rocks.

I even hate the big open sky that bends and darkens at the horizon.

In essence, I hate East Market—everything about it.

Plus, fishermen aren't good marks. They don't carry coins, rings, or anything valuable. They carry hooks, scaling knives, and fishing line. Not things I like finding in pockets. Fishermen are only useful because they smell like fish, and everyone hates the pungent smell of seaweed, sweat, and guts. As people dodge the smell, I step into their path and make quick work of their change purses.

But I'm not here on business today, so I keep my arms crossed as I head for the entrance to the ship-repair house. That's where Marcher sets up shop while his scoundrel children use the fishermen as decoys for running bump-grabs.

A bell begins to toll, and people slowly come to a halt, and I stop as well so I don't draw attention to myself. In truth, I feel rooted to the spot, as if the energy of the crowd is paralyzing me. A Royal announcer takes center stage. Behind him are three Royal guards, two of whom have black lapels and cuffs instead of white. Great. Guards in training—cadets, I've heard them called—are reckless, less likely to know all the laws, but more eager to dole out punishments. The two cadets are young, maybe my age. The girl has short brown hair swept behind her ears and a strong jaw. The guy has blond, short-cropped hair and keeps swallowing like he's thirsty. Rookie. He probably forgot to fill his water flask before heading out. Maybe I'll steal it from him.

The third guard is older, with a strong face, serene eyes that scan the crowd attentively, and a truly excellent beard dashed with gray.

Very few Royal guards actually guard the Royals. Most of them police the outer quadrants and markets. Some guards are more lenient than others, offering reprieve when others would offer an escort to the prison gallows.

The announcer is clean-shaven except for a thin mustache balanced over his lip. His smile is a fake, public show of teeth, and it makes me twitch. He could use lessons from a grifter on how to con with a real smile.

"Ladies and gentlemen, Legals and Royals," he says. "I am saddened to inform you that our beloved King Parson Rejoriak Fallow has passed away. Taken from us in his sleep, King Fallow whispered a name in his dying solitude."

I bristle, shifting with discomfort. Impossibly, the name he whispered was mine. I'm suddenly aware of the soreness of my arm. It feels like the tattoo is burning, that anyone, *everyone*, can see it. I don't even know if I believe it's real. What's worse, if anyone else finds out and *they* don't believe it's real . . . Getting a black tattoo or any tattoo that even resembles the sovereign's crown is illegal. Then it's either fire or amputation to remove it, and I doubt they'd waste their fire on me.

"None of the Royals from the five main families bear the tattoo, and neither do any of the Royals in the court," the announcer says, and another murmur flows through the crowd. "So it seems"—his fake smile reappears—"a Legal residing in the outer quadrants has been crowned."

Another ebb and flow of whispers swirls around me. The Fallow family had the crown up until today. Everyone in Seriden, including me, expected his daughter to get the crown next. I've never seen her up close, but people have said she's strong and would outstrip her father's accomplishments in her first year.

The announcer clears his throat. "We have searched the North and South Farms, West Market, and the Inner Ring that connects them all. East Market, dearest Legals and Royals, is the last public area to search. The next heir to Seriden's throne is likely among you."

My skin itches and burns, flushing with heat.

He continues, "If you will join us in this ceremony, we will uncover our shoulders on this beautiful spring morning and see who among you has been crowned."

Royals and Legals disrobing in public. I think some of them might faint. People pull down the shoulders of their coats, their dresses, their sleeves and suspenders. A Legal woman drops her basket of flowers and shoves aside her lime-green sleeve, exposing her smooth brown skin. Like everyone else, she finds nothing. The whole crowd is energized—or maybe it's me. My hands twitch at my side as I feel the rise and fall of expectations and disappointment.

As people start shifting around, they check each other's arms for any trace of ink, and I start moving again. I feel them all around me, like they're breathing on my skin. Their energy becomes my energy, and I'm suddenly desperate to be alone.

A small head of red hair bobs up and down, heading toward me. Hat. And Marcher is three steps behind, hot on her trail. Hat pushes through the pool of Legals and Royals.

I don't know why she's running or why he's chasing. Maybe he asked her to do something too dangerous. Maybe she told him she wanted to leave. Heat flares in my chest. Maybe he wanted her to pickpocket another Royal. Maybe he doesn't want her to leave the crew. Maybe he's just getting back at me. Either way, she's running. Toward me. I see my name on her lips: *Coin*.

She's afraid and calling out to me.

I rip off my own coat, exposing the Legal jacket beneath. I start toward Hat at a brisk pace, walking tall and hoping the beige fabric of the jacket will camouflage me.

"Hat." I'm six steps away as she bumps into a tall Royal with a monocle. The man, upset and off balance, grabs Hat's shoulder to steady himself.

Marcher eases off as we gather the attention of the nearby Royals and Legals. The Royal takes one look at Hat and his expression sours.

"Nameless thief!" Monocle Royal snatches Hat's wrist.

He calls for a Royal guard, and the closest one is the young blond cadet. He grabs Hat by the collar, and the people nearby stir angrily.

I race through the crowd, pushing. I'm still wearing the Legal jacket, so I only get rude glares instead of curse words.

"Arrest her!"

"Throw her in jail!"

"Hang her!"

Shouts ring louder and louder in my ears. The cadet should arrest her and put her in a holding cell overnight, but his eyes burn with a crowd-fostered fury as he unsheathes his sword.

What a fool! Street executions are rare, but they're supposed to be quick and clean at least. A blade means things will get messy—fast.

I shove the Royal in front of me so hard that he falls to the ground. I pull off the Legal coat, drop it, and grab the shoulder of my long sleeved green shirt and tear, ripping the sleeve off. I clear my throat and will my voice to be loud and clear.

"In the name of the queen, I command you to stop!" I shout, and the cadet falters.

I fight to keep calm as the cadet slowly lowers Hat, staring at my tattoo. My heart pounds.

The lieutenant at the gazebo is the first to recover, and he starts toward the cadet. The announcer, however, beams at me from the edge of the gazebo. He speaks loudly, broadcasting to the entire market.

"What is your appellation and designation?" It's his fancy Royal way of asking my name and class.

I could lie. Give a fake name, say I'm Legal. Even if they ask for citizenship papers, it'll give me time to get away. *My papers are at my home in the North Residences.* Yet my body is stone.

"She is Nameless!" The shout rings out in the silence. Marcher, that Nameless traitor. If everyone wasn't watching me before, they certainly are now. The announcer falters. He looks at me, really looks. I imagine he doesn't like what he sees: scrappy teenager, bony from hunger yet strong from fighting, shoddy clothes, dirty face. What he sees is me—one of the Nameless.

The announcer's voice booms. "Friends and strangers, Legals and Royals! I give you the impossible heir: the Nameless queen!"

The crowd shifts to shock, and it's like electricity tingling my skin. Everything loosens, the chill in the air evaporates, and I feel like I have control over my limbs again.

I don't know where the other guard comes from. He was behind me, and I missed him. I was so focused on Hat. I thought I could save her. Instead I watch as they place shackles on her wrists just before the same is done to me.

I'm about to hook his ankle to knock him down when he grips my left shoulder with a gloved hand. As his fingers tighten around my arm, a piercing, deep pain strikes through my shoulder to my chest. The tattoo is like an open wound—sensitive to every pressure and touch.

The guards haul Hat and me in opposite directions. Her

westward and me south toward the holding cells and the Royal Court. All the while, she's shouting my name—yelling it as she disappears.

Coin, Coin, Coin.

A swarm of a hundred bodies separates us, and I struggle to keep her in my sight—a glint of steel shackles, a wisp of red hair—and then she's gone.

CHAPTER 4

We're in the Royal Court when I realize they aren't taking me to the holding cells. They march me to the front gates of the palace. The guard with the excellent beard—they call him Lieutenant Glenquartz—pats me down. I don't object as he takes my favorite knife, a waxy candle stub, and a few stolen baubles and snacks from my pockets. I definitely don't object when he fails to find the two iron rings in my boot or the lockpick sewn into my pant leg.

As I enter the palace alongside Lieutenant Glenquartz, my fingers twitch at my sides, eager to refill my pockets. The corridors aren't busy, but we pass by several groups of Royals. One Royal has a change purse tied at his waist. Another has a set of gold rings on her thumb: currency worn as jewelry.

We pass a huge tapestry depicting the construction of Seriden that hangs from the ceiling to the floor. I'm hardly interested in a history lesson from something that really ought to be a blanket. But I can't deny its beauty.

We go down another corridor, passing statues and sculptures. Then one lined with oil portraits of people who all sport the crown tattoo around their arms. On them, it's a proud symbol of sovereignty.

I try not to be impressed. I try really, *really* hard.

But there are chandeliers dripping with crystals, artworks framed by sparkling gold, everything clean and shining and soft. Each room we pass is more oddly decorated than the last. One of the rooms stirs with the green glow from emerald glass windows. Another is filled entirely with candles and mirrors, reflecting a sparkling infinity. And there are so many empty rooms, easy spaces just waiting to be filled. Here, space is a luxury instead of a territory to defend.

I track every turn, mapping the palace in my head. I count the time it would take to run to the entrance, and I tally the rooms with windows big enough to fit through. We pass tables holding vases of thorny flowers and bowls of polished river rocks, the occasional bust of a probably dead person. How thoughtful of them to position makeshift weapons so conveniently.

They may have searched me upon entry, but by the time they lead me into a quaint sitting room, my pockets are filled once again. My best take is a kitchen knife from an untended platter of half-eaten food. Granted, it's difficult to make thefts when my hands are shackled, but I keep my hands moving and clinking so they don't notice when I snatch something. It doesn't even occur to them to search me again. Big mistake.

At the end of the quaint room there's a heavy stone door, which Glenquartz hauls open, and we descend steep stairs into what I quickly realize is the dungeon.

The world gets darker and colder the farther down we go. We pass by some holding cells, which are similar to the waiting room upstairs: large, with cushioned chairs and doors that barely lock. I imagine Royals getting tossed in here for a night when they get too drunk at a party or complain too loudly about taxes.

I move closer to Glenquartz so I'm sure he will hear me when I speak.

"I'm assuming my cell *doesn't* have pillows?" I say.

Glenquartz's shoulders tense, and he doesn't answer.

I shrug. "I mean, that's all right. I'd prefer having some, and proper blankets wouldn't hurt either—but I'm not going to complain when you're being so hospitable and giving me a place to sleep tonight."

I see the flicker of an almost-smile on his face.

"Let's be honest. I'm not upset," I continue, "but you seem to be neglecting your dungeon. Dust everywhere. And I don't want to seem too forward, but I am excellent at redecorating drab places. In fact, you scooped me up before I could gather my things. I forgot to douse the stove and close the curtains in my alley."

The angry cadet at my side—with his round face, dark hair, and delightfully inattentive eyes—keeps a firm grip on my right shoulder. When he pulls me to a stop, I bump into him. I can't steal anything as ostentatious as his rifle or pistol, but I quickly unsnap the metal ring of keys inside his jacket and twist sharply to the side and drop it in my boot, pretending that I've tripped.

It's over in an instant, and now I have my escape.

Angry Cadet keeps his hold on my shirt as Glenquartz removes my cuffs, but he lets go when Glenquartz prompts me to enter the cell.

I walk through the cell door as if I'm excited to enter my new home. I'm pleased to see Glenquartz use the same key to lock the door that he used to unlock my cuffs.

I give Glenquartz a coy look. "No pillows? Really? Very rude to your future queen."

Angry Cadet openly scoffs. "As soon as we confirm that your tattoo is a forgery, I'll escort you myself to the prison gallows, where you can join your little friend from the market."

Glenquartz is good at keeping a straight face, but I see him wince. "That's enough, Cadet Dominic. One more outburst and I'll have you report to General Demure." He makes a gesture, and the cadet departs—and I note an uncomfortable slant in his shoulder at the mention of the general.

"I'll be watching over you for the evening," Glenquartz says, dismissing the remaining cadets. They salute and depart.

I make a show of waiting until they're gone. I have a key, and I have a knife. All I have to do is get out of here and get to Hat. I size the lieutenant up. He's obviously formal. Gullible, too—what other people might call "trusting." He wasn't the guard who went after Hat. He was the one ordering him to stop.

"Her name is Hat," I say.

"Who do you mean?" Glenquartz asks, but with a glimmer of recognition.

"The girl your new recruit was going to kill," I say. "She's young. Too young for an unordered street execution."

"How old is she?" Glenquartz asks.

I pause. "Not sure. The Nameless often don't know. One

day I decided I was fourteen, and now, three years later, I'm seventeen. Hat hasn't decided yet, so she's twelve? Thirteen, maybe? Still too young to die, don't you think?"

"Is that why you did it?" He points at the tattoo on my arm below my left shoulder. I take a slow breath. He's already seen me desperate and angry, snarky and confident. To get his help, I have to show him I'm vulnerable.

"If you're asking if that's why I stepped forward and got arrested? Yes. But this tattoo? I didn't put it there. Can you . . . ?" I trail off and move farther into the cell to remind him that I'm trapped here.

He puts a hand on the bar and offers a consoling smile. "I can't get you any pillows."

I shake my head and bite my lip. "Can you make sure she's alive?" When the words leave my lips, I'm stunned by how terrified I truly am. "Can you go after that cadet from the market, and make sure Hat is safe?"

He seems sympathetic, like maybe he doesn't want to see Hat hurt any more than I do.

I remember the sensation and flash of memory that burst into my thoughts when I touched the Royal's hand yesterday. Glenquartz's fingers are wrapped around one of the bars. I put my hand on his. Suddenly I see a small, young face staring up at me.

She has black, straight hair and a scattering of freckles across her cheeks and forehead. She's smiling, with rays of sunlight settling on her hair and a gentle breeze stirring the sound of distant music. I reach out to cup her face in my hand, and my skin is dark and warmer, and there's a red sleeve and white cuff at my wrist.

I let go, and the memory vanishes, and I realize that the red-cuffed arm in the memory was Glenquartz's.

"You have a daughter?" I say, probing gently.

Glenquartz purses his lips carefully. "Her name is Flannery. She's with her mother, but they both left me a very long time ago. I miss her terribly." He stares past me as if toward the curving horizon at the edge of the ocean.

"You understand, then," I insist gently. "I sensed you're afraid of forgetting them. Think of what you'd do if Flannery was arrested."

"I can send someone to check on her," Glenquartz says, and he pats the bars of the cell. "It was brave of you to help her. But Cadet Dominic was right. That fake tattoo will get you killed."

I take a seat on the long stone bench. "Please check on her." I don't address his warning. If my tattoo is fake, I'm dead. But I'm equally dead if it's real.

Glenquartz nods at last and withdraws from the door of the cell. I count the seconds as his footsteps fade, and I give it an extra five seconds before I put the key in the lock. I consider for a moment whether I should take the kitchen knife with me or not. If I stow it in the waste drain, it'll be here if I get arrested again. They'll search me, and they'll search the cell, but I'm betting they won't search the drain.

Once the cell door is open, I stuff the key in my pocket, hide the knife, and head out. I count the turns I took on the way down here, and when I reach the stairs, I walk up them quickly. Soon I'm at the heavy stone. I place my hand on the cool handle. I can't get around a blind exit like this, so I have to take my chances.

Slowly, I leverage the door against its own hinge to keep it from making too much noise as it opens. As I move into the room, I see a woman standing near the opposite door, dressed in a sapphire-blue dress with ornate silver bracelets at her wrist.

I recognize her from parades in the city: Esther Merelda Fallow, daughter of the recently dead king, the former heir apparent. Her brown eyes are warm, but her expression is anything but. Her aura is like a cold mist that makes me shiver. She unfolds her arms, and I wouldn't be surprised to find steel claws in place of her fingers.

"I hear you're called Coin," Esther says.

I narrow my eyes. I regret not bringing the knife now.

"Didn't take you long," she continues. "I'd like to say I'm impressed, but . . ."

"But you're afraid the mere act of uttering those words would shatter you?" I offer.

Her eyes narrow this time, and she advances.

"Listen, I have an appointment to get to, and I'm late," I say apologetically. I step sideways, and she mirrors my movements, blocking my path to the door.

"The only appointment you're going to have is when I prove the tattoo on your arm is forged, and that will be an—"

"An appointment with the gallows?" I give her a disappointed frown. "That's never *not* a bad joke. And trust me, as a Nameless, I've heard it before."

Esther fumes, and she stomps even closer. I let her draw as close as she wants until she gets uncomfortable.

"You're making a fool of yourself," she says, putting a hand on my shoulder and pushing me against the wall. "You don't know the first thing about being queen."

"I don't," I admit as she stands a breath away. "I know how to survive. And the first rule: Getting close to someone?"

Esther looms over me.

I continue, "It makes you *vulnerable*." I reach up and curl my fingers around her throat, turning my ankle behind hers and bringing her weight down toward the wall. In an instant, I've spun her right around and thrown her into one of the waiting chairs. It's so fast that all I see of her thoughts is the image of high walls and peach stone.

She puts a hand to her throat, where her skin has flushed a faint shade of red. "You have no idea what world you've walked into." She glares at the tattoo on my arm as if to peel it off. "I think you'll find it's as dangerous here as on the streets." She rises to her feet, but she doesn't advance on me again.

I lock eyes with her. "See, the problem is you're trying to threaten me, but you're being polite about it. I grew up on the streets, so you'll have to do better than that. If you want to threaten someone, you do it like *this*." I step closer so we're almost nose to nose, my voice dropping to a dead, even tone. "If you ever touch me again, or if I ever feel threatened by you"—I allow a delicate, careful smile to overtake my features—"I will kill you."

Esther's satin sleeves bunch at her shoulders as she tenses, anger rolling off her like steam. I pivot on the heel of my boot and head for the door.

"You can't leave," Esther commands.

A flare of anger passes through me. "No. *You* can't leave." I imagine trapping her in the cell I just escaped, bars and stones surrounding her. I open the door and slip out of the room, then pull the door shut with a slam.

I'm surprised a moment later when I hear her pounding on the door and then the wall. She's muttering and shouting, a trace of panic in her voice. When I face the corridor, I find Glenquartz standing across from me, leaning casually against the wall. There are three Royal guards on either side of him, boxing me in. I curl my fingers into fists. Even if I had the knife from my cell, it would only be good to take out one or two guards.

"So this is a trap?" I grind my teeth. "I'd like to say I'm impressed."

Esther opens the door behind me and joins us. "Go ahead. No one's stopping you. And it wasn't a trap. It was a test."

"One that she passed?" Glenquartz asks, his forehead crinkling.

Esther runs a hand on the door frame. "The tattoo is real. I don't know how she knew to do it. Probably an accident. But it's proof enough for me." She appraises me distastefully, keeping her distance as good old Angry Cadet Dominic puts shackles on my wrists with a too-easy click.

"What proof?" I say. "What was an accident? That I almost had you dead to rights in there? That's nothing."

Esther's hand perches on her hip. "You really don't know." She looks me up and down with disgust. She says to Glenquartz, "She made me see stones over every surface, and metal bars blocking all the windows and doors. It was good. I believed it. The illusion didn't last long, though. It faded as soon as she got distracted by you."

Alarmed, I realize that when I imagined she was trapped in the room, I made her see something that wasn't there. "Wait, you're saying you *actually* saw a room filled with rocks?"

She exhales sharply. "A room *encased* in rocks. Do try to keep up, or else you'll have us all convinced you are the uneducated criminal you appear to be."

I shake my head, not sure how I'm supposed to respond to the insult—not even convinced it *is* an insult.

"The tattoo lets you cause hallucinations," she says, as though she's explaining to a child why fire is bad. "Whoever you are and whatever you want, at least we know the tattoo is real."

I feel insulted, for sure. Angry, of course. Embarrassed, just a little. What Esther said, though, overshadows everything else I feel. The tattoo is real, and I can make people hallucinate. That's going to come in handy.

Esther huffs, thoroughly annoyed, and she stalks down the hall. Glenquartz escorts me back down into the dark corridors of the dungeon, with three of the guards in tow.

"I expect you won't have to stay down here for long," Glenquartz says as we walk. He's trying to be comforting, but he's also a little smug that he and his guards have outsmarted me. "Now that they know you are the new sovereign, the Royal

Council will have to decide what to do next. If you hadn't escaped so quickly, I might have been able to convince them to let you stay in a proper room upstairs. But if you can escape the dungeon in five minutes, I doubt our simple palace quarters would give you trouble."

I remain silent, thinking through my next moves. They've reclaimed the key, and they search me more thoroughly outside the cell this time. I only have the lockpick in my pant leg. At least they're putting me in the same cell, where the knife waits in the drain.

The cell door clicks shut, and I place my hand on the bars.

"Will you still check on Hat?" I ask Glenquartz, ignoring the other guards. "I know I was using it as an excuse to get rid of you before, but I really mean it. I'm not sure which is worse: her getting arrested or her disappearing from the streets."

"Disappearing?" Glenquartz is puzzled, and I'm not surprised. There's no reason he would've heard about Nameless kids vanishing, because no one else cares.

"The Nameless have been disappearing lately," I say. "More and more, and right around her age. No one knows what happens to them. I'm worried. She could disappear from wherever they've stashed her—the prisons or the holding cells, or who knows where. Please check on her. But don't send that spetzing angry cadet who doesn't know Law Twenty-Two from Law Thirty-Six."

Glenquartz raises an eyebrow. "Those are the two most cited sumptuary laws."

Frustration overwhelms me, and I slam my open palm against the stones. "Law Twenty-Two: 'A citizen shall not dress out of their class, such as a Legal wearing clothes of a Royal or the Nameless donning the clothes of either.' Law Thirty-Six, the common exemption, where a Legal can wear a Royal's clothing on the day of their wedding to a Royal, at which time the Legal becomes a Royal. Of course I know the stupid laws! I've broken more than half of them. I'm already here behind bars, so go ahead and arrest me again if you want to! But, please, will you check on Hat? She's why I'm here. And if I can't make sure she's all right, she is why I'll escape again. If you can tell me she's safe, then I'll stay here as long as you want me to. Please. Think of Flannery."

I know it's a risk to say that. If I promise to stay here, he could lie just to pacify me. But he has a daughter named Flannery with freckles and a carefree smile, a daughter he's afraid of forgetting. He's troubled, like a distant storm cloud. He takes a decided step away, but by the way he looks at me, I know he's considering it. Then he leaves quietly, and I'm left alone, staring at the gray stones of the tunnel wall, which seem to shiver in the light of the lantern held by the guard who stays behind to watch me.

I press my forehead against the cell bars, letting the cool metal chill my skin. I told Glenquartz I wouldn't leave the palace, but I didn't say anything about leaving my cell. After all, I made Esther believe the door had vanished. There's no telling what else I can do. I have magic.

I stare up at the dark ceiling, imagining I can see the sky. What have I gotten myself into? Hat has been arrested. I don't know where she is. She could be dead right now or on her way to be killed. And all I can think about is what kind of magical powers I may or may not have.

Out in the city and with Glenquartz, I learned that I can see a person's thoughts or memories when I touch them. Here in the palace, I was able to make Esther hallucinate that she was trapped in a room, but to me everything was normal. Maybe my abilities work on other people but not me? I study the tattoo on my arm in the small trace of light afforded by the lantern, trying to decide if I feel any different.

In addition to seeing memories and creating illusions, there's something else. It was the storm cloud building when Glenquartz listened to me talk about Hat. It was the strange feeling of steel and ice that I sensed from Esther. It was the overwhelming pressure of the crowds in West Market.

I reach for it now. It's a small buzzing sensation, like an ever-persistent fly buzzing around at the edge of my mind. I focus on it and realize that what I'm sensing is the aura of the guard outside the cell. The more I reach for it, the more I sense. Then, somewhere far overhead, I sense another aura, like a swirling crackle of lightning.

These auras are the blurs in my vision when my eyes are closed. They are columns of smoke I can barely detect. They are a type of energy I don't yet understand.

As I search the dark ceiling, I can almost hear it. It's a rhythmic pounding, like a distant heartbeat of the city. Maybe it's the aura of someone else lurking in the depths of the dungeon: a prisoner long forgotten, a guard patrolling the darkness.

I don't understand it yet, just as I don't understand what happens to the Nameless when they go missing, or where Hat has been taken, or what awaits me tomorrow in this palace.

I don't understand yet. But I'm going to.

CHAPTER 5

Glenquartz returns hours later, and I sense his aura before I see or hear him. It's cautious and careful as he negotiates the dark tunnels with a flickering lantern and a tray of food.

He slides the food tray under the cell door—buttered flatbread and some kind of pink egg. Then he passes a thin metal flask through the bars. I examine both, balancing my hunger against the potential that either could be poisoned. He encourages me to eat, and I wonder if it's worth pointing out that if he cares so much about me starving, he could try caring about the hundreds of Nameless starving on the streets. But caution prevails for once, and I keep quiet.

"I tracked down the cadet who arrested Hat," Glenquartz says. "He passed her off to a guard who keeps watch over the northern holding cells, but it doesn't look like she's there. I haven't found her yet."

I curb my impatience that it's taking him so long to find Hat, and I thank him for the food. As he leaves, I shout after him, "Bring me a pillow next time, will you?"

I see the corner of a smile as he departs.

There's not much to do when I'm locked in a cell. I've searched every inch of it. Aside from the waste drain in the corner, there are sixteen broken pieces of stone from the wall, a tiny screw, and unpleasant evidence of rats.

The only thing I really know about my abilities so far is that they don't seem to work on me. When I made Esther think she was imprisoned, I couldn't see it. I can see into Glenquartz's memories of his daughter, but I certainly can't explore my own memories like that. So testing my new abilities will be tricky. In the evening, when Angry Cadet Dominic—I've grudgingly decided to remember his name—brings me dinner and collects the lunch tray, I focus all my thoughts on the tray as he reaches for it. I imagine a spider, hairy with a small dash of red on it. Slow-moving legs. A field of tiny shining eyes.

When Dominic reaches for the tray, he lets out a small yelp and slaps at it. I sit up sharply as if surprised.

"Spetzing spiders," Dominic mutters. "At least they've got good company." He glares at me. I put some effort into glowering, but I'm too smug with pride.

Aside from eating the food, which so far hasn't been poisoned, I pace around the cell. I'm not used to sitting. I'm accustomed to scoping out a crowd, running through alleys, ducking between rooftops.

By the time night rolls around, I've paced every inch of my cell. Glenquartz stops by to drop off a new blanket and pillow to soften the news that Hat is probably alive but still "somewhere in Seriden."

"If I was one of your guards," I say, "and I watched a Nameless girl step forward with the crown tattoo, I might be inclined to keep ahold of the girl that the queen tried to save. Keep her as leverage. Blackmail. A hostage, even."

Glenquartz winces. He isn't thrilled with the idea that one of his guards would do something like that. But the longer it takes him to track down Hat, the bleaker things become. When he leaves, his aura teems with puzzled frustration.

As Dominic settles into place guarding my door, I use my knife from the drain to quietly slice open the pillow. It's a mixture of chunked fabric and feathers, which I distribute underneath the blanket in the shape of a body. Then I sit quietly, breathing slowly, staring at the wall.

If I made a door invisible to Esther, I can make myself invisible too.

I imagine the textures of the dungeon wall on my skin. For a while I imagine my body not as translucent, but as a mirage of dark color. I get up after a while and approach the cell bars, where Dominic faces outward. I focus all my energy and thoughts on being exactly what is around me, on not being there at all. I use my metal lockpick to tap the bar behind Dominic's head. He swivels around, bored.

I hold my breath. He looks straight through me and scans the cell, spends an extra moment glancing up at the corners of the ceiling.

I sigh with relief, and Dominic's head immediately snaps back. I cover my mouth with a hand to keep myself silent.

Dominic may not be able to see me, but he can hear me. He stares at the cell for a moment longer, his eyes resting on the pillow and blanket. His lip twitches in disgust, and he returns his attention to the tunnel. I exhale. Slowly.

It's not difficult, I tell myself. My whole life, people have looked at me and only seen the alley and the trash around me. They see my circumstances, but they don't see me. *They don't see me.* I repeat the mantra in my head.

The guards change places every three hours during the day and then every two hours at night. If they were smart, they'd check my cell in person when they traded places.

I move to the cell bars once again, but I won't be able to reach around to Dominic's inside jacket pocket for his key, so I use the metal lockpick from my pant leg and the small screw pressed with my thumb for torque. When I get the lock to turn, I leave it unlocked and closed. I withdraw to the bench and silently curl up under the blankets, reshuffling the disassembled pillow into a ball at my stomach.

It'll be another half hour before the next Royal guard comes to relieve Dominic, and when they're trading places—if I can be quiet enough—I can slip through the unlocked door, and be back in two hours at the next trade-off.

It takes everything I have not to count the seconds aloud. I haven't been inside the palace before. Patrolling corridors in darkness and solitude is how I've explored countless homes. I may be an excellent pickpocket during the day, but at night I'm a rather splendid thief. In familiar shops in the Inner Ring, I know every creak of the floorboards. Here, not so much.

When the guards change places, no one notices when I slip

out of the cell. I move slowly down the corridor. It takes a lot of concentration to make myself invisible to them. That's why, even though I want to search for Hat myself—check the docks, the holding cells, the prison, even the crematorium—I don't. I can't. Not yet.

Besides, if Glenquartz is as trusting as he seems, then he is my best chance for finding out what happened to her.

At ground level, I move from room to room furtively, and in the first few, there's nothing unusual—just a storage room filled with cabinets of fanciful dishware. The kitchen isn't too far off when I see someone in pastel-blue clothing. A Legal working late for some reason. He wears a white waistband and small white epaulets, which mean he's a servant in the palace. The Royals can put as many walls around their court as they want to, but someone has to fix the drains to the sewers, scrub the stoves, and cook their fancy meals.

I don't have much experience cooking in a proper kitchen. I've only used a stove once, really, and that was to start a fire in a house I was robbing. That was hardly my fault, though. They came home early, and a distraction became necessary. What I know of food is limited to what I see in the markets. I know what's poisonous. I know what's cheap. I know how to sell a bag of near-spoiled potatoes for full price.

Over the next hour, I move through twelve rooms in the eastern wing of the palace, searching them and building a map in my head. There are closets filled with clothing and shoes, countless sitting rooms, and some spaces that are entirely empty except for a single podium or rug. I even come across a hall with a small elevated stage in front of several clusters of pews.

I've been gone for about eighty minutes, which means I don't have much time to get back into position before the guards change again. I head to the dungeon, moving a few trinkets along the way. I snag an artist's chisel and hammer and place them on the table nearest the dungeon. Always good to know where the nearest weapons are.

I stop off in a final sitting room. If I thought I could get away with it, I'd sleep in the horsehair rocking chair. But maybe . . . I run a hand along the decorative pillows resting on the couches. I've got maybe twenty minutes left until the guards switch places.

It'll be a risk, but I can't resist.

+

"Where did you get all of these pillows?" Glenquartz demands.

I can't tell if he's amused, aghast, or frustrated, but *I'm* certainly smiling.

Throughout the rest of the night, I stole seven pillows from the sitting room. Six of them are decorative and small, and one of them is actually quite plush. I've lined the edges of the cell with them, evenly spaced like decorations. Glenquartz holds his lantern as close to the bars as he can, as if he can squeeze more light into the cell.

"They brighten the place up, don't you think?" I say proudly. "Now, is that food for *me*, or are you going to eat that yourself? Don't take this the wrong way: you don't seem like a stale-bread type of person. But I am." I gesture at the plate in his hands.

"Did . . . did one of my cadets bring them?" Glenquartz asks.

I purse my lips, considering. "That would make sense, wouldn't it? After all, I am a Nameless grifter from the streets. Odds are, I'm smarter than your guards, and I've conned them into doing my bidding. Or bribed them. Or threatened them. Though the pillows could just be hallucinations, couldn't they? I could've invented them. Do you think I did?"

I press down on one of the pillows. "It's quite soft. Hard to tell. Could be either."

I throw the pillow up in the air, and before it falls down, I concentrate on making it disappear. Glenquartz rubs his eyes in shock as the pillow vanishes before it can fall. Of course the pillow landed in my lap, but he doesn't know that.

"Now," I say, "did I make a real pillow disappear? Or was it never really there to begin with?" I frown pensively.

Glenquartz shakes his head as he slides the plate underneath the door. I bite into the bread. Not quite stale, but close.

"Have you found Hat yet?" I ask.

Glenquartz shakes his head. "Not yet. The Royal Council has been meeting almost nonstop since you arrived, trying to decide what to do about you."

"That's probably for the best," I say. "I shouldn't be the only one locked up through all of this. And now that they've verified the tattoo is real, they'll want to know why I'm Nameless as well. Was it a mistake? Do I really have a name? What is the purpose of magic, anyway?" I roll my eyes. In fairness, the questions do plague me. The tattoo can only be passed on by name, which means that somehow, I *have* to have a name. And the king knew it. Vexing.

"What do you think is going to happen?" I ask. As I speak, I make the pillows disappear one by one. The only way I know it's working is that his eyes follow the pattern around the room. I feel a bit crass testing him like this, but the alternative is spiders.

"They'll be hard-pressed to admit you're Nameless. They're scared about what it's doing to the city."

"What do you mean, 'what it's doing to the city'? *I'm* not doing anything to the city. I'm in prison, in case you forgot."

He waves his hand and hums under his breath. "They should have a decision by tomorrow, certainly."

"We should be friends, you and me," I say.

Glenquartz nearly laughs. "Friends with a grifter? Is there such a thing?"

I brush his comment off. "You're the only one who cares about Hat. We both want her to be safe. We both want to make sure I don't die down here. Need I mention our shared fondness for pillows?" I spread my arms out at my colorful collection of mostly real pillows.

Despite his obvious amusement, he appraises the pillows with a critical gaze. "I'm having your guards rotated more frequently."

I flash him a winning smile. Excellent.

Glenquartz is true to his word. He increases the guard shifts so that they change every hour instead of every three, and I hardly see the same face twice. If I was trying to build a relationship with one of them to run a con, that would make it more difficult. But I'm strictly in theft mode, and more faces means fewer people who get wise to my actions. I'm able to practice on more and more people, sneaking up on them while making them unable to see me.

By the time Glenquartz shows up the following afternoon—day three in prison—I've fished twelve oddities from the pockets of my guards. I keep the four copper coins in my pocket and a handful of writing utensils under a small pile of rocks in the corner. I've started keeping the knife hidden under my one remaining sleeve, ready to wield at any moment.

"What can I do for you, Glen-beard?" I ask.

He raises an eyebrow. "Glen-beard? Just Glen is fine." He absently runs a finger down the jawline of his crisp, graying beard. Then he does something I don't expect. He unlocks my cell door, opens it, and steps aside. He's as somber as can be, and my immediate thought is that something terrible has happened to Hat and this is his way of showing remorse.

"Not that I don't appreciate you saving me the trouble," I say, "but what's going on?"

I keep my shoulders and posture loose, but my legs are

tensed to run if he so much as utters a single word that sounds like "gallows" or "execution."

"The Royal Council has been debating since you arrived about whether to execute you or not."

I'd be running already if it wasn't for the gentle gray fog of his aura.

He gestures for me to leave the cell and he doesn't reach for his cuffs. He simply stands aside as I join him tentatively.

"And?" I ask, gripping the kitchen knife.

"They've made up their mind."

CHAPTER 6

Glenquartz leads me through the palace in the northern corridor. I've been this way before, but I make a show of looking around curiously as if I'm trying to figure things out.

"We're meeting the Royal Council in the north assembly room," Glenquartz explains. "There will be ten of us, not counting you. General Demure, head of the Royal Guard, will lead the conversation. It's not far from here."

"A left at the bronze bust and a right at the lion statue, yeah?" I say.

Glenquartz regards me skeptically. "We . . . didn't come through this way when you were escorted to the dungeon. . . ."

"Your cadets love to talk, dearest lieutenant." I get a certain kind of satisfaction from his bewilderment. Obviously, I can get to the assembly room on my own, but I can't resist flustering Glen-beard.

Now he's trying to give me a brief tour. "Here is where the second sovereign was assassinated—there's still a snowflake splinter in the green stained glass where the bloody arrow tip pierced the window. Here is where citizens who have left their cities or been exiled can petition Seriden's sovereign for citizenship. Farther along is the palace's Med Ward. Down that corridor is the kitchen, where the Legal servants work, and down this corridor is a private library."

He's so nervous that he actually points the wrong way for the kitchen, and I stop myself from correcting him.

"Your friend, Hat," Glenquartz starts. "I was able to track her down, finally."

"Where?" I almost pull to a stop.

"She's in the prison outside the city." Glenquartz twists his hands together in knots.

"Why would they take her there and not to one of the temporary holding cells inside the city?" I've been in my share of holding cells. It's where guards throw us when they want us off the streets for the night or under control but they're not willing to cart us to the prison for a permanent stay.

At first Glenquartz doesn't answer. Finally, he says, "I don't know, but the people in this room have the most power in the city—second to you, technically." He slows down as we approach a double set of wooden doors. "This is it. Now, if things end up going poorly, I'll be the one to escort you. That way, if their decision is to . . . um . . . I can help you . . ."

My heart pinches. If they sentence me to execution, he's willing to do what? Help me escape? Give me a head start before the chase begins? Give me a quick end?

I put my hand on the shoulder of his uniform, and his aura is like a bell on the edge of tolling. He fidgets.

I gesture at the door. "Shall we?"

He doesn't make a move to enter quite yet. "As long as they focus on the simplest solution, everything should be fine."

"What's the simplest solution?" I ask.

"That you aren't really Nameless," Glenquartz says almost eagerly. "That you were lost and forgotten, but you still have a name."

I wonder if it's true, or if I even want it to be true.

He continues, "Their biggest concern will be that you'll want to change the legal status of the Nameless." He fixes me with an expectant gaze.

Let's say the Nameless start working jobs and learning skilled trades. Let's say they get small houses on the outer edges of the residential quadrants. Would that be so terrible?

But I've spent my life listening to the Legals complain that the Nameless would take away jobs that the Legals struggle to keep. The Nameless would swindle their way through the markets and trade would collapse. The Royals maintain a delicate hold over the city, established by peace treaties and sustained by prejudice. The names that unite them just give them a reason to hate the Nameless.

"As of right now," I say slowly, "my concern is staying alive and finding out what happened to Hat. And I want to stop people like her from vanishing from the alleys. I mean, gaiza, there's a lot of craziness out there that no one here knows about."

Glenquartz nods as if he understands, but he doesn't. He's never had to choose between robbing a Legal woman on her way home from East Market and tiptoeing between the tails of vicious sleeping dogs to get at the butcher's latest cuts. He's never had to pretend to hate the Nameless in order to run a long con on a shipman, or stare down the endless barrel of a Royal's musket and hope to escape before the trigger is pulled.

I sigh angrily. "The dead king. Could he see the illusions he created? Could he sense his own aura?"

"Yes," Glenquartz says.

"Then here's the real problem. I *am* Nameless. I can't see my own illusions. The simple solution they want is a lie."

Glenquartz considers this. "Simple solutions often are." He grips the handle of the door now, and I feel his aura pulsating. He's torn between two worlds: one in which he opens the door and one in which the door stays closed.

The truth is heavy inside my chest. I am Nameless. Really and truly Nameless. But then how did King Fallow name me queen?

"Allow me to give you some advice," Glenquartz says. "For you. And for Hat."

"I love advice," I say. I even sometimes pay attention to it.

"They know about your talent for sensing auras and creating illusions. You can use that to your advantage. Give them the proof and comfort that they seek, but keep in mind that even though they're willing to hear you out, they can choose to kill you today."

A weight presses down on my shoulders. Suddenly I'm supposed to understand the inner workings of the Royal world. It's as if someone has handed me a watch and, instead of asking me the time, is asking me to understand how all the gears fit together.

He waits expectantly.

"The Nameless have been going missing. For months. Years, really. But more and more frequently. You're part of the Royal Guard here in the palace. Are the Royals deporting the Nameless? Killing them? Using them as slave labor? Selling them to other cities? If these people are a part of that, I need to know."

Glenquartz is troubled. "I don't know. I'm sure that the Nameless vanish all the time, but . . ." He shakes his head when he sees my sharp glare, and he winces in apology. He starts to pull the door open. "Just, please, make me a promise?"

I appraise him warily. "What?"

"Promise me that while we're in this room," he says, "you'll do your best to present yourself like a lady. Let them know that you can lead them. Don't let them disregard you."

"I'll behave as best I can," I say. "I promise."

With that the door opens, and we enter a room that is sharp and imposing. The ceiling is severe, with steep support arches that look as if they're designed more to fall and decapitate us than to support the heavy stone ceiling. At the center of the room sits a glossy wooden table. Twelve chairs surround the table, nine of them already filled. As the council members rise from their seats, a sour scent of body odor wafts and then lingers, which tells me they've spent a lot of time here over the last three days, no doubt discussing what to do with me.

As I move toward one of the empty seats, everyone watches

me with the attention of alley rats following the scent of discarded food scraps. I come to a stop behind one of the unoccupied seats, and there's a long moment when no one speaks. I stand awkwardly, wondering if they're waiting for a secret signal or handshake that will commence the meeting. After a minute, I realize everyone is waiting for *me* to take my seat.

I clear my throat and sit, trying to sense their auras. Sometimes an aura jumps out at me like an unpleasant smell or a bright light, but most of the time I have to reach for it. It doesn't take my newfound ability to sense their displeasure. Only one person is excited to be here: a man with scruffy white hair and a beard that thins to a point at his chest. I recognize one face aside from Glenquartz's: Esther Merelda Fallow sits at the far end of the table.

Esther is annoyed, her arms tight at her side as she sits with perfect posture.

Beside me, Glenquartz radiates calm energy. While I'm patient from the waist upward, my legs jitter, and I pick at my cuticles beneath the table. This could be the place—the very moment—where they decide I'm unfit to be queen.

A woman stands up, collecting everyone's attention. She's on edge, her aura as sharp as the decorative sword beneath her Royal Guard uniform, which bears crisp white-and-black decorations on the sleeves and lapel. She clearly outranks Glenquartz. She's the general of the entire Royal Guard. What did Glenquartz say the general's name was? Demure. She seems anything but.

"Good afternoon," General Demure begins. "Today we

gather to discuss our impossible heir, who I am pleased to see has joined us."

Saying that I've joined them is a bit of a stretch. There may not be handcuffs on my wrists, but that doesn't mean I'm not a prisoner. And it doesn't escape my notice that she says "our heir" instead of "the heir," as if she's claiming me as property, which, since I'm Nameless, might be how she truly thinks of me.

In my head I hear what Hat would say: *They aren't claiming you; they're including you.*

The Royal who is wearing a silver-plated pocket watch and sitting on the other side of Glenquartz speaks up. "Come now, I refuse to accept she is Nameless."

Right to business, then. I figured they'd spend a few minutes being official and introducing themselves. But as a woman speaks up next, I realize that these people are all about getting to the heart of the matter.

"She must not *be* Nameless if the late King Fallow named her the heir," the woman says. She wears a purple-and-gold bow in her hair that is encrusted with small amethysts. The bow matches her amethyst and quartz jewelry. Overall, she's mostly purple.

The Silver Watch Royal scoffs. "If she doesn't know her own name, she is as good as Nameless."

The Amethyst Royal counters, "Being Nameless and not knowing one's name are two different things."

"Is it?" General Demure says.

"She could be an impostor," Silver Watch says.

Amethyst Woman shakes her head firmly. "The test performed by Esther was conclusive. The only question is whether her loyalties belong with Seriden or with the Nameless."

An older woman decked in pearls speaks for the first time. Her voice is quiet and smooth but with an edge, like a glass feather. "My family hasn't seen the throne in seventy years, and I will not tolerate some worthless street sleeper taking power. The crown should go to someone who knows how to bear its weight. To the Vesania family." Pearl folds her hands together, and Silver Watch agrees with a slap to the table. Obviously, they are both from the Vesania family.

"Then why not the Demure family, or the Rident family, or the Otiose?" says Amethyst Woman.

I realize that I'm categorizing and remembering people based on their possessions, on what I could steal from them. Amethyst Woman, Pearl, Silver Watch.

Old habits.

It goes on like this for a while, and this is obviously the argument they've been having for the past days. But one thing they all have in common is that they never meet my eye. They're talking about me as if I'm not even here. I'm the same as I was on the streets: a shadow on the wall. I gather that this council is made up of the heads of their areas: the head commerce keeper, the general of the Royal Guard, the senior judge, and others.

The only people in the room who haven't spoken are Glenquartz and me. His facial expressions give him away. He sides with Amethyst Woman and the general, who are on the opposite side from Pearl, Silver Watch, and Esther. The rest of the room, based on their auras, is divided.

"She is a child among adults," Silver Watch says at length. "She is obviously outside her class here." He gestures snidely at my ratty, stained clothes.

"She was in the dungeon for three days, where we put her," Glenquartz clarifies, shaking a finger.

Glenquartz is a good man, I think. Maybe he even believes I can be a successful queen, or perhaps he pities me enough to defend me.

"Her loyalties are what is in question," Amethyst Woman says. "The security of Seriden is what's at stake. The Nameless have been growing more and more restless over these past years. This could be the start of a revolt. We must address the protests."

Protests. That must be what Glenquartz meant when he talked about what was happening in the city.

Silver Watch's aura sparks with interest. "You talk about her loyalties as if we don't have another option."

A swell of confusion rises through me. "What other option?" I finally break my silence. I'm not going to be invited to talk. Being patient won't win me anything.

I run my finger against the flat side of the blade pressed against my arm, keeping a smooth expression on my face even though I can feel the whole room trying to read my features for any reaction. Glenquartz places a cautioning hand on my arm. I feel a ripple of concern and kindness, like cool ocean breeze mixing with warm wind. He wants me to restrain myself. Calm down. Act like a lady.

"This"—Silver Watch looks me up and down—"*anomaly* is not the breaking of a pattern or the beginning of a new pattern. Nothing extraordinary will be tolerated, and there is a time-tried tradition for resolving this sort of inconvenience."

My nerve endings fray as he continues talking *about* me instead of *to* me.

"You think I'm extraordinary," I say, pretending to be flattered. "That's so sweet."

"That is *not* a compliment," Silver Watch stresses, pointing at me.

"Isn't it?" I say casually.

"Belrosa," Silver Watch says to the general, "will you please explain to this impossible girl that her best chance at surviving the next five and a half weeks includes that she sit quietly, keep her head down, and listen to the plan?"

I open my mouth to make a scathing retort, and Belrosa Demure holds up a white-gloved hand. "There is an event called the Assassins' Festival. Are you familiar with it?"

I grip the knife under the table and tell myself that cutting out Silver Watch's tongue wouldn't actually improve my situation. Instead I give a half-hearted shrug. I don't know much about the Assassins' Festival, only that it happens each time a new sovereign takes the throne, and there hasn't been one in my lifetime.

"The Assassins' Festival is a traditional event," Belrosa says. "In the six weeks after you acquire that tattoo, your magical abilities and the connection with your subjects will grow stronger. At the end of those six weeks, you'll be at your strongest, and you will have the ability for a single day to peacefully pass the tattoo to someone else. This is the only day you'll be able to give the tattoo away without dying. You will duel your challengers throughout the day, and if a challenger succeeds, you'll transfer the crown tattoo to them. Are we correct in assuming you have little desire to retain the tattoo?"

I don't want to nod enthusiastically or anything, but I incline my head to show that I understand. "As long as you meet a single condition, General Belrosa." I say her name carefully, trying to convey respect instead of impatience. "You may have heard the story of how I was arrested in East Market. An overzealous cadet was about to execute a child, and I stepped in to save her. What sort of authority do I have during these next weeks? I'm guessing that the city doesn't suddenly stop working in the meantime."

There's an exchange of uneasy glances in the room.

Belrosa herself hesitates. "The crowned heir does have many of the authorities that an in-power sovereign has, with a few exceptions."

"And those exceptions are . . . ?" I ask.

"You cannot pass any laws that aren't already under consideration with the judiciary," she says, indicating the man with the pointed white beard, who has remained a silent observer— the senior judge. Belrosa continues, "Nor can you broker any new trades or treaties with other cities. And you cannot travel to any other cities as an ambassador of Seriden."

I steeple my fingers together. "I didn't hear any mention of not being able to issue a pardon." I brandish a courteous smile. "I would like to issue one for the Nameless child who now sits in the prison outside Seriden's walls."

Now their auras feel like marshy mud, and no one is willing to speak first. They obviously don't like my idea.

Esther speaks up. "There are a couple of complications with that, Your Highness."

"Such as?"

Esther continues, "You cannot issue a pardon for the Nameless. They don't have rights and therefore can't be pardoned."

"But they can be imprisoned," I say. "And, apparently, they can be queen."

Elbows shift on the tabletop and people move uncomfortably in their seats, and I can sense that another argument is about to rise. Am I Nameless? Am I queen? I breathe out slowly through my nose.

I focus on a tight sensation in my chest, and I imagine steam rising from the table. For a second I'm not sure it's working, but then I hear the murmurs of confusion across the table. Then, as if I'm flexing a new muscle, I imagine tongues of silver fire with the strength of lightning, crackling in the air above the steam and arcing to the high ceiling above. I hear a couple of shocked gasps. Good. If they want proof I am queen, they have it.

"What are the other complications?" I ask as I let the steam and sparks dissipate.

Belrosa grimaces as though it pains her to share this with

me. "For a Nameless such as yourself, there are far more restrictions than the council has discussed."

"If I can have this tattoo on my arm," I say, "then explain why I can't have its power."

"The council isn't even sure how you *acquired* the tattoo," Belrosa says, and there are several words of agreement through the room. Esther glares at me as if contemplating the best way to separate my arm from my body.

"So what *can* I do?" I ask. "It sounds like that is a much shorter list."

"You can stay here in the palace," Esther says, and though I see the welcoming smile on her face, it isn't in her voice or her aura. "Lieutenant Glenquartz will act as your personal bodyguard and escort you to your sleeping quarters. You will enjoy every luxury the Royals have to offer . . . for the next five and a half weeks."

"And at that time," Belrosa says, "whether it is by peaceful council election or cession through a duel, that crown will find its proper home."

"Yes," Silver Watch says. "If the council is in consensus on who should take your place, then the Assassins' Festival will be preempted by a short ceremony to transfer the tattoo right away, and then the rest of the day's celebration will continue. The council may speak if they disagree, but I believe our top two contenders are the former heir apparent, Esther Fallow, daughter of the late king, and the next highest-ranked member of the council, General Belrosa Demure. All in favor of the heir apparent?"

About half the hands go up. Silver Watch then says, "All in favor of the general?" The other half of the hands go up.

Esther bristles, as though she expected this but still isn't pleased.

I grin. "All in favor of the Nameless thief?" I put my hand up. No one joins in. Shocker. I shrug and lower my hand.

"The festival is in less than six weeks," Silver Watch says, ignoring me. "Between now and then, anyone can sign up as a challenger for the duels, but given the split vote, I think it will probably be two duels of note: one with Esther and one with the general. The sign-up sheet will be posted outside the dining hall within the hour."

"It seems as if the only thing you agree on is that I shouldn't have the tattoo." I frown pensively. "Now. It sounds like it is in your benefit for me to go along with this plan. Believe me, I want to get rid of this tattoo as well, but"—I hold up a finger—"my request stands. For my compliance until the festival, that girl will be released from prison. Now, if you, as the council, would like to be the ones to issue the pardon, then so be it. Have the moral high ground, if you want it. But I will see that girl released, or you'll never see this tattoo again."

After a long, tense silence, everyone turns to the general. Belrosa considers it, but Silver Watch scoffs loudly, drawing the room's attention.

He's obviously gearing up to speak, so I cut him off and say, "I am the heir to Seriden's throne, like it or not. Your only question is whether I can live peacefully here in the palace or if you should stick my head on a pike outside the Royal Court."

Esther grimaces at the gruesome image.

"Yes," answers Silver Watch.

I didn't expect that. I was trying to put him off, playing to his noble disposition, but his aura is as cold as his eyes.

I'm not the only one who's surprised. Everyone is either appalled or shocked. Even Esther is nervous, as if the situation has gotten away from her. Guilt, I think. She doesn't like me, because I have her crown, but I don't think she actually wants me dead.

I wonder how many of my assumptions of her character are coming from what I see of her across the room—sitting in her chair, leaning forward with her fingers tense against the wooden table—and how much is from the aura that I struggle to distinguish in the swirl of auras in this room. Hers is fervent and quick, like the unnerved cicadas of high summer.

"Come now, you can't really mean that," Amethyst Woman objects, but he cuts her off and continues.

"Yes," Silver Watch repeats. "We are here to decide whether or not a scrawny, dirty, Nameless orphan can successfully preside over the entirety of Seriden without allowing the city to descend into chaos and riots. Where do her loyalties lie? With Seriden or with the Nameless?" He turns his sour gaze to me. "We are not in the business of doing favors for the likes of you."

I want to stuff Silver Watch's silver watch down his stupid throat, but I have to control myself or I'll prove his point. His aura teems with indignation. He wants to trip me up, catch me off guard. He's angry. My best defense is to speak calmly and turn his words against him. Let *him* be the petulant child with a temper.

Belrosa stands up before I can. Her chair screeches against the floor, regaining everyone's attention. "That is enough. We are civilized citizens of Seriden. We do not stoop to threats or insults. Corwin, you do not speak for this council. You speak for your temper alone, and I'll not have that be what drives us. Dear, your agreement and willingness to negotiate garners goodwill with us. As long as you keep your head down and attend Royal etiquette lessons—to learn our manners and customs, which will help you adjust to life here—I see no reason we can't meet your demand."

It's at this point that I realize no one knows what to call me. I've been "Your Highness" and "impossible heir." Belrosa even called me "dear." Esther and Glenquartz must not have told them I go by Coin.

"I will submit a formal request on your behalf for her release," Belrosa says. "It may take a week or so to convince the prison guards that the request is genuine and then for the request to be processed through the judiciary. During that time, you can stay here in the palace, proving you can coexist with the Royals and not cause any problems, and I'll make sure she's released. As long as you agree to pass the tattoo along peacefully during the Assassins' Festival, there is no reason your stay here should be unpleasant." She places an arm across her chest, as if a salute means anything to me.

"Agreed," I say, rising and extending my hand. I ignore the

feeling of everyone watching me as Belrosa walks around the edge of the table toward me.

She removes her white gloves as she pivots around the corner of the table, and she takes my hand and shakes it.

Then my whole body turns to fire. It's like what happened with the Royal in the market and with Glenquartz in the dungeon: I'm inside someone else's memories and thoughts. Except this time, I'm trapped. Fire and fear coil around every bone and muscle, every sinew and strand of hair.

Images flash through my mind as fast as Belrosa thinks them: a Nameless man hanging from the gallows, a Nameless woman tied with chains and thrown into the harbor, and a Nameless child having her fingers smashed with the butt of a rifle after picking the wrong pocket. Then, something worse than memories: the image of Royal guards by the legion, stomping and marching down the streets, rounding up the Nameless and shooting them with expensive rifles. Hundreds of Nameless, killed in droves.

I return to my own body, and Belrosa offers a kind smile, and even her eyes reflect the same joviality, but her hand is ash in my grasp.

That's when I lose it.

I twist her hand inward toward her body, putting pressure on the joints in her wrist with my thumb. Belrosa gasps in pain.

With a single strike, I could send her sprawling, dislocate her wrist, or snap a bone. A dark flare in my chest wants to do it, to rip her down from her pedestal.

With my only measure of restraint, I push her twisted arm up against her torso. Beneath my fingers, I feel a muscle spasm radiate through her wrist and arm. I let go, giving her one last shove. She stumbles into the jovial Royal behind her, sending them both to the floor.

"Highness!" Esther scolds, on her feet, her aura sharp with alarm.

Glenquartz's smooth, supportive aura is buried by the rising auras of shock, fear, and anger from the rest of the room. Belrosa hobbles to her feet.

Silver Watch appeals to the council members. "She is *obviously* not suited for this."

"Obviously?" I question.

"You are, as far as I'm concerned, a magical fluke and a Nameless cretin who is prone to violence," he says. "I don't know what you did to get that tattoo, but we will not sit here as an illegal Nameless takes the throne."

"So stand. Face me," I command, and he doesn't move a muscle. Silver Watch chews his lip as he considers my words.

This is all a game. A con. These are the players, the marks. They'll do anything to put me down. Silver Watch with his threats, Pearl with her snide insults, Belrosa with her cruel thoughts. At least on the streets, when someone has a problem with me, they just take a swing at my jaw. Here, everything hovers above the skin, like flies above a corpse. No punches, no swings, only a building buzz of energy.

The room waits for Silver Watch to speak, to rise or respond.

Belrosa gets to her feet, giving an apologetic gesture to the room. I almost snarl. She's pretending to *forgive* me, as if it was an accident that I shoved her to the floor.

"There's a reason you haven't killed me yet," I say. "Two, actually. One: I'm Nameless, and you have no idea what that means for magic. If I die, maybe the crown disappears forever. Maybe Seriden's magic vanishes entirely. And the second reason you haven't killed me is that I am Nameless." I pull the blade from my sleeve and stab it into the table. "Go ahead and try." If they're accustomed to polite Royals and formality, they won't get it.

I remember my promise to Glenquartz. Be a lady. Well. The general is still clutching a sprained wrist, there's a knife sticking out of the table, and everyone's gaping at me. If I can't show restraint, I'll show strength.

I square my shoulders, stand up straight, nod pleasantly to the room, and stride out through the doors just as gracefully and as ladylike as I entered.

Let *that* be their first impression of me.

CHAPTER 7

I stomp down the hall in my boots. I've made them afraid of me—which is great—but I'm terrified too. And angry.

Hurried, heavy footsteps catch up to me at an even jog. I sense who it is before I see him: Glenquartz. He matches my stride.

"Aren't you going to say anything?" I stop short and turn on him.

His leather boots squeak against the marble floor as he comes to a sharp stop. "Why would I, Your Highness?"

"Because I screwed up Royally in there." I pace the corridor. "Make a good impression, you said. Be a lady, you said. I failed on every count."

Glenquartz doesn't say anything for a while, watching me pace, and even his aura is patient. "If you don't mind my forwardness, we might need to work on how you express anger, my lady."

"I swear by everything Nameless," I say, stopping in front of him and pointing in his face, "that if you call me Highness or my lady one more spetzing time, I'm going to punch you right in your excellently bearded face." I pause, collecting myself. "And I mean that . . . in a . . . *not* violent way? Yeah, I'll work on it."

Glenquartz's grin compresses into an uneasy grimace. "At least you got them to agree to release Hat from the prison."

Her name crawls into my chest and burns. Everything in my body—the tremulous ache of my heart, the twitching of my legs—wants me to run to her. "They better. I meant what I said in there. This crown on my arm might as well be a noose around my neck. At some point, I may die because of it, but I will not let Hat die. Let me be blunt: if she becomes a martyr, I become a soldier. And I don't think the Royal Council wants a soldier as queen, do you?" I back off, realizing I've essentially just threatened him.

He blinks a couple of times, spinning a button on the cuff of his long red sleeve. "I understand. You can be scary when you want to be. You can be strong. That's good. You'll have to be strong if you're going to survive Eldritch's infamous etiquette class." He tries to give a good-natured laugh. Then, more seriously, he adds, "You will have to get along with the general if you're going to win over the council."

"You didn't see what I saw when Belrosa touched my hand," I say. "What she was thinking about the Nameless and about me! Murder by the *hundreds*. It was awful. She's awful. And she knew what she was doing. She *showed* that to me."

"Her family—the Demures—held the crown as recently as three generations ago," he says. "It stands to reason that she'd be unhappy that you have it now. She'd want to undermine you in front of the council. To all appearances, though, she was on your side. Even after what you did to her. It didn't look too bad, though. I'm sure Med Ward will patch her up."

"What am I supposed to do for nearly *six weeks*? Tell me straight. Is Hat alive? Or were you just conning me into attending that meeting?"

"What I said is true," Glenquartz says. "She's in the prison, and she's alive. I wasn't lying to you."

I take a shaky breath and lean against the wall. I point down the hall toward the assembly room. "That was terrifying." I trace a pattern on the wallpaper with an idle hand, trying to calm my heart.

Glenquartz looks at me, puzzled. "You didn't seem scared when you were talking to them."

"That's part of the grift," I say. "How you make people see you isn't necessarily how you really are." I shake my hands, loosening the tension in my body, almost laughing. Glenquartz's aura is in pieces like a puzzle—part curious, part confused, part amused. No anger or annoyance. Of all the people on the council, if I have to trust one person, it's Glenquartz.

"You're terrified, but you're laughing?" he asks.

I shrug as if it's the most normal thing in the world.

"You'll make a great queen," he says. "Now, I know you told the council you don't know how you got the tattoo. . . . Is that true?" He starts down the corridor, and I follow at a dragging pace.

"I understand this as little as anyone else," I say. "Because, believe me, if I knew why I was here, I wouldn't *be* here. If I'd had any say in this, I would've said no. But I wasn't given a vote. I was given a magical crown tattoo that gives me weird illusion and mind-reading abilities! And in the course of discovering that, I ended up in a palace dungeon, and I lost my . . ." I stop. My what? My friend? My best and only friend? My responsibility. My failure.

I don't know how to put what she is to me into words that make sense.

"Hat," Glenquartz says. "You mean your friend?"

I sigh sharply. "'Friend' isn't the right word. I don't even know what to call her. What do you call the most important person in your life? The person you promised to protect but refused to take responsibility for. And what do you call it when that person is dragged away from you in handcuffs after nearly being executed in front of you? When that person is on the edge of disappearing, and you can't do a single thing to save them?"

"I don't know," he says. "That sounds . . . difficult. Impossible, even. One of those terrible things we have to live with, where living isn't quite the same as surviving. It's heartbreaking, and painful, and . . . I guess there isn't quite a name for it." His aura prickles as he shakes off his own painful memories.

I scoff. "How poetic. Everything about us is Nameless, even our tragedies."

✦

I consider it a dazzling success that I haven't been killed yet. As Glenquartz leads me through the palace, we're quiet. Exhaustion sets in, my feet dragging and head clouding with fog. He opens a set of burnished red doors, revealing an extravagant room. All the drapes are orange and gold, making the room seem bright even though the only light comes from the oil lamps in the hall.

"These are the guest sleeping quarters," Glenquartz explains, "where we house foreign dignitaries, queens, kings, and ambassadors when they visit. It should suit you."

Six ample beds are separated by individual wardrobes and bedside tables with oil lanterns. There is a trunk at the foot of each bed, presumably for storing travel items and clothes, but they definitely look big enough to hold a body. The beds all have comforters with gold-thread embroidered designs. I choose the bed that has a design of constellations and rests beneath a skylight.

Glenquartz is still standing in the doorway as if he isn't allowed to enter, and he points up at the skylight. "If it gets too hot, you can open it."

I wave my hand dismissively as though I'm not concerned about the heat, when I know full well that he has just pointed me to my best avenue of escape.

Framed drawings of Seriden cover the walls. Hanging in the middle is a document. I can't read it, but the page is filled with small blocky letters surrounded by a series of handwritten squiggles.

"What's this?" I ask, picking my way between the beds to get a closer look.

"That is a copy of the City-State Peace Treaties," Glenquartz says proudly. "It outlines the trade agreements and alliances between Seriden and the other cities. The border holds the signatures of the original fourteen sovereigns."

I'm impressed. "Of course they'd hang it here in the guest quarters to remind foreign officials of their pacts. Clever. I appreciate a well-framed manipulation." I hold my hands up in a frame shape, studying how the diagrams of the city surround and support the treaty.

Glenquartz regards the treaty apprehensively, as if he hasn't considered it before.

I remove my jacket and set it on the bedside table. The surface of the table is polished and dusted, but the lantern's wick is hardened, and there's a layer of dust on the curved glass. The room has been maintained, but no one has used it recently.

"When's the last time anyone stayed here?" I ask.

"It has been a while," Glenquartz says. "King Fallow was dealing with some political . . . difficulties. We haven't hosted our neighbors in quite some time."

I observe the five empty beds. Hat would love it here. I inhale the dust of unfamiliar fabric, trying to summon the scent of cinnamon and salt, dirt and sweat.

I throw a half glance at Glenquartz. He's watching me.

"How exactly do I get to the prison?" I ask. "It's one of the only buildings outside the city, right? It's to the west, but then what? North? South? It has to be close by."

Suddenly I wish I'd paid attention to all the times that a Nameless was dragged off to prison. Mostly, I was busy getting as far away as I could.

"I can't think of any reason you'd want to know that," Glenquartz says, entering the room and fiddling with the lantern on the nearest table, "unless you were planning on going there.

The prison is no place for the queen. The guards stationed there are not kind toward the Nameless, but I do have one friend who has agreed to watch over Hat as best she can. I wouldn't be able to guarantee your safety if you went to the prison, let alone Hat's. General Belrosa has agreed in front of the council to issue a command for her release."

"Not a command. A request. She promised to *ask* for Hat to be released," I say. "I need *you* to make sure they actually do it."

Glenquartz agrees. "Of course, my lady."

"Call me Coin," I say with an incline of my head.

"Coin." He says my name gently, almost reverently. "I'll do everything in my power. Just remember that even though you do have some leverage as the heir, you'll have to make concessions to the council and fulfill your role until the Assassins' Festival."

I sit on the foot of a bed. I peel off my outer green shirt with its torn sleeve to reveal a short-sleeved, once-white shirt. It has a few torn ruffles—it was once a dress shirt belonging to a Legal—and a few huge streaks of black. To prevent the Nameless from filching discarded clothes and pretending to be Legals, a lot of people either burn their old clothes or stain them with black dye.

Glenquartz blushes and busies himself organizing a stack of books, looking anywhere but at my face.

"Such a gentleman," I say. "Do I offend your modesty? So, why do they call it the Assassins' Festival, anyway? That doesn't sound very good. Not for me, anyway."

"The Assassins' Festival used to be a weeklong festival, but now it's only a day," he explains. "Throughout the day, you duel the highest-ranked challengers. Like the council explained, if any of them wins, you pass the tattoo to them willingly."

"Then why don't they call it the *Dueling* Festival?" I say, glaring at him.

His lips pinch together. "Historically, the duels were to the death, and a lot of times the sovereign was assassinated before the duels could be completed."

"When's the last time a sovereign was assassinated?" I ask.

"Four generations ago, I think," Glenquartz says. "Fallow got the crown from his parents, who got it from the Demure family. Three generations would've been the longest time the crown has been in one family. I mean, until now." He catches himself and winces apologetically, as if I'm supposed to feel bad for breaking their streak. I sigh in frustration.

"It wasn't me who named me queen," I say. "Now. Where's the bath? Two nights is a long time to spend in a dungeon, and I don't think you're standing that far away just because of my temperament."

Glenquartz points to the water closet, and I'm already halfway to it when he adds, "There are some clothes in the wardrobes, and it's a shower, not just a tub."

"It's a what?" I say, and my mouth drops open. I stop with one foot inside the doorway.

"A shower," he repeats sagely.

Running water is common throughout Seriden, and most houses have it now—but it's usually only installed in two

places: a sink for the kitchen and the toilet with a complicated high reservoir and chain. When someone wants to take a
bath, they cart water in from the kitchen after boiling it on the
stove.

"Here at the palace, the water is heated," Glenquartz says.

"Seriously?"

Glenquartz's eyes light up when he sees what must be the
biggest smile I've ever smiled. "Would you like me to show you
how it works?"

I dash into the room, and he totters in after me. Though
the controls aren't complicated—a valve for the water and a
chain for the drain—he enjoys teaching me. He fiddles with
the controls, and when he turns around, I've already changed
out of my clothes and I'm wrapped up in a towel. He bursts
out laughing and slips, catching himself on the edge of the tub
before he can fall over.

"You sure work fast," he says.

I grin. "Now, Glenquartz, I say this with the utmost care . . ."

"I'll be outside," he says, and he's barely containing his
laughter.

+

The next morning, I wake up on the floor. At some point during the night, the bed was too soft and hot, so I dragged a layer
of blankets to the floor and curled up between two of the beds.
I lift myself onto the edge of a bed, stretching and enjoying
the fact that my fingers and toes aren't stiff from the cold or

from clutching a weapon. I yawn lazily and realize that what woke me up was the sound of approaching footsteps. The door handle twists.

"Wait!" I shout, but it's too late.

The door opens, and a small glass bowl falls and shatters. Glenquartz pauses, halfway into the room. He inspects the graveyard of glass shards and twine.

"What's this?" he asks.

I slap a hand to my forehead. "An alarm." I slide to the edge of the bed. "The glass bowl was netted with twine and looped over the door handle. Open the door, and the glass falls."

"Clever," he says, swallowing uneasily. "You're an early riser." He steps carefully inside, boots crunching the glass.

"Got to be," I say, "if I want to get to the markets early to scope out marks."

Glenquartz shifts uncomfortably, and Esther enters the room behind him. She glares distastefully at the glass on the floor.

"An irreplaceable, hand-blown vase from the city of Tuvo," Esther says, appraising the damage. "But as long as you got to sleep soundly . . ." She sucks at her teeth and turns her glare on me.

I nod, rising to my feet, doing a smooth curtsy in the bedclothes I scavenged from a wardrobe last night.

"Can I help you?" I ask in a too-sweet voice.

"Today will be your first time meeting the Royals en masse," Esther says, "and your first etiquette lesson with Eldritch Weathers is tomorrow. I've brought you some proper clothing. If anything doesn't fit, the tailor will pay you a visit sometime in the next few days." She sets down an armful of brightly colored clothes. From the pile, she picks up a vibrant red bundle.

A small, displeased sigh escapes her lips as she surveys me as if I'm a dusty bag of rice for sale at West Market. I feel an old impulse, like a prodding weight at my back, telling me to simply walk out and leave.

Esther unfurls the bundle with an overzealous flourish. It's a dress.

I give it my darkest glare. *Hell, no.*

Despite my profuse complaints, within ten minutes I'm more offensively bright than a red flame.

"This isn't a dress. It's a blanket with sleeves." I hold up the excess of crimson fabric that hangs at my ankles.

"This dress is worth one of the sloops in the harbor," Esther says as I tie the sash at my waist.

I deadpan, "Okay, it's an *expensive* blanket with sleeves."

Esther's thick eyelashes flutter as she resists rolling her eyes at me. "You could at least try for a little decorum. You could even try for some grace and strength, if you liked."

Her words sound suspiciously like advice hidden inside an insult. I want to play this game like the grifter I am, but I can't seem to hold my tongue around her. I don't know if it's because she's exactly what I expected of all of the snooty Royals or because she's so immediately judgmental of me.

I give the dress a more careful inspection. Before today, the only thought I gave to clothing was whether it was warm, durable, and had enough pockets. Now, as I examine the fabric, I wonder for the first time what it would be like to feel beautiful. I suppose that, before now, I've never been brave enough to really try.

The broad neckline slopes down around the shoulders, and small shimmering beads cover the bodice. It doesn't have a single pocket. Esther adjusts the fabric around my waist, carefully avoiding touching my skin. I thought the Nameless had a healthy sense of immodesty, but Esther didn't even blink as she banished Glenquartz from the room and hurried me out of my my bedclothes and into this dress.

The streets. I'm surprised to find I miss them already. Back in the market, I pulled on a Legal coat to try to save Hat. As soon as the pale fabric covered my skin, I was different. Walking strong, standing tall, on equal ground with everyone I passed. Will it be as easy to put on this dress and become a Royal?

I smooth the red fabric, turning to Esther. Her gaze starts on my hair with a slight frown. A smile tugs at her lips as she observes the dress, but when she gets to my ankles, she frowns again.

"I guess there's not much we can do about the shoes for now," she says. "I'll have to put a call out for a cobbler to visit you."

"These are *boots,* not shoes," I say defensively. "There's a difference. Maybe I could just make you hallucinate that I'm wearing fancy shoes. That'd work, right?"

"As if you have enough focus and strength to maintain such an illusion," Esther says with a drawn-out sigh. She spins me like a doll and tugs on the sleeves, which fall short above the tattoo. Then she pulls tight the tie around the waist, and suddenly the dress fits *too* well. "I wish the crimson was a bit brighter," Esther says. "With your skin tone, you really are suited for bold colors."

I can tell she pities me. And while I want nothing more than to be prideful and turn down her help, I have a lot of experience weighing pride in my hands. Do I want pride, or do I want to eat? Do I want pride, or a safe place to sleep? Do I want pride, or do I want to escape the guards chasing me?

Surprisingly, pride doesn't win very often. That's how I've ended up eating mold, being the monster in a small child's closet, and half covered in fish guts—respectively, of course.

Esther hands me a smaller bundle of clothes, and I pick through them, a faint blush rising to my cheeks when I realize what they are.

"How many pairs of undergarments do I need?" I say.

Esther stammers, "You . . . A lot." I can tell she's coming to the realization that this, too, is a luxury the Nameless are not afforded. "Every time you take a shower, you put on a whole new set of clean clothes. Every day is best."

I frown. "Are you saying I'm supposed to bathe more than once a season?"

She squints. "You're joking, right?"

I break out in a sly grin. "You're quick. Well, you're clever at least. We can work on quickness later." I push the clothing to the side.

Esther is not as amused by my quips as Glenquartz is.

"I'm sure this is more than sufficient," Esther says. One last look over and she sighs. "That is the best we can do, I suppose."

Squaring my shoulders, I stand straight and tall. Be Royal, be confident. Esther opens the doors to the corridor to let Glenquartz back into the room. She turns around and does a double take when she sees my posture.

I bet she wasn't expecting me to act the part. I need to find a balance between independent and obedient. If I can't trust my temper to stay in check, I need to decide when to use it to show strength. For now, I need to show her I can stand tall and walk gracefully. I clasp my hands delicately in front of me.

Glenquartz reenters the room and has a delightful look of surprise when he sees the dress.

"I'll see you at dinner tonight." Esther offers an imitation of a curtsy, and I suppose I have to give her credit for making a show of being respectful.

"Did you learn anything?" I ask as she walks away.

"Pardon?" she says, pausing in the doorway.

I point to the clothes and dress. "Certainly this is something that would be managed by a servant of some kind. You wanted to come to size me up. Both literally and figuratively. So. Did you learn anything?"

She glares at me. "You're quick. And clever." She disappears into the corridor, and even though her words were phrased like compliments, they linger in the air with the sharp sting of insults.

I sigh dramatically and look forlornly at Glenquartz. "I don't think Esther wants to be my friend."

He chuckles. "I think you're probably right about that."

In the hours until lunch, I do my best to create the illusion of dress shoes instead of my boots. Glenquartz commends me on them, but I can barely make it thirty minutes at a time before the illusion falters. Esther was right—sustaining an illusion requires constant focus, but it also requires mental energy. By the time we adjourn to the dining hall for dinner, my mind is weary. I pause outside the door to gather my thoughts, and I find a corkboard hanging beside it. On it there are four pieces of paper pinned up. They're filled with different-sized scribbles and lines.

"What's this?" I ask.

"Ah, it's the list of people who've signed up so far to duel you at the Assassins' Festival," Glenquartz says. "It's more ceremonial than anything else. If you cede to Esther or Belrosa, you won't have to worry about the remaining duels. Take a look, if you like. I see Belrosa's name on it already—no surprise there. Doesn't look like Esther has signed up yet, though."

I regard the list of names. There are at least twenty of them. I retreat to the table across the corridor to untie and retie my boots.

"What, not interested?" he says, teasing, but he stops when he sees my annoyance. He puts an apologetic hand on my shoulder.

Burned, I step away from his touch. "I can't *read*."

"Oh." His hand hovers for a moment before falling to his side.

In his Royal world, I'm sure learning to read is as natural as studying which silverware to use and how to dance.

"The Nameless aren't *taught* to read," Glenquartz says.

My shoulders tense. "Thanks for reminding me."

"No," Glenquartz says, wincing. "What I meant is that it's not your fault."

"I could have learned if I wanted to," I admit, my shoulders slumping. "If it really mattered to me, I could have found someone to teach me." What I don't say weighs more heavily: that trying to learn to read was like deciphering planets from flickering stars. I gave up long ago.

"You're still so young," Glenquartz consoles me. "You have time to learn if you want to. You're only . . ." He trails off when he realizes he doesn't remember how old I am.

"Seventeen, if it's up to me," I say. "But in truth . . . I don't know." I cross my arms. It's never really bothered me before that I don't know these few and vital things about myself. I created truths as I needed them. But now these things matter, and I have to look at the facts and realize I'm a stranger in my own life.

I approach the dining-hall door again and place a hand on it, running a finger along the polished grain.

"You know," I say softly, "before now it didn't bother me that I can't read, that I don't have good posture, or that I don't know how to make a good first impression."

Glenquartz stands beside me, letting me speak.

"I don't have proper clothing, I've spent my life stealing, and I don't know how to be around cruel people without punching them. I mean, I don't know if those things *bother* me, but I've never had to worry about them before." On the other side of the door, there is an entire room filled with people bustling, feasting, and socializing.

"If I could walk through these doors and, I don't know . . . just *be* one of them . . ." I curl my fingers into a fist, the smooth wood leaving traces of oily polish on my skin. I let my fist fall to my side. I relax.

Glenquartz is staring at the door as pensively as I am.

"I served King Fallow for nearly my entire life," Glenquartz says, "and my family has served the sovereigns of Scriden for generations. I'm not going to say that learning how to interact with the Royals isn't important, because I know it is. But King Fallow wouldn't have named you queen without a reason. You're concerned about being different from all of the people in that room. Don't be. You're not meant to be their friend or their equal. You're meant to lead them."

I scoff. "I'm meant to keep my head down and not cause trouble for the next five and a half weeks. What do I know about leading people?"

"From what I've seen so far," Glenquartz says, "you're pretty good at telling people what to do."

I pout playfully. "Are you calling me bossy, *Glen-beard*?"

He puts a hand to his chest, feigning offense. "Me? Would I say that, *my lady*?"

Still, I hesitate, staring at the door as if I can see through it.

"Of all the people in this city," Glenquartz says, "I think there is at least one person who doesn't care how tall you stand or how bad your manners are. Or how bossy you are. I'm guessing that's the person you care about most?"

Hat. My chin turns up with pride.

"I'll make sure the request for her release is sent as soon as possible," he says.

"Shall we?" I say, but even I can hear the reluctance—the *fear*—in my voice.

Glenquartz opens the door for me, then stands to the side to let me go first.

With fear and bravery in equal balance, I square my shoulders, and I enter.

—✦—

No one tries to assassinate me during dinner, but that doesn't mean they're not thinking about it. On my path through the dining hall, several people touch me before I can sidestep them. If they hold on for more than a second or two, I feel a tidal surge of memories and images. From some people I see the last time they saw the king or the first time they saw me in a corridor. I see hands wrapped around my throat, poison-dipped food slipped onto my tray, and—most creative of all— a spring-loaded blade propped under my pillow. None of the images, though, are as hate-filled or horrible as the thoughts Belrosa pushed on me yesterday during the meeting with the council.

Needless to say, when I take my seat at the high table,

everyone's watching me. It doesn't help that the table has eight empty cushioned chairs and that the entire setup is on an elevated platform—quite literally a stage. After seeing several imaginings of my death, all I want to do is lock myself in a quiet room. I miss the dungeon. As the Legal servants bring out trays of food, all I can think about is what might be poisoned. Glenquartz takes a seat beside me as the food is brought out, and it doesn't *smell* poisoned. It smells fantastic. Even though fresh fish is common in a coastal city, I've only had it a couple of times, and the breading and spices make my mouth water.

But when dinner is placed before us, Glenquartz makes a point of slowly switching food with me over the course of the meal. It's one excuse or another to trade with me: His is too spicy; green vegetables don't agree with him; I just *have* to try the coffee cake. He thinks he's being subtle, but I'm not fooled. I am impressed, though. Everyone in the room sees Glenquartz trying my food before me. If anyone wants to poison me, they have to go through him. My bodyguard indeed. And while people's auras stiffen or sharpen in my presence, they are kind and soft in his.

When the meal is done, I watch a group of Legal servants prepare silver trays of food for the Royals to take with them to their rooms in the palace or to their homes out in the court. I watch a boy—a couple of years younger than me, in a Legal servant's uniform—sort through the dessert table, cleaning a splash of raspberry liquor, wiping crumbs from a tray of small cakes. When I see him swipe a piece of cake, wrap it in a cloth, and tuck it in his pocket, it piques my interest. When genuine kindness lingers in his smile after he meets someone's gaze, I slip through the thinning crowd and join him at the table.

"It must be difficult," I say to him, "serving the Royals like this, working in this fancy world that you don't quite belong in."

The boy assesses the red Royal dress I'm wearing. He must figure me for the daughter of a Royal family.

"Could be," he says in a polite tone, but he does a double take when he sees the crown tattoo on my arm. His aura spikes silver with fear.

"Your Highness!" He does a clumsy bow and looks me up and down before adding, "You're . . . Is it true that you're Nameless?"

I sigh serenely as if this is my favorite question to answer in the world.

He hurries to regain ground. "If you'd like to take some food with you, I can prepare a tray, or I can leave word with the kitchen staff to have something sent to your room." His whole body is angled to keep his stolen cake a secret. He is not a good thief. Not yet, anyway.

I shake my head. "That's not what I want. I want to *do* something while I'm here," I say. "I've got . . . a little over five weeks? Until the Assassins' Festival. I can't solve every problem, but maybe I can help with just one. At least one." I reach around him for a piece of fruit, but instead I pluck the cake from his pocket. I set it in front of him, and his cheeks turn scarlet.

"It's for my little brother," he says. "My family can't afford to . . . We don't have cake like this out in the North Residences."

His shoulder is pinned up in a shrug, and he takes the cake when I nudge it toward him with a conspiratorial wink.

"If I give you a place and a name, will you be able to divert some of the food being prepared out into the city? Not so much that it goes noticed, but *something*. Since you live in the Legal residences, it could very well be on your way. Queen-sanctioned theft, what do you say?"

He chews his lip. "For who? To where?" He doesn't say no.

"For people who are starving. The Nameless."

He stares at the food for a while. "Yeah." Then, excited: "Yeah! Where do you want it taken? How do we do this?"

"First you have to get a lot better at stealing," I say.

It doesn't take long to talk him through the basics, and I make a show of picking at a tray of skewered vegetables while we talk so that no one finds our discussion suspicious. I describe the part of the Inner Ring that Devil frequents, and when I give him her name, he scrunches his nose in confusion. I reassure him that, yes, Devil is the right name. Yes, she's a woman. Yes, I'm sure.

If I had a silver ring for every time a Legal or Royal looked at me funny upon hearing one of the strange names of the Nameless, I'd have enough to buy a house in the North Residences.

The Legal writes down the details on a pad of paper from his apron pocket. He keeps agreeing enthusiastically.

"This is good. Confusing, but good," he says.

"If you think Devil is a confusing name, there's a man who lives near the docks called Narms. It's because he has no arms and a habit of slurring his words."

"No, I meant confusing in a good way. It's good to have a sovereign who cares about people outside the Royal class, about both the Legals and the Nameless. We've never really had that in a sovereign before." He adjusts the straps of his apron. "I mean, I've heard that in the past, if a Legal got the crown, things would get better for a little while—lower taxes, fairer laws—but *you*. You're something different."

"Check with me tomorrow morning," I say. "I want to know they got it safely."

"I'll bring you some breakfast," he says, delighted. "Any special requests?"

I shrug, not wanting to feel as if I'm taking advantage of his goodwill. "Something with a lot of protein, but be careful not to tell anyone you're preparing my meal. I'm sure I have no shortage of enemies here."

"You can count me among your allies," he says. "And once the other Legal servants hear of this, you can count them among your allies too."

"If you can keep this between us," I say, "the fewer people who know, the better. I don't think the council would take too kindly to our actions."

"Well," he says, "I take kindly to it, and so will your friends out there." He stows his pad in his apron and hurries off with a tray of leftover food.

I watch him go, wondering what he must think of me. He assumes they're my friends, the Nameless out on the streets. I trust Devil with this, but I wouldn't quite call us friends. She may keep some of the better food for herself and sell it to those who can afford it, and she plays at being a hardened smuggler and fence, but she's as soft as the pillows I left in the dungeon. She'll get it in the hands of those who need it most.

I return to the guest quarters for the rest of the evening. I'm sapped of energy, and it's all I can do to sit still when the tailor visits with his measuring tape. I threaten his fingers when he comes too close to my boots, but he manages to take my measurements anyway. The next morning, the Legal servant brings a meal of strips of beef alongside slices of gravy-soaked bread, and I'm in heaven.

Glenquartz outlines a day of tours through the palace, and he promises to have news of Hat's release within a week. I half suspect it's a ploy to put me in front of more Royals. Mostly, we pass undisturbed. Occasionally, someone wants to shake my hand, and I have to take a moment to brace myself for whatever images or imaginings are coursing through their mind. Two people dodge me entirely, ducking into rooms to avoid me, their auras sharp and clear with fear and disdain. As much as I want to be frustrated that there are people literally running away from me, I have as little interest in interacting with them as they do with me.

It's as if I'm a disease they can catch. If they get too close to me, they'll be stripped of their titles and names, and cast down from their towers. Fools.

I count the days.

CHAPTER 8

It's been a week since I asked the Royal Council and General Belrosa Demure to intercede with Hat, and I've finally settled on a proper definition of hell. Hell is sitting in an etiquette class with a prim and proper teacher named Eldritch Weathers, and dear old Eldritch, with his rich aura as smooth as purple velvet, is lecturing me on the difference between posture and poise (apparently they're not the same thing), and all I can think about is Hat slumped in a cell; and then he's describing the types of food you shouldn't eat in public, and I know Hat is probably starving right now; and then he argues for the twentieth time that I should wear proper ladies' shoes instead of my boots, and all I can think is that Hat won't be wearing shoes in the prison—the floor at night will be cold.

On and on like this for days. And every day, in between lessons with Eldritch, I meet with new Royals. I learn their names, but the only thing I can vaguely remember is the blur of their auras. Every day, someone wants my response to whatever is happening out in the city. Someone wants to know if I really do have a name and I'm only pretending for some inane sense of drama.

Eldritch isn't unpleasant, but he isn't patient. Part of me wants to meet his every challenge, the same way I once met the challenges issued by Marcher. Pickpocket a Royal, rob a dock shipment, dress out of class, spend a week clearing out the attic of a wealthy Legal. I have experience with people like Eldritch, and I have one advantage over him. I'm less pleasant and even more patient.

Plus, I'm his queen, more or less.

Eldritch has seen enough of my snarky behavior and anger to suspect I have no interest in learning, but he's wrong about that. As a grifter, I make my way conning people, which means I study people and learn to imitate them. They've assigned me etiquette lessons as if they're a punishment or a challenge I won't meet, when in fact they're equipping me with the tools I would have acquired anyway by observing Royals at dinners and lunches. I'm a quick learner, but I have no interest in letting Eldritch know that.

"Are you perhaps not capable of sitting up straight?" Eldritch asks as we sit at a formal dinner setting, discussing wine-serving ceremonies and the proper use of cutlery. According to Eldritch, wine is for ceremony and celebration, not everyday consumption. And cutlery is for eating food and definitely never ever for threatening the well-liked daughter of a recently deceased king. If nothing else, I'm glad stories of my resourcefulness have circulated.

After I've sat through the first two courses of a pretend formal dinner, he has added to his list of displeasures. "Are you perhaps not capable of holding a knife correctly? Are you perhaps not capable of maintaining eye contact? Are you perhaps not capable of holding a cordial conversation?"

"I am perfectly capable," I say, sitting with slumped posture. "I am *perhaps* not *patient* enough. You know what these lessons are missing?"

"A dedicated student?" Eldritch offers gently, a pencil jutting out from behind his ear as he straightens the pocket square in his formal jacket.

I grit my teeth. Nothing's worse than someone stealing the punch line of your sarcastic quip.

"In fact, yes," I say. I grab my thin white shawl from the curving arm of the ornately carved wooden chair, wrap it around my shoulders, and head for the door.

"If you cannot tolerate me," Eldritch says in a lofty tone, "how do you ever expect to tolerate the Royal class as a whole?"

I pause at the door. I don't know whether he's insulting himself, insulting the Royals, or insulting me. I try not to care.

I'm about to leave, when I sense an aura approach on the other side of the door. Angrily, I pull it open, ready to push past the visitor and stalk the corridors. Seven days I've been coming to these lessons. I've learned a lot from Eldritch in that time, but I'm too angry to be anything but stubborn. When I open the door, Esther is standing there in a sterling blue blouse and long black slacks.

Eldritch rises to his feet. "Ah, good, I heard you'd be joining us today."

Esther skirts around me. "The Royal Council has been

receiving updates from Eldritch, and they thought my presence might spur some improvement in you, since we don't have months to train you. If you would sit, we can continue the lesson."

I plop down in my chair with overly exaggerated obedience.

She rolls her eyes. "You know that's not what I meant."

"Wait, are you telling me there's a difference between the letter of the law and the spirit?" I say. "Oh dear, I think I've been exploiting laws incorrectly all this time."

She opens her mouth to retort, but Eldritch cuts in and says, "A thing to learn—which Esther herself is still learning—is that when conflict presents itself, the appropriate and regal thing to do is keep your head, keep your temper, and keep control."

Part of what he's saying is correct. If you stay calm and collected during a fight, you have the advantage. But the detail he's missing is that my version of calm and collected doesn't match Esther's. I calmly and collectedly drive everyone to frustration. Or, if tempers rise, I calmly and collectedly punch someone in the face. It's about context, really.

"I think this will go splendidly," Eldritch says. For a moment I'm annoyed at his sarcasm, but then I realize he's being sincere, which is worse.

Eldritch starts guiding us on how to have a conversation during a meal—the biggest tip is to avoid talking while food is still in your mouth.

On the list of things I didn't want to learn: the seventeen different types of cups arranged on the side table, and the myriad ways you should and shouldn't hold each one.

At some point we start going through an entire, rehearsed seven-course dinner. First a dry wine coupled with a discussion of how to hold the stem of the wineglass. Then some kind of small, layered bread-and-meat snack, drizzled with oil, coupled with a discussion on how to handle crumbs and coughing. Then, through the next three courses, various vegetables and proteins with countless notes about silverware and hand placement. Despite the delicious food, it's tiresome.

As we wrap up the sixth course, a lobster bisque, I'm pushing the spoon around the bowl and thinking of Hat. I've eaten past the point of hunger, which is something I'm so unaccustomed to doing that I feel sick.

As Eldritch compliments Esther on her excellent posture, I work on balancing a kitchen knife across the rim of my wineglass. When Eldritch departs to see why the dessert course hasn't been delivered yet, Esther turns to me. She slams her own silverware to the table in frustration when she sees what I'm doing.

"I don't know how you expect to learn when you treat everything like a mockery," Esther says, pointing at my wineglass. "Not because you can't do it, but because you don't care enough to try." She shakes her head. "I'd love to be an advocate for you, because you're alone here and could use the help. And the way we treat the Nameless population is one of the longest-standing shames shared across all the cities. But you? As a representative of all of Seriden's Nameless, you're not making it easy."

I stare her down for a moment before straightening in my chair and picking up the flute of sweet wine. I hold it delicately.

"If you don't mind, Ambassador," I say coyly, "I know we've barely started the ground-spice meringue, but we really must talk about the import tax your city has levied against the pre-defined trade goods. And might I suggest a white sapling-shade wine to pair with the meringue? It's absolutely perfect for soothing the heat of the Lindragore ground-spice."

Esther is slack-jawed for a moment.

"I think the napkin has fallen off your lap, dear," I say. "You should pick it up off the floor, along with your jaw."

"How did . . . You've been paying attention this whole time." Esther frowns. "Then why do you act so crass? Why not allow Eldritch to pass on good news of your etiquette training? It's like you have no appreciation for the opportunity you've been given!"

I feel my face grow hot and—annoyingly—I hear Eldritch's voice in my head. *Be calm and collected.* Yet the smile on my face disappears.

"The *opportunity* I've been *given*?" I repeat slowly, my anger building. I set the flute down. "What do you think this is to me?" I point to the crown tattoo on my arm.

"*That* is the highest privilege of Seriden!" she says. "It is *power,* and you treat it like it's gaudy jewelry to be stolen and sold!"

I let out a slow breath. Calm and collected. Calm. Collected. "You think this is a privilege for me? Maybe for you it would be. Gaiza, if you had this crown, your life would be perfect now. You think this is a chance to save Seriden. You think it's a gift! That I should be proud. My only friend is in prison right now. She was nearly executed, and to save her, I gave myself up and got locked in your dungeon for three days. This tattoo is going to get me killed. It's not power—not for someone like me. It's not jewelry. It's a shackle. You want me to take this seriously? You want me to act like the queen you think I'm allowed to be? I'll start doing that the moment you tell me how having this tattoo on my arm is going to do anything but get me and my friend killed." I hunch over the table angrily. To her credit, she doesn't say anything.

She reclines in her chair and stares pensively at the wall. I know I've given her something to think about, but I don't know what she *actually* thinks. I reach out to sense her aura, but it's constantly shifting and unsettled. Eldritch finally returns with a silver tray in his arms, but neither of us makes a move to correct our posture.

When Eldritch sees my knife still balanced on the wine-glass, he sighs. "Are you perhaps incapable of—"

"I am more than capable!" I shout, slamming my hand on the table. The knife falls from the rim of the glass and clatters onto my plate. As it settles, I say more politely, "But that's not what this is all about, is it? These etiquette lessons. The Assassins' Festival. It's not about proving I'm capable of being queen. It's about proving who I am and who I'm not. I am Nameless. I am not a Royal. And that makes everyone nervous."

Eldritch doesn't seem the least bit offended by my outburst.

I imagine he's seen his fair share of outbursts over the years. He sets the silver tray down, and I let out a long, slow breath.

Esther asks pleasantly, "What is it that you've been so kind to grace us with, dear Eldritch?"

He gives us a knowing look. "If not manners, then dessert."

Underneath the tray is a toasted, braided pastry. Scents of cinnamon and sugar waft upward. Delight fills Esther's face and she seems to forget or forgive our dispute now that there's a sugary dessert involved.

Eldritch places a pastry on Esther's plate and one on mine. I couldn't possibly eat anything else, but it does smell fantastic.

Eldritch gestures to the remaining pastry before him. "This dessert is called the weaver's basket, so named because of the braided dough. Often it is served inverted and filled with fruit. Looks like the kitchen sprinkled some extra sugar on top. Perfection!"

I think about my visits to the dining hall over the past week. There was a tray of these, presented in a similar fashion, but the sugar was sprinkled on in a spiral.

Esther selects a puny fork and knife and starts carefully cutting off one of the woven strands of bread. I lean down and carefully smell the pastry.

Eldritch nods as if I'm appreciating the cinnamon scent. I lick the tip of my finger and touch it to the sugar. When I touch the white powder to my tongue, an overwhelmingly sweet taste strikes me. I immediately spit it out onto the floor. For good measure, I rinse my mouth with the sweet white wine.

Eldritch gasps as though I've insulted his firstborn child.

"My lady!" Eldritch shouts.

"Put that down immediately," I say, pointing at Esther's fork. "It's poison."

"It's *what*?" Esther says with an incredulous laugh.

Annoyed, I focus on the fork in her hand and the one in Eldritch's. I imagine their forks turning into snakes.

Esther shouts in fear, dropping her fork like it has bitten her, and Eldritch throws his to the floor.

"It's salite poison," I clarify, letting the illusion of reptilian cutlery disappear. "It comes in two forms, and one of them is a very sweet white powder that's deadly if you ingest it." I point at what we all thought was powdered sugar on the dessert.

Eldritch jumps up, aghast, and Esther pushes back from the table with a screech of her chair. I check their desserts as well, confirming the presence of the overly smooth salite powder.

"Congratulations," I say. "You just survived an assassination attempt."

They gape in horror at me.

"What?" I say. "You should be happy. You don't seem happy. I did say *survived*, didn't I?"

They exchange glances, and Eldritch sits down.

I continue, "The poison is a bummer, though, because I really wanted to try this dessert. Well . . . I mean . . . since the poison is on the top, I *could* come at it from the bottom." I tilt the dessert.

Esther's lids drop to half-mast, and she glares at me.

"No, you're right. You're right. Bad idea. Definitely not worth it." I set the weaver's basket onto its plate.

Esther points at the dessert. "I should speak with the Royal Council immediately. They need to know."

"Know what?" I scoff. "That someone isn't patient enough to wait until the Assassins' Festival? Remember, it's not illegal for anyone to kill me."

"They can't just do that, though," she says. "They can't just kill you. It would upset the balance of everything in our city, and magic is too fragile after what we've done to it."

I cock my head to the side. "What you do mean, 'after what we've done to it'?" I know I've caught her off guard, but she adjusts her features to a professional calm.

"The tattoos were used to bind magic to the fourteen sovereigns all those years ago. . . . Magic was free once, and now it's controlled. The tenets we've put in place to protect and control it are delicate. If you are killed before the festival, we don't know what will happen to magic." Esther rises from her chair, but she rests her hands on the edge of the table and leans forward. "When I said that tattoo is power—power that you aren't prepared for—you said that being able to have power is a privilege. You say it's dangerous for you. Power always, *always* goes hand in hand with danger. Even if power isn't a privilege given to you, Coin, it's still something you can possess." Esther pushes off the table and strides to the door. "I'm going to let the Royal Council know there has been an attempt on your life. I presume you can have this disposed of properly, Eldritch."

"Shouldn't I be the one giving orders?" I say.

She squints at me. "Would you like to?"

I purse my lips, knowing it would be foolish for me to repeat what she's said.

"It won't dissolve," I tell Eldritch as Esther heads for the door, and I can tell she's listening. "The poison. It doesn't dissolve. Not in water. Tell the kitchen to use oil."

For a moment, Eldritch's aura flickers with indecision, but he agrees.

Esther departs, but I'm quick on her heels.

"Something has been nagging at me," I say as I chase her down the corridor.

Esther's aura twists as she bites back a retort.

"The list of challengers posted outside the dining hall," I say. "Your name wasn't on it. The general had *her* name written there in a heartbeat, but not you. Why?"

Esther quickens her pace but then stops short. I move around to face her.

"I am not careless with my words or my actions," Esther says. "When I write my name on that paper, that is when you will know with absolute certainty that you will never be queen." With that, she picks up her quick pace, and this time, I don't follow.

I check on Eldritch to make sure the poison is disposed of safely, and then I pace the corridors. It's not every day that someone tries to kill me, but I wager it will be commonplace soon enough.

What Esther said during the lesson sits with me as I move

through the palace. I don't know how to dream big. I don't know how to help *everyone.* I can barely keep myself afloat.

I take a moment to assess myself. I've been at the palace for ten days. My abilities, according to the Royal Council, will continue to grow stronger until six weeks have passed. Am I stronger? After sensing the auras of strangers and avoiding skin contact since I arrived here, I'm not sure.

I wonder if I'm strong enough to break Hat out of prison myself. I can sense auras, see memories, and cause hallucinations. But I have barely practiced the latter since settling into the routine of meals and etiquette lessons.

As I take a sharp turn and head down a short corridor, I feel a prickle on my neck. For a moment I can't tell if it's my usual paranoia or if it's someone's aura. Out of instinct or intuition, I glance behind me. There's a flash of bright orange cloth, and a Royal ducks into a room behind me.

I try to reach out to sense the person's aura, but I can't. I backtrack and enter the room.

When I see the orange cloth, I push the Royal up against the wall, arm against his throat, saying quietly, "You think I can't spot when someone's following me?"

The slick black hair tickles my arm on his throat. I would know the cold green eyes anywhere.

You have got to be kidding me.

It's Marcher.

CHAPTER 9

"What the hell are you doing here, Marcher?" I demand.

"Tut, tut," Marcher says, waggling a finger as I press my arm against his throat. "Language, Highness. We're of a better class here."

Not only is he wearing Royal clothes, but they fit him perfectly. The orange dress shirt is tucked into a pair of dark blue trousers. Either he happened to steal a set of perfectly tailored clothes, or he has posed as a Royal before. His hair is combed neatly, most of it tied back, revealing a couple of graying streaks. No dirt smudges, no fish oil, no lingering spices from the markets.

"What is this?" I press him harder against the wall. Is Marcher really a Royal? No. I can't sense his aura, so that must mean he's Nameless.

"Let me guess. You demand to know what I want or else blah blah some kind of threat," Marcher says. "First, I want your gracious gift of freedom." He grips my right arm like a prison bar. He glances down at the crown tattoo. I doubt he knows that the tattoo is still sensitive to the touch, a built-in vulnerability displayed on my arm, but I don't want to take the chance.

He carefully slides along the wall, and I let him.

Of all the things I have to worry about in the palace—execution, Royal injustice, being poisoned, losing Hat—this is the one thing I hoped to leave behind.

I back up to a safe distance. "I don't want to make a deal with you, if that's what you're after."

He grins. "The only thing I want from you is for you to honor the deals you *do* make. For instance: I could have led the Royal Guard to you on the night that you were discovered as queen." In response to my skepticism, he adds, "You were at Devil's. You spent the whole night there. In exchange for not selling you out, all I ask is that you let me walk out of here today. Unless you were planning on killing me. What do you say?"

He may be dressed up in Royal garb, but he's still the same bastard.

"So go," I say, answering his question without saying yes. "Leave." He also kept Hat and risked her life, nearly getting her killed. But I can barely stand to be in the same room with him anymore.

He straightens his collar. "Don't you want to know what I can offer? I can tell you who to trust." He sidles closer.

I push him firmly away in disgust. "I'm sure you'd be on that list."

"Of course not. You know me better than that," Marcher says, adjusting his sleeves. "Look at me, Coin. Clearly I've been here before. I know the ins and outs of this world better than you ever will. When the time comes, you'll need to know who to trust. I have information on the Assassins' Festival."

I cross my arms, refusing to accept anything he says at face value. Anything he has to offer, I don't want.

He smirks. "So contrary. But I've known you your entire life, since the day you were abandoned on the streets. No matter how selfish you think you are, or how fiercely alone . . . there are always people you care about. Think. I can tell you who to trust. More importantly, I can tell you who *not* to trust."

That's a list I'm more inclined to believe.

"Why?" I demand.

Marcher tries to speak kindly. "Would you believe me if I told you it was because I care about you?" He draws close.

"No." I hold my ground.

He smirks, easing off. "Too right. It's because, unlike the other players in this game, I'm not underestimating you. I understand how intoxicating it can be to stand above all the Royals who spend their lives crushing the fingers of the starving Nameless. I see all the moving pieces, Coin, and I see where it'll fall apart."

"Anything you want to share out of the kindness of your heart?" I ask.

"That would be playing fair." The gleam in his eyes tells me that he knows something. "You never want to play fair— not if you want to win. I am not without ambition here. It's in my best interest if you remain an active participant in this game. Let's go with a piece of advice, then, shall we? You might want to check on Devil tomorrow. I hear the streets are getting dangerous, and you need to understand what's been going on since you left." He strolls to the door. "Have a lovely day, Your Grace." He bows. Then he's gone.

"Wait," I order, following him.

Glenquartz takes his place in the doorway, blocking my path. "Everything all right, Coin?"

Marcher disappears down the corridor. Glenquartz has already seen the frustration etched on my face. I can't pretend nothing happened.

No, I want to say. *Nothing is all right. The man I hate is offering me his help, and I may never see Hat again.*

"Absolutely," I say, smiling. "I met a Royal, and I didn't catch his name, but he was in a hurry."

Glenquartz frowns. "I didn't see his face, sorry."

Throughout the rest of the day, I'm consumed with what Marcher said. I remind myself: *Never say no to a deal until you hear the terms, and never ignore advice—but always be willing to turn down both.*

By evening, the events of the day—nearly being poisoned, running into Marcher, not to mention sensing everyone's auras of stress, fear, indignation, and anger—have made me feel as if I've spent hours buried deep underground. The minute I'm in my sleeping quarters for the evening, I close the door, embrace the silence, and take a shower to rinse away the day.

As water pours through my long hair, runs down my body, and collects around my feet, I let it drag away the sweat and the dirt. But it can't carry everything away.

I thought my biggest worry would be avoiding execution and rescuing Hat from prison. But the auras press all around me, and a single touch can propel me into someone's darkest thoughts, like Belrosa's cruel imaginings of Nameless slaughter. The memory of sweet poison still lingers on my tongue. And Marcher is here, walking confidently among the Royals.

A bead of water tracks along my shoulder and down my arm, and I'm struck with a memory: a finger trailing from my shoulder to my wrist, staking a claim to me. Kind and caring, and more terrible because of that.

I slap away the itching bead of water and duck into the warm stream from the showerhead. Immerse myself in it. Drown in it.

I can hardly breathe.

Marcher would put a gentle hand on my shoulder when he asked me to do something dangerous. Steal charts from a ship, or run a one-woman con on a Royal guard while he broke into a shop. Every request coupled with that warm hand on my shoulder, the hand trailing down my arm when I walked away. Saying yes wasn't a question of force. My answer was always yes.

Worst of all: that same hand on the shoulders of the other kids, the only people I ever considered calling family. All of them. They said yes. Always.

I slam the heel of my hand into the water spout. It wrenches to the side, the mounting bracket snapping, and pain shoots up my arm. Water sprays everywhere, and I quickly turn the valve and let the water ease to a drip. I stand in the inch of draining water, which smells faintly of peppermint, copper, and dirt.

I said no. Finally, I said no. I walked away. Then I think of all the ways and times I should have said no to Marcher, and of the others who didn't say no, who *couldn't,* because they didn't know how. All the almost-family who said yes and walked off to their deaths.

I still feel the coil of rope itching in my hands, though it was four years ago. I still feel the breakneck race of my heart, the stiffness of my clenched jaw, the cold chill of midnight and fear. Knowing that no one else would have to say yes . . . as long as I could find the strength to ruin what was left of my good heart. Live the rest of my life with blood on my hands, or live my life watching Marcher exploit others with that same kind touch.

I tried to kill him, and I failed.

I don't live with my mistakes—I survive them. Barely.

I fumble with the broken bracket, rig it in place with a hand towel. I'm as damaged as the things I break, and there's nothing that can put me together again.

I turn the water back on, and even though it's warm, a certain numbness overtakes me, and it sinks into me like fear. Fear that four more years won't be enough to distance myself from the pain of saying yes.

Fear because I said no and it still hurts.

✦

When I'm out of the shower, the lantern flame struggles to cast a feeble glow in the sleeping quarters. It sends dim shadows dancing between the beds, but they do little for the shiver that settles on my skin. Marcher suggested I check in with Devil tomorrow, but I see no reason to wait. I'm going tonight. Besides, if anyone has a way in and out of the prison, it'll be her. Hopefully, I'll have garnered enough of her goodwill by having food sent to her.

I don't want to wear Royal clothing if I'm going out into the city. In the wardrobe, I dig out the clothes I wore when I first arrived. The sleeve is still torn off, so I pull on a long tan Lindragore coat over my outfit. In the dark of night, it'll seem gray.

By the time I'm dressed, I'm itching to get out of the palace, not only to check in with Devil but also just to spend some time on my own.

I like Glenquartz, and I want to trust him. I almost do. But I don't think trust matters unless it's wholly given. Or maybe there are different versions of trust, like how I trust a Royal to overreact to being pickpocketed and a cadet to overreact in a crowd. I trust Hat to meet me every morning at the corner. I trust Marcher to be self-serving. And I want to trust Glenquartz to have my back. But I'm not there yet.

I move the wardrobe underneath the skylight, climb on top, and push it open. I heave myself up and onto the roof. I follow the slanting patterns of the mostly flat roof until I get to a gutter system, where I climb down to ground level. It isn't until I'm scaling walls and ducking down the streets of the Royal Court that this begins to feel like a mistake.

I hoped that dressing as one of the dark-clad Nameless would be like slipping into my old skin, but I'm annoyed to find that the clothes are more uncomfortable than I remember. I'd always thought the Royals looked pinned together and their outfits would be uncomfortable, but their clothes are warmer and smoother, and they fit better.

At this late hour, the gates out of the court are closed, and a guard paces the length of the front gate. I watch him, timing his path. It's a fifteen-step trek each way, which takes him about ten seconds to walk. But sometimes he walks more slowly or quickly, putting his time anywhere from eight seconds to twenty-three.

On the streets, all I have are steps and time to measure my cons and thefts. I can always walk away when the numbers don't add up. I don't have that luxury here.

I take a breath and focus.

Empty space. Empty space. And then . . . an aura pulses beyond this wall like a column of dust hanging in the air, shifting on a breeze, trembling with a heartbeat. Another aura is closer by, low and calm.

A faint smile shadows my lips. High above, a night of shielding clouds protects me from the faint sheen of distant starlight, no moon to be seen. Perfect for a night of sneaking through the shadows, slinking to the alleys.

The second guard sits in a chair beside the gate, but his aura is calmer, like the drooping fronds of limp beach grass. As I draw near, I realize he's asleep, head slumped forward.

The pacing aura moves away, and I walk quickly to the gate itself. When the aura slows down, I focus all my energy on being invisible. I remain motionless as he walks by again. Then I push open the gate and slip out as soon as he's past. I rush down the road until I'm out of their sight.

Now that I'm in the Inner Ring, I'm beginning to feel like my old self again. No one is watching me or measuring my movements. No one is waiting for me to make a mistake or assassinate me.

It's freeing.

It doesn't take long to get to Devil's. I'm as discreet as I can be outside her alley, but pulling on the string doesn't do anything this time.

I call for her over the wall, and she tosses over the rope ladder. A quick climb, and I'm descending the stairs into her alley.

"Coin!" Devil says. "What in the vittin hell are you doing here?"

I'm struck with a sudden desire to hug her, and the image in my head is so startling, I stumble down the last step. Devil's here, and she looks almost exactly the way I left her. Not much has changed, except that there are more half-burned candle stubs across her table.

"Have you been getting the food deliveries?" I ask.

"They were good for a while," she says, "but the last couple have made people sick. I was going to send a message to you through the Legal boy. Things have been getting more violent out here since then."

I start to correct her with the Legal servant's real name, but I'm shocked to realize I don't know it.

Instead, I ask the question that brought me here, Marcher's question: "What's been happening on the streets since I've been gone?"

Devil's eyes darken, and her fingers curl into bold, angry fists. "Ask a different question."

"Things aren't good, then."

"No." She flexes her fingers and rolls her neck. "The Nameless are getting killed in the streets. Bodies are turning up every day now."

"What about the ones who've disappeared over the past months? Have you heard anything new about them?" I hate the almost-hope that edges my voice, as if a mysterious disappearance is better than certain death.

Devil shrugs. "The answer is the same as when you asked the first time. I don't know. Why are you so interested? We have bigger problems out here than a Nameless vanishing every few weeks."

"We don't know exactly when or why they disappear," I stress. "Maybe they've been arrested?"

Devil sighs. "Chances are, you're not going to find out. They could be anywhere. Shipped to another city that still deals in forced labor or simply killed and dumped in the ocean. Are you sure you want me looking? I hate to be the bearer of bad news, but I'll do it if you ask . . . and if you pay me." She flashes a bright set of smiling teeth at me.

"Yes. I tried to ask at the palace, but either they don't understand or they don't care. I just . . . I haven't wanted to care in a long time. It hurts, you know? To care about things I can't change. It's easier to ignore them, because then I can say nothing I'd do would make a difference . . . but I'm not so sure anymore. After the Assassins' Festival, I could just go back to being me. While I have this tattoo . . . shouldn't I *do* something?"

Devil scans my face. "You're good, Coin. I didn't think you'd con yourself into thinking you could make a difference, but I suppose if anyone could . . . it would be you."

"If anyone could con themselves, or if anyone could make a difference?" I ask.

She gazes serenely into the empty orbital sockets of a wolf skull on her shelves. "I'll do what you ask. I'll look into it."

"As long as you get paid?" I grin.

"As long as I get paid."

"Let me guess, just the rings?"

"Of course. But also find me something *interesting* from the palace. I love a good trinket." She strokes her bookcase delicately.

Before I can think of a smooth way to say goodbye, I feel a strange wispy sensation on my arm as if the wind is changing direction, and I sense three people rounding the corner near the alley.

"There are three Legals nearby . . . but there's something wrong." I shake my head, a sense of dread rising up inside me.

Devil sees my panic and checks her flip-book watch. "Gaiza!" She immediately goes to the opposite wall and presses on one of the bricks.

"Gear," she says, and her nostrils flare.

She pushes on the brick wall, and it opens up into the

millinery next door. That explains how the sawn-in-half couch got into the walled-off alley.

"What?" I shout, chasing after her.

She rushes through the store, knocking over a rack of hats.

"Gear! He was supposed to return five minutes ago," she says. "And he's never late!"

There's panic more than fear in her voice, and I can do nothing but follow.

When we barrel out into the street, the three Legals have rounded the corner and are almost close enough to see us in the shadows. They drag beside them a young man. I don't recognize his face, beaten as it is, but he's one of Devil's runners, who help her move goods around the cities. He's young but not reckless. Kind but not soft.

"What in the vittin hell is this?" Devil says, starting toward the Legals.

I put a hand on her shoulder, and her eyes flash like lightning.

"Groups of Legals like that," she says to me, pointing at them, "have been killing Nameless on every street from here to the western gates."

Two of the three Legals have muskets on their shoulders, but I stay close to Devil. She pulls the rifle from her shoulder and heads toward them. By the time the Legals notice us, Devil has them in her sights.

"Drop him," Devil commands, and her arms are steady with the rifle.

Devil's shirt rises up above her hips as she faces down the Legals, and I see the silver handle of a single-shot pistol. I tap her arm so she won't be startled as I take the weapon. Then I'm standing beside her, and now both of us hold guns on the three Legal men, with Gear still at their side.

The three Legals are my subjects, but I'm not about to issue a proper decree while holding a pistol. Yet if they are my subjects, maybe I can use my abilities against them. I should be able to make them see a hallucination—something that will stop them in their tracks.

I try to imagine a wall building up between the Legals and Gear, but I can't focus on the idea without thinking, *Are there bullets in this pistol? Am I really going to shoot someone? Are those footsteps behind us?*

I'm not sure where they come from, the other Legals. Suddenly there's a crowd upon us from the west. They're marching in protest, and their auras are like a hundred oak trees folding into the wind, strong and united. A few of them hold large signs with who knows what written on them in bold strokes.

Things are horrid and tense for a half second. Then, amid the mob of Legals, I spot a Royal in bright colors. He's pointing at me, mouth agape, and in that instant I know he recognizes me. I don't recognize him. How could I, when I've met hundreds of people I'll never remember over the past week?

He starts shouting, "The Nameless—"

And the Legals in the group pick up the charge before he can finish, all of them shouting for the Nameless. His cry for me is lost in the roar of the mob.

There's shouting and rushing. Movement on all sides. Screams. Slapping shoes and slamming doors. The sound rises in my body like steam. The rage and fear of their auras—they infect me.

Devil still has her rifle leveled at the Legals, but there's a crowd charging the space between us.

The sound of a gun cracks through the air, and somehow I wish it was louder. I wish it hurt. Then it would feel real. Instead I watch what happens next with a sense of detachment.

Gear falls over, as if his body fell asleep without permission. It's so violent and sudden. I thought he'd be blown backward, but he simply tips and collapses to the ground, the life emptied from his body. I know Devil has seen it when her howl of rage fills the street. That is how the world shakes.

When a Legal man grabs onto Devil from behind, she pivots sharply as the charging crowd races around us, and she slams the butt of her rifle across his face. She doesn't hesitate as she raises the weapon, pans across the far edge of the street, and pulls the trigger. The Legal man who shot Gear falls to the ground, dead.

The Legals are surging and screaming now. There's a woman calling for her child.

Devil fires another shot at one of the Legals who were dragging Gear down the street, and he falls to the ground.

As Devil turns her smoldering gaze across the rest of the crowd, I reach her, grab her hand, and drag her away, certain that if I left her there, the whole street would fall.

We almost don't make it out. Bodies crash into each other;

feet stomp and kick; shouts buzz through my mind as if the voices are inside my head.

Devil eventually falls into step with me, and I'm not sure at first where I'm taking us. I'm just going *away*.

We head far enough north that we pass the network of alleys and reach the edge of the Royal Court. I lean heavily against the wall, and Devil paces. She picks up a loose brick and hurls it angrily at the wall.

"How did you know to come?" Devil demands. "Or was this a coincidence?"

"Marcher."

"That bastard. If he sent you, then he knew this was going to happen." She snarls, hatred coiling through her tense body.

"Those three Legals walked right past your alley with Gear," I say. "How could that have been planned? And that mob?"

Devil props her knee up on a broken barrel, and she removes the bullet from the rifle's chamber, tucking it in her pocket. "Chance is a cop-out for when you don't understand something. There's always a why." The emptiness in Devil's eyes fills with rage. From experience, I know it's easier to fill the hollowness with anger than to let it slowly fill with something as painful as grief.

"What do you want to do?" I ask her plainly.

For a moment, I think she wants to return to the fight. If she does, I will follow her. Then, with a controlled motion that seems to focus her, she slings her rifle over her shoulder and begins free-climbing up the Royal wall. I follow, and soon we're on top of the wall, feet dangling over twenty feet of open air. It takes a long time for Devil to break the silence, but I wait patiently for her to speak.

"I didn't say thank you," Devil says at last. "For sending food. I give you a hard time about changing, but the city needs change. Things like *this* need to stop happening."

"You said people were getting sick from the food. Did—" My voice catches. I don't know if I can take more death tonight.

She shakes her head. "Not yet. There's two of them who are really sick, though. And since doctors only help the Nameless when they want to test new medicines and procedures, their chances aren't good."

The rooftops of the Royal Court are neat and orderly. I swivel and lie down on the cool bricks, staring up at the sky. The world is too much to handle. I study the dark clouds.

"I think someone recognized me," I say.

"Recognized you as Coin, the thief and grifter? Or recognized you as the impossible sovereign of Seriden, or whatever it is they've been calling you?"

"When the riot started, it's because one of the Royals recognized me from the palace. I think he recognized me as queen." I press my hands down against the cold brick. "This is not good."

"Are you returning to the palace?" she asks.

"Unless you know a better way to get Hat out of prison and get this bloody tattoo off my arm," I say.

"I can ask around and see what kind of rumors are out

there," Devil says. "I do have *a* plan. Not for breaking someone else out of prison, but for getting *me* out of prison. I have a standing plan to escape if I ever get arrested."

"Will it work for Hat?" I ask. A chilly breeze rushes past us, and the ocean horizon turns to ash, and I know that sunrise isn't far off. I should have come to Devil first. I've wasted my time in the palace, waiting for General Belrosa to hold up her end of the deal.

"It might," she says. "I'll talk to some people. That Legal who brought me the poisoned food? I'll send a message with him tomorrow if I can work things out."

"Just let me know what you need," I say to her. "Any money or anything I can steal for you from the palace, tell me."

Devil is tempted, but then her shoulder twitches. "Nah. That little redheaded scamp used to visit me every morning . . . and I miss seeing her. She smiled. Not a lot of people do anymore. I'll see what I can do."

I imagine Hat's face—her frizzy red hair and freckled cheeks, and her dizzying array of hats. I spin up into a seated position.

"Do you have a lot of friends?" I ask Devil after a long silence.

She stares sideways at me. "I wouldn't say that you and I are friends, exactly."

"I don't mean me," I say. "Not really. Anyone. Do you find it easy . . . or impossible to make actual friends?" I kick my heel against the wall, and dirt flakes off and falls to the ground. "I don't think I ever have. Except with Hat . . . I'm so worried about her, and I can't tell if it's guilt or responsibility or friend-ship. I'm not even sure if there's a difference."

Devil kicks out her feet. "Well, you're coming to the wrong person if you're asking about friends. I'm a smuggler, which means anyone is my friend if they're useful to me."

I shrug. "Did you ever think that we could be . . . ?"

"More than friends?" Devil proposes, nudging me with a shoulder.

I laugh, and my cheeks heat up. "Just friends at all."

"Well," Devil says, surveying me, "you're certainly smart and resourceful. More than that, even. You're"—she wrinkles her nose at me—"kind. I think that's more than I'll ever be. They call me Devil for a reason. Do friends need to be kind? Is it enough to be loyal or present when the moment calls for it? I see what you're trying to do for the city, Coin. I see things that you don't see. I see what it's doing on the streets."

"What? Getting people killed?" I jerk a thumb behind us, where the distant shouts of the riot can still be heard.

"It's definitely having that effect," Devil says, "but it's also making people pay more attention to each other. The Nameless have spent generations on the streets without rights. That's not something that gets fixed overnight. But for the first time in a long time—ever, maybe—people are starting to think it can get fixed at all. They don't want something immediate. They just want . . ."

"Hope?" I offer.

Devil nods slowly. "They have hope. They are clinging to it with everything they have. But hope is a kind of fear, and that's what makes it dangerous. That's all this city is right now—a place of reckless hope and fear, and it's killing people. Gaiza, I'm going to miss Gear. He was good. *Good* good. Like Hat."

I put a hesitant hand on her shoulder, and I'm relieved to feel nothing but smooth warm skin—no aura, no memories.

Devil looks at my hand, and I withdraw it, worried I've overstepped.

"If you're walking back into that Royal nightmare," she says, "it's the least I can do to try to help Hat. We'll get her out of prison one way or another."

I say goodbye to Devil. She climbs down the wall into the Inner Ring, and I make good time returning to the palace. I think about everything she said. The only thing I've ever wanted was for the Nameless to have a place within the city. I've been so consumed with escaping the death sentence of this Royal tattoo and rescuing Hat that I haven't really considered if I should fight for the throne. I have power, and most people I've come across have told me that I'm not suited for it. They've told me I'm unprepared, unqualified, and simply *impossible*.

Maybe I've been making the mistake of believing them. Maybe I don't belong on the streets in the same way I don't belong at the palace. Everything that was *mine* about the streets is gone: the quiet anonymity of being a Nameless pickpocket, the smile of a girl called Hat, and the idea that I could leave Seriden any day I chose.

As I make my way along the roof to the skylight of my sleeping quarters, I realize that going out to the streets and returning to the palace—neither really feels like coming home.

CHAPTER 10

Dominic knocks sharply on the door, startling me awake. Without waiting, he opens the door and leans into the room.

"Can I help you?" I ask in a monotone.

Judging from the sun coming through the skylight at a sideways slant, I've gotten maybe two hours of sleep. Not nearly enough.

"I'm escorting you to breakfast this morning," he says.

I groan and bury my head under a pillow. "I'm skipping breakfast today." *Need more sleep.*

"You really ought to come," he says, and he makes a small effort to phrase it as a request when it really isn't a request. "The general will be present. Something about a riot out in the city last night."

I groan again.

"Shouldn't you, as the sovereign, care about a thing like that?" he asks impatiently. Then after a beat, he adds, "Ma'am."

I stuff the pillow under my arm and stare at him hard. He shouts in fear after a moment and slaps at the bridge of his nose. "Ugh! Why is it always spiders with you? Fine! Don't come!" He slams the door, and I can still hear his angry grumblings as he retreats down the corridor.

I grin smugly and mutter, "It was an impatient, inexperienced guard like you who tried to kill Hat. It'll be a hundred spiders a day for you until your death." I consider briefly if I have enough patience to hold a grudge that long. Maybe not.

An announcement about the riots. My grin fades. Despite my complaints, I should attend. In ten minutes I've taken a fast, cold shower and changed clothes. I wear white slacks and a flowing green shirt. Today I want to appear soft and non-threatening. If Belrosa plans on identifying me as a rioter in front of everyone, I want to appear as nonconfrontational as possible. People will easily believe a Nameless girl could sling guns in a riot, but I want to give them a tough time reconciling that idea with the calm, perfect-postured version of me in this grasshopper-green shirt.

Then again, if she does accuse me in front of everyone, I may need to defend myself. In the end, I settle for not taking a weapon but staying close to the buffet of breakfast food, where I can snatch a serving knife if needed.

In the dining hall, Dominic is posted near the door. When he sees me, he rolls his eyes. It takes a certain amount of self-control not to send spiders his way again.

Belrosa stands at the head of the room, behind my seat at the sovereign's table, every bit the military commander.

"My friends!" Belrosa calls out. Farther off, most of the Royal Council is gathered near the north exit, and they already seem prepared for the speech. This can't be good. "You may have heard the terrible news already: that there was a riot in the Inner Ring late last night." Her frown is like sculpted glass: carved, cold, and completely transparent. "Two Legals were killed."

I grind my teeth. Two Legals died and one Nameless died— at least. I consider interrupting to correct her, but I don't.

"I am pleased, however," Belrosa continues, "to share that we have identified the Nameless instigator of the riot."

My blood goes cold. I shift my weight so I can slide a small serving knife from the table. It's not the best weapon, but if she points the finger at me, I'll need to make a quick exit before they can arrest me.

Belrosa's eyes rest on me for a moment, piercing, but they move on dismissively. "It, as you would expect, was a Nameless criminal. She has been sentenced to execution."

I freeze, trying to piece together my thoughts. She means Devil. Belrosa has been waiting for any excuse to remind me that she is the one really in charge of Seriden.

My arms shake with anger and my stomach churns, but I can't stop the small knot inside my chest that loosens when she doesn't speak my name. I chastise myself. They're going to execute Devil.

"And of course," Belrosa adds, "as is required in a situation like this, and to put all your troubled hearts at ease, the heir herself will attend the event. Together we will ensure that this Nameless quarrel is settled once and for all." Her gaze fixes on me now. "Won't you?"

I ball my hands into fists and stuff the serving knife into my pocket as the attention of the Royals turns to me.

A nearby Royal echoes, "Won't you?"

I'm not close enough to sense the auras of Belrosa and the council members, but I know what they would feel like: salt and ego. They must be proud of themselves, addressing me publicly so they can avoid talking to me in private, where they know I'd be less than supportive.

I fix an unassuming, regal smile on my face. "Of course."

The room eases, as if everyone was standing on their toes before.

I will not let Devil be executed, but there's nothing I can do right now except play along.

They've arrested Devil, though I'm not sure how. I wonder if Marcher knew. Certainly he knew there were roving groups of violent Legals. Surely he would have known that Nameless were being plucked from the streets by rampant murderers.

"It is good to hear you are in agreement," Belrosa says with poorly concealed triumph. "Because the execution is scheduled for this morning at the gallows, and we are departing immediately to attend it."

My heart seizes, but the calm smile on my face betrays nothing. The Royal Council expects me to keep my head down and fulfill my role until the festival. Glenquartz told me that I'd have to make concessions. But concessions, when they hurt, are sacrifices. And I won't sacrifice Devil.

I nod again. "Lead the way."

Keep your head down, they tell me.

Keep your head down, they tell me.

What they don't tell me is that I'm underwater and if I stay down long enough, I'll drown.

I tell myself: *This is Devil. She told me yesterday how she has a plan for escape if she ever got arrested. Here's her chance.*

"Is there anything I can do to stop this?" I ask Glenquartz quietly as we walk with the Royals and the council members parading out of the palace, through the city, and toward the prison.

"You can *pardon* someone who's about to be executed," he whispers.

"How?" I say. "They wouldn't let me pardon Hat from prison; why would they let me pardon Devil from the gallows?"

"I think you should take a page from their book, then," he says. "If they're willing to spring an announcement on you in public so that the publicity of the statement protects it, then you should do the same."

"I wait until the execution," I say, thinking it through, "and then I pardon Devil in front of everyone?"

Glenquartz nods.

"What does a pardon look like?" I ask.

"You use your abilities," Glenquartz says. "It's an old tradition. If you're able to sense their remorse and true repentance, then you can grant them a pardon."

"But Devil is Nameless," I say. "I won't be able to sense her."

Glenquartz runs a finger down the jawline of his beard. "You could try pardoning her without your abilities. And if it comes down to it, no one except you can prove she isn't a Legal."

My hands jitter at my sides.

I have a terrible thought: if Marcher were to present himself now, and said he had a way to get Devil and Hat out of the prison and to safety, I would accept in a heartbeat. Regardless of cost.

The gallows, like the prison, is outside Seriden's walls. It's beside the prison, in fact. A door from the prison opens into a small, stone-filled arena. There's a waist-high wooden railing that surrounds the gallows arena, where spectators are invited to observe.

For the most part, executions are quiet affairs, with a smattering of people present. I attended one once. A Nameless orphan in Marcher's crew had gotten caught stealing. She was fourteen. I was nine. She was killed the very next day.

The Nameless don't typically last long in prison. If they did, there would be more of us there. Who doesn't want a free bed and meals? No, Seriden prefers we die on the streets or the gallows. It's a testament to Glenquartz's intervention and my threat to the council that Hat has survived there.

That was the first and only execution I ever attended. And here I am, as queen, and it's my *job* to be here. If I had my way, no one would hang from that noose ever again.

After trying to kill Marcher four years ago, with the rope in my hands . . . I couldn't do that again. It's ghoulish and cruel to everyone involved. There's a reason the executioner wears a hood.

I scan the onlookers. There are a lot of Legals and Royals here to watch the Nameless heir oversee her first execution of a Nameless criminal. There are some Nameless here too. A group of them at the south end of the arena, all watching me. They don't have auras for me to sense, but I see their anger in the tight twist of their crossed arms and the angry upward tilt of their chins. I can't blame them. I'd hate me too. I want to rip the soft green sleeves from my arms and shout at them: *Yes, I'm here. Yes, I'm Nameless. Yes, I'm every bit the monster you think I am.*

The executioner takes his place on the gallows. I expect him to move smoothly, like the shadow of death itself, but he lumbers up the stairs, and I can see that he has a bad knee and dark hair on his bare forearms. His whole outfit is black. It's the only time a Legal or Royal wears something outside the colors of their class.

Glenquartz touches my shoulder. It's a gentle movement, but I flinch. He points toward the prison, but something in the audience of Nameless catches my attention: Devil. She pushes her way to the front of the crowd, and she leans onto the rail with her arms bent and tense as if she wants to grind the rail into splinters and dust. I rise from my chair, confused. If she's not who they arrested for instigating the riot, then who?

I look at the figure being escorted from death row who Glenquartz is pointing at. Female. Short. Black clothes: Nameless.

She's small, young.

Too young. Too familiar.

Then I see the flash of red hair and the thin, trembling

arms. The chains are cuffed to her wrists, so big that they nearly fall right off. They march her toward the gallows as a stir rises in the crowd.

"Hat," I whisper.

Glenquartz's hand is on my shoulder again, gripping tightly. Through my sleeve, I can't read his thoughts to tell if he's trying to hold me back or urge me forward.

They're going to kill Hat.

The onlookers grow quieter, and it's not a hushed anticipation of a violent execution. Or at least, that's not *all* it is. There's a shift in the collective auras around me. Excitement wanes and discomfort rises, and I feel it like whispers on my skin.

Hat may not be a child, but she's certainly not the organizer of a riot, not the instigator of multiple deaths.

I sense Belrosa as she draws closer to me.

"The trick you used in the market won't work again today," she says. "There is no saving her 'in the name of the queen.'" Her voice drips with acidic pride.

I clench my fists at my sides and quickly decide that punching her in the throat won't improve the situation.

"The guards have been well informed that the queen doesn't have a name and therefore doesn't have any say in the events that transpire here today," Belrosa says. "Your word means nothing." The Royal guards urge Hat up the stairs of the gallows, and one of them throws a long glance at Belrosa, who gives him a firm nod. Of course they are working for her. They each keep a hand on one of Hat's shoulders since she's too short for them to hold at the elbows.

"Now, *my* word, however," Belrosa says, "is powerful. At my word, her life could be spared or severed. At my word, a war could start or end."

"What do you want?" I seethe.

Belrosa smiles as if that's all she wanted to hear, but she says, "Nothing. Nothing except for you to understand that you'll give me that crown. For you to understand your place and power: you have neither. You are a vessel carrying the tether to magic, but you are otherwise empty and meaningless. Not even worth your own name: *Coin*. Just think what this does to you. The Nameless are about to watch as the only queen they've ever known lets a child hang. Crushing your bright spirit and killing your friend is a bonus. So go ahead. Try and save her. You may win the favor of the Nameless, but you'll lose it with the Royal Council, and they will *insist* I take the crown from you."

She adjusts her posture so I can see the Royal Council sitting in their gilded chairs. Instead I scan the crowd. Devil has disappeared from their ranks, and most of the Legals and Royals are still shaking their fists, eager for the Nameless perpetrator to hang. But some of them, *some of them* have the same unease and fear etched on their faces that I feel raking through me.

I can't pick the executioner's aura from the frenzy around me, but I see him adjust his grip again and again on the lever.

I think about the bell that rang at East Market when the announcement caught us in its grasp. I imagine them now—bells filling the air and growing louder and louder. And I imagine a veil of black night swallowing us up.

I know it works when everyone around me claps their hands

to their ears, shouting. But the noose is already around Hat's neck.

Belrosa lunges blindly in my direction, but I've already launched myself forward. I step on a gilded chair and hurl myself over the rail and into the arena. Belrosa shouts, "Kill her! Kill her!"

With the mad beating of my heart, I imagine bells louder than Belrosa's shout, clanging in their chests and pounding in their heads. The guards curl over on the gallows stairs.

The executioner's hand is still on the lever as I race up the steps, pushing past the incapacitated guards. His grip is tight enough, strong enough. All I need him to do is hesitate. And he does.

I charge past him to the platform. Hat's arms are chained behind her, and she's wild with fear. I wrench the noose forward, when I hear a heavy thud as the lever turns, and then the floor gives out beneath me.

I throw the noose upward and off, and I pull Hat into my arms as we plummet through the trapdoor. I'm ready for the impact of a ten-foot fall, but she isn't. We topple to the side, and it's now that I realize the shouts have stopped from the crowd. I stagger to my feet, pulling Hat with me, and everyone in the viewing arena is staring at us. Distracted, I lose hold over the illusion of bells. We're only three paces away in our sprint from the gallows when the shouting and gunshots begin.

We race toward the rail where the Nameless have gathered, and, impossibly, they are jumping over the rail and running toward us. I don't know what to expect: that they've seized the opportunity to come for me or that they're after Hat. But something in my heart soars as I realize they're rushing to protect us from the guards.

I lift Hat as we get to the rail, and a tall, burly Nameless man in a heavy jacket and crooked cap reaches for her. Any other day, I might have been scared of this man. But he takes Hat from my arms and sets her on her feet on the other side of the rail as I clamber over myself.

Belrosa is shouting something incoherent behind me. The crowd is surging. Legals and Royals flee the area as bullets rip through the air. I run toward the open city gates, and I don't dare look behind me. I grip Hat's shoulder to keep her moving forward to the nearest building, needing to round a blind corner so that no one can get a fix on us with their rifle sights. I try to focus my thoughts enough to make Hat and myself invisible. But all I can think is *run faster, run faster*.

As we careen around the corner, someone else skids around the other side. It's Glenquartz, holding his rifle in his hands, face red from exertion. I pull Hat up to a short stop, twisting her behind my body, wishing I had a weapon, any weapon. Glenquartz's shoulders slacken when he sees us unharmed, and he gestures for us to follow him toward the city.

Of course, Glenquartz. *Of course.*

A large stretch of empty space stands between us and the city—a lot of open ground. But we don't have any choice. We race onward.

One of Belrosa's guards is gaining on us. I glance behind me. He's pulling his pistol from his holster. A gunshot cracks, and the man collapses, blood spurting from his leg. My attention snaps forward, and I see Devil standing at the gate to the city, peering around the corner with her long rifle in her hands. The bodies of two posted guards are at her feet, and I don't have time to ask if they're alive or not.

As we rush through the gates, Devil abandons her post and joins us. "I knew you'd escape. You care about that one too much." She gestures at Hat. "I thought I'd give you some cover." She grins.

I smile back.

Together, we run.

CHAPTER 11

Once we're inside the city, my first instinct is to run to the abandoned library at the western edge of the Inner Ring. In stead, I follow Glenquartz. He leads us through West Market and into the Royal Court. Everything in my bones burns at the idea of returning to the palace, but it's the last place they'd search for us. Yet Glenquartz leads us to a collection of simple brick houses on the outskirts of the Royal Court. I hold Hat close as we walk. Glenquartz has draped his jacket over her shoulders so that no one can see her shackled wrists behind her. As soon as we find a concealed alley, Glenquartz fumbles through his pockets until he finds his keys. He frees her and throws the shackles angrily down the alley. I take quick note that even the alleys in the Royal Court are cleaner. Neat, tidy drains that funnel water into the sewers.

Glenquartz leads us down another couple of streets before he opens the door to a small house. He ushers us into a bright living space. Devil stays outside, saying that she'll keep watch on the streets for a while to make sure no one is following us. As soon as Glenquartz shuts the door, he rushes to close the curtains. Dim shade fills the room like silence.

He checks the bruises on Hat's wrists. "You're all right?" he says, more a sigh of relief than a question.

She nods, choking back tears. She's been in Seriden's prison longer than most Nameless. I raise an eyebrow in concern, and she won't meet my gaze.

My heart tightens, and I pat Glenquartz's arm. "Can you bring her some water and food?"

He doesn't want to leave her side, but Hat's hand flutters to her stomach, and the hungry pinch of her lips sends him fumbling his way into the kitchen.

I sit beside Hat and gently put my hand on her shoulder. "Tell me."

Instead she shows me.

Her ribs. Her ankle. The back of her neck. Cracked, twisted, and bruised. She tells me about her cell, the food she could hardly eat, the water she was scarcely given, and the fight with another prisoner that she barely survived.

At last, she looks up. I can tell she wants to wrap her arms around me, but I hold off for a moment.

"Don't look down," I say, and my voice cracks. "When you tell the truth, don't ever look down. Don't be ashamed and don't be afraid. The truth isn't something you control. It's something you live with, and if you want to let it make you stronger, it has to be something you own."

Silently, tears slip down Hat's cheeks. She looks up at me and nods. I pull her against me, breathing the scent of sweat and dirt from her hair.

"Things happen to us," I say, "things we can't control and

things we don't want. But we are more than what happens to us." I say it as much to myself as to her.

She sniffs, pulling out of the embrace. "There's something else. It didn't happen to *me*. It was someone else." She takes a moment to steady her hands. "There was a Nameless boy in a cell near mine. Not quite across. I couldn't see his face. I could see his arm if he reached out, but . . . he was arrested sometime before I was brought in, and three nights later he was taken."

"To the gallows?" I ask gently. "Or . . ."

"No. Some kind of soldier took him in the middle of the night. They kept it very quiet, and I saw it because I couldn't sleep anyway. They took him, and they walked out and never came back. I don't know what happened to him."

"Was it the Royal guards?" I ask.

I sense Glenquartz's aura sharpening in the kitchen, and I know he's listening. I ignore him.

"I don't know," she says. "They had weapons like the ones I've seen the guards carry. Rifles or muskets, I'm not sure which. They were wearing similar clothes, but it was too dark, and I couldn't see whether it was the Royal Guard uniform or not. I don't think they were, though."

I pat her shoulder. "Everything will be okay." It feels like a lie, but it's the best I can do.

The soldiers she's talking about could be foreign soldiers from another city. But if I had to guess, it makes the most sense for them to be Royal guards, which means they're probably answering to General Belrosa.

Glenquartz returns into the doorway. "I've warmed up some

vegetables and corn bread for you." He brings a plate to Hat and then me.

"Thank you." I scan the room quizzically as Hat scarfs down her food. "This is your home."

"Yes?" he says, confused by my confusion.

I shake my head. "I knew you lived somewhere, but I didn't think of you as actually *having* a home. Like, these are your walls."

He smiles. "You thought I lived in the barracks?"

"No," I say. "I just . . . I've never had one of these before. An actual home, I mean." I place a hand on the wall behind the couch and gesture with the other hand at the mantel, the hat rack, and the bookshelf. "These are your walls. This is your space. It all belongs to you."

Glenquartz softens, and suddenly he's as exhausted as I feel. "Coin?" he says. "You will always have a place here. A home. Wherever I am, whatever happens to us, consider my home to be yours."

For once, I'm honestly speechless.

"And for you, too," Glenquartz says to Hat. "You never have to leave these walls again if you don't want to."

Hat bites her lip.

Glenquartz pinches the bridge of his nose. "I . . . I wish that I had a house big enough for everyone who needs one."

I think maybe I'm starting to understand what this crown tattoo really means, and why King Fallow gave it to me in the first place. I think *Seriden* is supposed to be my home. If I can find the strength to be as brave as Glenquartz, then my home *can* be big enough to fit everyone.

Glenquartz takes some food outside to Devil, and when he comes back in, he sits in an old chair. Hat is getting drowsier by the minute, and she keeps squirming in her clothes as if she wants to burn everything she's wearing. I show Hat to the water closet, and from my time in the palace, I show her how to use the bath. There won't be any hot water, but as the tub fills, Glenquartz heats some water on his stove and pours it into the bath to raise its temperature.

I lean against the rough, gray-brown cupboard as Glenquartz washes the dishes. He's very careful and precise about it.

"I thought you'd have a shower," I say. "Don't most of the Royal homes have them now?"

He lifts a single shoulder in a shrug. "Maybe the Royals do."

I frown. "But . . . you're a Royal guard and you're living in the Royal Court. Are you not a Royal?"

"I'm a Legal," he says. "Like most Royal guards. It's one of the only ways a Legal can live in the Royal Court without actually being a Royal. Us and the doctors—the Royals like having us close at hand."

"Is that difficult? Living here, but not belonging here?"

"It is. I'll never advance past my current station. As a Legal, the highest I can rise is lieutenant. The ones who outrank me are all Royals, and it's not that they don't deserve it. They're more trained than I am and have more experience. They attended the military academy in Tuvo. So it's not that I'm more qualified. It's just that . . . I *can't* become more qualified. I know I shouldn't complain. With all the things I take for granted in my life, to complain about not getting enough privilege must sound like I'm comparing luxuries." He gestures toward the running water at his fingertips.

He's not wrong, except the problems he's facing are similar to what the Nameless face. We aren't afforded things like homes or jobs or legal rights, and so—by and large—we are criminals. In a similar way, we can't rise above our stations. "So . . . does your family visit you here?" I search for any sign that his wife and Flannery visit: toys or shawls or shoes. Surprisingly, though, I don't find any.

His aura grows uneasy and fragile, like a brittle piece of driftwood being bent and ready to snap at the slightest pressure.

He shifts and turns his gaze to me. "Ah, you sensed that, didn't you? You're getting better. When we first met, you didn't quite pick up on it." He does little to stop the tears from building. "When I talked about Flannery—that beautiful sweet girl—and when you saw my memory of her, you sensed my fear of forgetting her. You picked up on the fear, but you misinterpreted it. I told you my wife had left me with our daughter, but that's a lie I wanted to believe. My wife was taking Flannery to visit the orchards of Lindragore for the summer." He clears his throat and turns off the running water, and the dish trembles in his hands. "I was supposed to see them off at the harbor. It was storming. The sailors told me that my wife slipped on the docks, hit her head, and fell into the water. Flannery—that precious girl of ours—jumped in after her. They both died." With the sleeve of his shirt, he wipes his eyes.

I don't know what I'm supposed to say to comfort him. It's different from comforting Hat. If I put my hand on his to comfort him, I'll be rocketed into his memories—no doubt to the moment he learned of their deaths—and that wouldn't help either of us. His aura alone is troubled like deep, dark waters.

I take the plate gently from his hands and begin drying it with a dishcloth.

He sniffs. "I don't want you to think that the only reason I care about you and Hat is because of them. I think, maybe, it's because of them that I *can* care. Does that make any sense at all?"

"I think so." In truth, I don't quite understand. But everything in me—maybe because of everything in him—*wants* to understand.

When Hat is finished with her bath, she wears an old dress of Flannery's. Glenquartz makes Hat some more food, and in the warmth of midday, all of us are ready to sleep. Hat curls up on the sofa and rests her head on my lap, drifting off as Glenquartz and I talk.

"I think they'll get suspicious if I don't return to the palace," Glenquartz says. "If I don't report to the general, she may look for you here."

I agree with him and I don't like it. With Hat resting on me as she sleeps, I feel trapped.

"You need to go back," I say.

He rubs a stiff shoulder. "I'll keep my head down."

"Don't do that," I say. "Grifter lessons: if you try to appear like you have nothing to hide, that's when they'll know you're hiding something. What would you have done if you hadn't caught up with me and Hat outside the city?"

He considers it. "I would have searched for you in the markets and the alleys. If I still hadn't found you, I would have suspected they captured you, and I would have returned to the general. She's my superior officer, but I couldn't help being angry."

"And if she hasn't found us?" I say, motioning to the fact that Hat and I are safe on his couch.

Glenquartz clenches and unclenches his fists. "I'd yell, I'm sure. It's my job to protect you, and I don't know where you are! I'd demand that every spare guard be sent on the search for you. I'd demand to join them."

I beam with pride. "So that's what you do."

Glenquartz blinks in surprise, glancing at his clenched fists. "That is . . . devious and clever. You're very good. What if she knows I'm lying?"

"You tell yourself, *convince* yourself, that you didn't find us," I say. "You searched for hours. You're tired, worried, feeling like you've failed us."

He regards me as if he's trying to see if I'm wearing a second skin or something. He moves to the front door, and I can tell he's hesitant to actually leave.

"I'll be back tomorrow," he says. "When I can."

Glenquartz stands at the front door. For the first time, I'm asking him to leave me. I've sneaked away from him before, but this is different. I can sense it in his aura. It's as if there are threads tied to his body preventing him from leaving. I imagine that those threads are connected to us. One rests in my hands, and another in Hat's. Maybe another is held by the ghost of his daughter that he sees in Hat.

"It's okay," I tell him, in the same way I spoke to Hat earlier. "Everything will be okay."

"I tell myself that leaving is what will protect you," he says. "Keep them off your trail. But that doesn't stop me from thinking I'm abandoning you here."

"You're not abandoning us," I say. "You're leaving us in the safety of your home." Then I add gently, "*Our* home."

His face lights up.

"Go," I urge.

And he does, mustering up the strength to leave at a quick march. Devil comes in before the door can close behind him.

"What's the plan? Where did the Beard go?" She jerks a thumb at the front door.

"We're staying here tonight," I explain. "Glenquartz is heading to the palace to play his part and pretend he doesn't know where we are. Even so, we should leave tomorrow."

"I see," Devil says, casting a sour glance around the room.

"I thought it was you," I say suddenly. "I thought it was you they were going to march out of that prison. Then I saw you in the crowd and I realized it was Hat, and I definitely lost control."

"If it was me, you were going to let me hang?" she teases. "Gee, thanks. And I thought we were, what? Not quite friends? I'm hurt."

"I didn't do anything before then," I explain, "because you said you had a plan for escape. I guess I was counting on that."

"Too late," she says airily. "I'll never forgive you now." She starts perusing Glenquartz's shelves. She plucks up an item and slips it into her pocket.

I glare at her. "Really?"

She fishes out a small glass bowl. "I hardly think he'll miss this. He doesn't even use it for anything." When I don't let up, she grumbles as she returns it to its place.

I watch her for a little while before I work up the nerve to be honest.

"Thank you," I say. The words seem so small compared to what I want them to mean. I want them to mean *thank you* for helping me distribute food to the Nameless, for fighting alongside me, for not brushing me off when I asked about friendship. *Thank you* for having my back, for showing up at the execution, and for helping us escape.

"You're welcome," she says. And maybe it's only me, but her words feel just as weighted.

I clear my throat.

"You're more than welcome to stay," I say. "I'm sure Glen-quartz wouldn't mind."

She doesn't answer right away. For the first few seconds, I'm convinced she'll say no. For a while longer, I'm convinced she didn't hear me at all.

But she finally swings her rifle up across her shoulders and rests her arms over it casually.

"I'm taking a bath," she says. "And then I'm sleeping in the largest bed here. I will do my best to refrain from stealing that mantelpiece clock when I leave, but I make no promises."

She retreats upstairs, smiling in response to my glare. I imagine Glenquartz's clock finding a home in Devil's alley, and I can think of no better fate for it.

Hat is asleep, leaning against me. She's heavy. After a while, she rolls over and I tuck her folded jacket underneath her head. Then I slump down, lean my head against the cushioned couch, and fall asleep.

At some point, I groggily become aware of a tickling sensation on my upper arm. I don't know how long I've been asleep, but I know that the warmth of the sun is gone, and I don't want to wake. The foreign touch is near the crown tattoo. I figure it's a spider or ant. Too small to be a rat. I ignore it. If I woke up at every creepy-crawly, I'd never get a good night's rest.

The pressure on my arm changes. It becomes a deliberate point of pressure tracing the tattoo.

It's not a bug.

It's a person.

My eyes fly open, and my right hand shoots out and grabs

at the pale exposed throat. I grip the vocal cords, prepared to squeeze if the hand doesn't move instantly.

It occurs to me that it could be Hat, up in the night after sleeping all day, trying to get my attention. Or Devil wanting to trade favors to get me out of the city.

Then I see the dark green eyes, and I dig my nails into the soft flesh.

Marcher.

A faint sheen of moonlight cascades through the front door, which has been edged open.

Marcher whispers, "Peace offering." He leaves his fingers gently pressing on the tattoo. With his other hand, he holds up a small wooden container.

"What is it?" I demand quietly, more breath than word. At any moment I could reach for Hat, but something stops me. I don't want her to know he's here, if I can help it.

He just smirks, a faint wrinkling under one eye and a faint yellow of a healing bruise under the other from when I punched him nearly two weeks ago. I glare hard before relaxing the pressure on his throat. But I won't let go. Not until he moves his hand from my arm.

He delicately increases the pressure on the tattoo with his finger, and I respond by squeezing his throat tighter. He scoffs and pointedly removes his hand.

I rise to my feet, keeping my hand on his throat. "What is it?"

"I have a surprise for you," Marcher says.

Hat is asleep on the couch. She hasn't woken up yet.

"Relax," he says. "I'm not threatening you. Not yet, anyway. Come on, let's talk. Unless you prefer I stay." He walks backward toward the door, freeing himself of my grip.

Hat lies motionless on the sofa, a thin frown on her lips. I rise to my feet, and as I leave the room, I check my coat pocket to make sure the serving knife from the palace's dining hall is still there.

If I have to, I'll use it.

And unlike when I tried to kill him four years ago, this time I won't hesitate.

─+─

Marcher leads me outside Glenquartz's home, to the dark patch of stone that provides a walkway from the door to the road. There's a garden I didn't notice before, and a small wall of bricks lining one side. He hops onto the brick wall as if he owns it. Really he wants to stand over me and be taller and stronger.

How hard would it be to pull this knife across his ankles and cut him down to size?

"How did you know I was here?" I demand. I scan the nighttime street, but there are no legions of guards or rioters storming toward us.

"I didn't," he says. "I thought you might be, and I was right. I saw the way the dear lieutenant chased after you. It took some asking around to find out what part of the Royal Court he lives in, and then it's just a matter of doors, and you know better than most that locks are more like suggestions than barriers."

"What do you want, Marcher?"

"Like I said," Marcher says pleasantly, "to bring you a peace offering." He flips open the box. It's half filled with purple, grainy salve.

"It's for Red," he says. "For her wrists. Those prison shackles can be rough on the skin. I'm sure you saw them. This'll help them heal."

I advance angrily. "Her name isn't Red. It's Hat."

"She can change her name as often as she likes, but she'll always be Red to me. You kept the name I gave you—didn't seem to bother you much. Wait . . . that's not your name anymore, is it? Little Coin has a *real* name somewhere." He stands on the very edge of the wall.

I don't like hearing him say my name. It's the name he gave me before I knew what names were. Even though I've been on my own for four years, I haven't gotten away from that part of myself.

"Back off," I say.

He rubs his neck. "You couldn't kill me four years ago. Care to give it another go with that knife you're fiddling with in your pocket, or do you want your present?"

"I don't want your salve."

Marcher flips the lid closed. "Shame. It'd be a pity if your pride let Hat get an infection."

My face grows hot. Somehow, I feel three feet tall around him. I frown and snatch the wooden box.

"Why did you bring me this?" I open it up and survey the purple salve. It's hardly used.

Marcher taps the side of the box. "I feel bad about almost getting Hat killed at East Market."

"You feel *bad*?" Anger bubbles in my chest.

"A little." Marcher shrugs. "I was acting from frustration. It was impulse. From what you did to me." He gently strokes the faded bruise at his temple. "But you always did have a way of getting under my skin."

"I'm supposed to believe that something has changed since then?" I snap the box lid closed.

"Something? Try *everything*." He gives me a swooping bow.

My neck heats up and I change the topic. "In East Market, when you got me arrested, why were you chasing Hat?"

A twitching smile flickers on Marcher's lips. He nods slowly. "She wanted to leave. Like you did. Do you think you saved Red—sorry, *Hat*—because she was in danger, or because she reminds you of yourself? Ready to take any risk and ready to risk everything."

I shouldn't answer him. It'll feed him. Yet I can't make myself walk away. "If you've forgotten why I tried to kill you"—I brandish the knife—"I'll refresh your memory."

"Oh, I remember," Marcher says, rubbing at his throat reminiscently. "Don't insult yourself. You couldn't kill me then, and you certainly can't now." He spreads out his arms to show he has no weapon, as if, even unarmed, I couldn't beat him. He spins on his heel and leaps off the wall, heading toward the road and leaving me fuming, but then he turns around as if remembering something.

He points at the wooden box. "That wasn't the surprise.

That was the peace offering." He waits for me to ask what the surprise is.

I won't do it. I won't play his game. I'm stronger than that.

He turns away, and I can't stand it.

"What is it?" I ask in a tight voice. So much for being stronger.

He turns back with victory plastered on his face. "It's not that simple, Coin. The salve was a gift. This is not."

I grind my teeth. "What will it cost?" *Don't turn down a deal without hearing the terms.*

"You are in a position of power," he says. "More or less. Mostly less. Oh, that lovely hexagon of a palace, it has a lot of answers and even more secrets. What kind, you ask? Your name, for starters. The long, glorious, bloody history of the Nameless vanishing from the streets. Running water for showers, I hear."

I scoff and don't answer.

"I know you've been gone from the streets for a while," Marcher says, "but I've got a pretty good setup out here. Have you even thought about what happens if you manage to keep the throne? A Nameless girl leading the city? You could start an insurrection inside Seriden. Or, if the other cities refuse to trade with you, the peace treaties could crumble."

I have thought about it. I can hardly stop thinking about it.

He continues, "What do I want from you? I want you to remember this moment. I want you to remember *every* moment. Every moment I saved your life or taught you a skill that helped you save yourself." He glances at the towers of the palace in the southeast. "I want you to remember how I helped you and how I left. I want your protection for me and my crew if you survive the Assassins' Festival. In exchange, I'll give you a hint about your biggest puzzle: what has been happening to the Nameless."

"You're trying to tell me you know where they've been disappearing to?" I challenge.

"Of course," he says. "That's the surprise: I know. I can't have anything threatening my crew or my plans, so of course I found out."

It makes sense. I hate it, but it makes sense.

Marcher's crews are typically kids up to the age of about twenty. Most of Marcher's scams involve cons with "sick kids" and small hands that can brush through a mark's pockets.

From the confident glimmer in his eyes, I can tell that Marcher knows what is happening. Or he *thinks* he knows. Or he wants me to think he knows.

"Mull it over," he says. "Let me know if you're willing to deal. Me and my crew get your Royal protection, and you get to finally understand what's been happening to the missing Nameless."

Before I can contemplate whether to accept the deal or spit at his feet, he departs with a swooping bow.

As soon as I'm inside, I lie down on the floor next to the couch where Hat is sleeping. I pull aside the long curtain and stare up at the night sky, tracking the patterns of constellations.

So, Marcher is back. With a gift, a surprise, and a deal.

I want nothing more than to push away every word that

comes from Marcher's spetzing mouth, but I don't have the luxury of ignoring the darkest parts of my past. Those memories helped forge me. They are the iron veins running through me.

Every time I see Marcher, it's as if I never left and I'm still a kid, running wherever he points, sitting huddled with the other kids on old mattresses tucked in the corners of abandoned houses. At night, I would stare through the last unbroken window, barely able to distinguish starlight from the glowing air of Seriden.

Part of me will always be staring out that window, seeing the city but wishing for starlight.

I can't see the stars the way Hat does. She feels their warmth like a barrel fire. They inspire her. They shine inside her eyes. To me, lights from a distance are cold. They are everything I cannot have. When I wish for starlight, I want the freedom to see it. To be somewhere far outside the city, where Seriden's lights are faint shivering flickers against the horizon.

On the night of the riots, Devil asked me if I wanted to stay in the palace. She was offering me the same thing she had when I first came to her after I found the tattoo on my arm: a way out. But it's hopeful and selfish to think that leaving Seriden will make anything better. Hat was nearly executed today just because General Belrosa wanted to prove a point. What happens to the rest of the Nameless if I leave? And abandoning Seriden will mean I'm walking away from the only chance I've ever had to find my name.

If King Fallow died and made me queen, then I must have a real name, given to me at birth. Whoever named me, father or mother, died and left me Nameless. Fallow somehow found it and spoke it before he died, giving me this tattoo. No matter what the crown means—that I'm meant to rule or to speak another name and die—my name is out there. An ache fills my chest as I imagine a whisper—barely a breath—passing through the king's lips.

Maybe, with a name, I'll finally learn how friendship works when it's more than the alleys you share, the blood, the secrets, and the food. I'll understand courtesy and common kindness, smiling on the streets instead of slipping through the shadows to avoid reproachful glares.

Then there's Hat, who stares at me with all the impossible optimism that I can never understand. When she looks at me, she sees everything she thinks I can change about Seriden. What's stopping me from proving to the Legals and Royals that the Nameless have worth?

What's stopping me? Aside from this trembling ache inside my chest? Aside from fear?

I stare up at the stars, trying desperately to feel their warmth, trying to understand how hope can fuel me instead of crush me.

By morning, I've made up my mind.

CHAPTER 12

The shadows are soft against the ceiling when I wake. The curtains are closed again, so I'm not sure how late it is. There's a quilt tucked around Hat and an afghan draped over my waist.

Devil is sitting in the middle of the kitchen table, drinking something steamy from a teacup.

I smile suspiciously and point at the blanket on me. "Did you?"

"No," she answers curtly, and I hardly believe her, but I let it rest.

"Listen," she says after a moment. "I've asked about the Nameless going missing, and so far no one knows anything. It's like they vanish overnight. I'm sorry I don't have anything for you."

I whisper over Hat's sleeping form. "Hat said a boy disappeared from the prison in the middle of the night, that maybe it was a Royal guard who took him."

Devil considers this. "Could be. The lack of information is telling. If there's no sign of what's going on, either something very organized is happening, or nothing is happening and we're just reading into it."

But we know that's not true. They're going missing, and we don't know how or why.

Hat yawns and stretches, and as she sits up, it's clear that her hair has gone from a tangled mess to an unrivaled frizz ball. She fixes the problem by grabbing one of Glenquartz's hats from his rack and pulling it down tightly over her head.

She springs to her feet, full of sprightly energy. "I could have slept for days!" she says. After being in prison for that long, I'm surprised she didn't.

"We're not staying here," I say to Hat. "I need to get to the palace. I've been letting them dictate the terms of my reign until the festival. But they're stuck with me. They don't get to control how I act and what I do. Not anymore."

"If you want to keep her safe, the best way to do that is to keep her close by," Devil says. "You should take her into the palace with you. It's the last place they'd search for her, especially if you tell them she left the city. Tell them she left on . . ." Devil counts on her fingers. "It's a Wednesday? Tell them she left last night on a ship called the *Delicate Crest*. It's an old schooner headed around the south coast toward Olefar. That type of ship is fast enough that they wouldn't even think about chasing it down. Not to mention that its captain occasionally dabbles in . . . untethered acquisitions and transport."

"You know a pirate?" I ask.

"A *part-time* pirate," Devil says. "But it works as a cover story. Just remember: southbound schooner, *Delicate Crest*. Then all you have to do is get Hat into the palace unnoticed."

I peek through the curtains. It's early enough that the streets won't be filled, but we will still be seen if we aim for a casual stroll through the Royal Court.

"How do you suggest we do that with no one noticing?"

Devil downs the rest of her tea in a single gulp. "You forget so soon. I'm a smuggler. It's what I do."

＋

Devil's plan involves two scaled walls, a padlock to pick, and the loading entrance near the kitchens for shipments from the South Farms. We make our way without incident, which in and of itself is a feat.

I can't take Hat to the guest quarters. That's the first place they'd look. I know I can't conceal her indefinitely, but I need to keep her safe until I can confront the Royal Council. I take her to Med Ward. It's the best chance to keep her safe.

As we enter, I spy the doctor on the far side of the room at a workbench. She's mixing some chemicals in a flask, and there are four teenagers grouped around her.

I nudge Hat to the nearest unoccupied cot. We've gone over the plan enough that it goes smoothly. Hat will feign illness if anyone gets suspicious. I promise her I'll return as soon as I can. I can't help feeling anxious; I'm leaving to protect her, but I can only hope she'll be safe without me.

After I leave Med Ward, I move along the outer corridors before heading inward toward the dining hall. Sharp turn left, a quick pace down a long corridor, and I'm there. It's breakfast time, and the scent of greasy sausage and citrus dominates the air.

I slip inside and steal the first thing I find: a stack of pancakes and a bowl of fruit. I toss the pancakes into the bowl and walk out with the whole thing.

I eat as I make my way to the Royal Council's meeting room, where all the Royals go to collectively panic when something goes wrong. Me disappearing with an almost-executed Nameless girl would certainly qualify as "something gone wrong."

I knock crisply on the door four times and open it.

"Good morning," I say in a cheery voice. I raise the bowl of fruit as if I'm giving a toast.

"My lady!" Glenquartz says, shooting straight up, relief and excitement plastered on his tired face. "Where have you been?"

"This is a delicacy, my friends," I say, ignoring his question. "Fruit *inside* a pancake."

I count the faces in the room. A little under half of them smiled. Three of them scowled. It's good to get an initial count of who will be on my side and who won't. Belrosa herself is furious, but with an edge of triumph. She thinks that I'm making a fool of myself and that she'll have the upper hand here.

"Your Highness," Belrosa says, reaching for the cuffs on her belt, "I'm afraid that—"

"Are you going to try to arrest me?" I say, thoroughly amused. "That'd be a neat trick. What for?" I take another bite of the pancake.

"You interrupted the due course of an execution and went on the run!" Belrosa says with an incredulous laugh.

I tilt my head and look at her questioningly. "Do I look like

I'm running? Now, I'll remind you—and this is a fact I'm sure you haven't forgotten in my absence—that I am Nameless. If you can cite for me which law I've broken, I will surrender myself to the chains." I put my wrists together in front of me. "The Nameless have absolutely no rights within the city. My interference with the execution of another Nameless has absolutely no consequence as far as the law is concerned." I pull my wrists apart as if breaking free of the imaginary chains.

"She was the instigator of a riot," Belrosa argues. "A riot that killed two people!"

"No," I say, "it killed at least three people. Two of them were Legals, who were torturing the third—a Nameless boy. And that young girl you wanted to hang? She was in prison the entire time. She's little more than a child. Some of you may be so heartless that that doesn't mean anything to you. You made a mistake when you tried to pin the riots on her, General.

"The Nameless don't need to be organized to be dangerous. They only need to be afraid and empowered. What empowers them? I do. The crown on my arm does. You can let the Nameless die on the streets, and you can try to execute a child to prove your strength, and you can lock me in chains for saving her, but that would give them the injustice they need to become brave. I don't want to be the martyr they fight for or wage war over. But I will be if I have to."

The room is silent. I give it a beat for the weight of my words to sink in.

"I need you to understand this." I lean onto the table with both hands, recalling my threat to Glenquartz after my first council meeting. "If you kill that girl, I will no longer be your queen. I will be a soldier. An enemy. There will be no refuge in unfair laws or status. Now. Who has a problem with saving a little girl's life?" I look around the room, at each of them in turn. None rise to challenge me.

Belrosa is too furious to formulate an argument.

"I'm not going to storm out this time," I reassure them. "When we all leave this room, we may not agree, but we'll understand each other better. You have me for another four weeks. At that time, I've already agreed to pass on the tattoo, but until then, I think we can all expend some effort to get along. Like it or not, the city out there doesn't care if we hate each other or like each other. They only care if the city falls apart or comes together. Whoever gets this tattoo after me will have to bear the weight of whatever happens. As for me, there's no way on the spetzing blue earth that I'm going to let this ship crash while I'm at the helm. That was a joke, because we're a coastal city."

I check to see who is smiling. Five of them now.

"Regardless," I add, "you have questions. I will answer them, if I can."

We spend the next three hours in that room. I feed them the lie of Hat on the southbound vessel, and they swarm with questions. Of course Belrosa challenges my authority at every turn, but when all is said and done, we at least agree on this: The city needs to hear my voice as the heir, as Nameless.

"They need to know my story about what happened at the execution," I say. "I should give a speech out in the city. It will not call anyone out by name or address the fact that the Nameless helped me escape. My speech won't challenge the Royals in any way, but it will explain that the wrong prisoner was brought out and an otherwise innocent girl was about to be executed. I get to be a hero, and no one on the council will have to be the villain."

The council is about to agree when Belrosa adds, "You must also renounce your loyalties to the Nameless entirely. You showed them too much sympathy when you saved that girl. The Nameless, as you said, are dangerous. They need to know that you're not on their side. You're on *our* side. You're on the side of Seriden itself."

I pause. "You're suggesting I denounce who I am. But then, in four weeks, I'll be one of them again. You see how that's a problem for me, don't you?"

Belrosa shrugs. "Surely you must understand," she says, "that while you hold the position as the heir, your first and foremost obligation is to the city itself. It has to be. Otherwise we cannot support you as the heir a moment longer. Now, you've proven to us that rectifying the mistake with the Nameless girl is in the best interest of the city. That's why we'll allow this course of action. However, if your loyalty is clearly with the Nameless and against the proper, loyal citizens of Seriden, that poses an even greater danger to the city."

Six council members nod in agreement.

"You must renounce your ties to the Nameless," Belrosa insists. "You must do so with the speech. The people need to hear from you to know the city isn't going to fall apart on your watch, that it isn't going to crash like a sinking ship, as you said. I think you must go out as soon as possible to address them. Tomorrow. Today, even!"

Esther frowns. "Come, now. When my father gave speeches, they were never less than three days after the announcement."

The woman bejeweled with amethysts—Ariel—weighs in with a kind voice. "I believe the matter is much more urgent than those of your father's days."

"Then two days," Esther says, speaking as though the decision is final. "That's enough time to write a speech, I think, and get it approved by the council."

"With the city how it is," Belrosa says, "the sooner the better."

As they talk about the speech, my chest is slowly tightening like a constrictor knot. Glenquartz watches me, knowing something is off. I feel my face heating up, and I rise to my feet.

"Then it's agreed," I say. "I will see you at the speech."

A few of them murmur in assent, but most of their auras flicker with nerves and fear.

"Now that we've resolved the course of action for the matter of the execution," I say, "I have another issue to present to you. Nameless are disappearing off the streets. I need you to help me find out what's happening and stop it."

Silence reigns through the room.

"If these were Legals going missing, or Royals, you wouldn't hesitate to start an inquiry," I scoff. "You let something as silly as a name be enough to change your conscience. Seriden can have its treaty that protects magic and stops the cities from declaring war on one another, but that doesn't mean anything if you won't actually protect *everyone* who calls Seriden their home. As much as you don't want to think about it or admit it, the Nameless are as much a part of Seriden as the Legals and Royals. Am I not proof of that?"

What I sense from them is worse than fear and worse than anger: it's discomfort. Fear and anger drive people to act. Discomfort drives people to nothing except avoidance. And all of them feel the same unease, except for one. Esther.

From her I sense something like pride.

"Now, I'm perfectly content," I add, "to give this speech you want. I only ask that you listen to my request and give it due consideration."

"The Nameless go missing frequently," says Belrosa. "It would be irresponsible of us to assign resources for this inquiry when there is such turmoil present in the city, when everything is so politically charged and fragile."

"Where is your evidence?" Esther asks.

I'm startled to hear her speak with a harsh conviction and criticism in her voice that don't match her aura at all.

"Pardon?" I say, buying myself time.

"You say the Nameless disappear at a frequency and quantity they haven't before. I simply wonder how you know this and how you can confirm its accuracy before you ask us to act. As we know, actions without basis are directionless and, sadly, a waste. I have no doubt that people go missing occasionally. But offer us proof."

I twist my hands into angry knots beneath the table.

"I've heard personal testimony from several Nameless," I say.

Esther listens with a serene expression that gives nothing away. Her aura is soothing.

"Given that the city doesn't track the Nameless the way it tracks Legals and Royals for taxes," I say, "this is the only proof I can offer."

"Perhaps when you bring us evidence," Esther says delicately, "of where these Nameless are going, then we would have a solid foundation for action."

I pinch the bridge of my nose. "You're telling me that if I want the Royal Guard to assist in finding out what's happening to the Nameless, I first have to find out what's happening to the Nameless?" I do little to conceal my frustration, and Belrosa's aura dances with amusement.

Most of the remaining council members are firm in their refusal to help now that they've been given a voice of reason to hide behind. Their auras close in on me, closer than the tight walls of an alley, and they feed into me like water collecting in a drain. My frustration grows.

Belrosa chimes in. "The Royal Guard is not a search party, unfortunately. They are here to protect and police Seriden under my command. Regrettably, Your Highness, I can offer no assistance."

I close my eyes for a moment, remembering my first encounter with this woman. I crave another confrontation, but every moment I'm here is a con. I have to play my part. I open my eyes and give a firm nod.

"Understood," I say. "Thank you for hearing me."

Belrosa's smug aura is like a foul scent from a trash bin.

I reach out to sense Esther's aura. While I expect to find a similar sense wafting outward, I find an insistent regret, as if she's pushing an apology at me. I look at her, and there's a brief flicker of a remorseful frown. I seethe silently, trying to stay calm. I don't want an apology. I want an explanation.

The rest of the Royal Council meeting goes by quickly. I've lost a lot of my fire. My energy wanes. They only barely mention the fact that Esther still hasn't added her name to the list of challengers, but even if they unanimously voted that Belrosa should get the tattoo peacefully, it sounds like they *want* me to lose the duel in front of everyone. That way, the Nameless are reminded of their place and I am dethroned in defeat instead of peace. As the meeting wraps up, I tuck the empty fruit bowl under my arm like a stack of papers, and I push away from the table.

Esther stares at me while I head for the door. She could only advertise her intent better if she shouted it. She wants to talk to me, and she's trying to get my attention. Rookie.

I hurry from the room, angry and disheartened as the Royals start to discuss dinner plans and tax collections and preparations for the Assassins' Festival. Esther is five steps behind me as I walk the corridor, which gives her ample time to see me enter a room four doors down. She pokes her head in experimentally. I'm sitting on a desk across the room, my feet on the chair.

"What was all that about?" I demand. "You're the one who told me I had to care about the city. And when I try to put a foot forward to care for the Nameless, you shoot me down like that? Explain! I can sense your guilt all over you."

Esther gently closes the door behind her. We're in some kind of postage room. I have to push aside three different-colored inkwells to sit on the desk, and I'm not anywhere near certain that I'm not actively getting ink stains on my clothes.

"You can't immediately start speaking for the Nameless," Esther says. "Not to the Royals and not like that. They won't give you anything you ask for. You have to wrap your request in something more palatable."

I scratch at some melted wax on the edge of the desk. "You mean like when people give medicine to children. Or so I hear."

"Exactly," Esther says. "Think of the Royals like imperti-nent, impatient children. If you tell them the Nameless are missing, they won't care. If you tell them there's a threat to the Nameless that also threatens them, they will listen. When I took a stance against you, I was giving you a way forward. If you get any indication at all of what's happening, you can position it as a threat against them. Then they'll act."

I sigh. "That's stupid. Something terrible is happening to people in Seridan, and they'll only care about it if it's someone they know."

Esther grimaces. "The truth may not be preferable, but it is still the truth. That's the system we currently have. But giving the speech will be a great step forward with them."

A wave of anxious energy rises through me. A speech. I have to give a speech in front of all the Nameless, denouncing them. And the council expects a handwritten copy for approval.

I squint up at the ceiling, and Esther peers at me.

"Here's the thing," I say. "I can't read." And now that I've said it, I look at her more directly. "I'm sure that delights you. I'm every bit as unqualified as you believe me to be."

She studies me for a moment and then sighs as if she has given up trying to understand what I'm thinking. "You're not unqualified. Or at least . . . you're not as unsuited for this as I thought you were. The way you discussed terms with the Royal Council today was impressive. Did you get everything you wanted? No. But you got them to meet you halfway. Everything you've learned from Eldritch, everything you've learned from . . . wherever you learn things . . . let you *lead* for the first time."

"Here's the second thing," I start. "I need to make this speech. I know that. But I'm afraid that if I give the *wrong* speech, I could make everything worse. Will you . . . ?" I pause for a long time.

Esther's confusion slowly transforms into amusement as she realizes what I'm trying to ask.

"Will you *help* me?" I force the words out.

"Did it hurt you to ask?" Esther says.

"Only my very soul," I respond. "I practically feel faint. Are you going to help me or not?"

"While my stance on your position as the heir is quite clear, I believe we share a genuine concern for the well-being of the city. It is in Seriden's best interest for me to assist you."

I appraise her for a moment. "See, now you have to help

me, because you just admitted that you don't like me, but you also kind of complimented me. You're very good at saying two things at once."

"Meet me in the palace library," she says, "and I'll help you write your speech."

I study her aura, searching for any sign of deception. Her aura reminds me of a wrought-iron gate—the kind I've seen protecting gardens in the Royal Court. She is firm and cold, but protective. She cares about Seriden more than I ever could.

I cycle through a couple of sarcastic remarks before speaking. "I'll join you within an hour. I have to stop off somewhere first."

She taps a fingernail against the edge of the shelf she's standing beside. "She's not really on a schooner called the *Delicate Crest*, is she?"

"I'm sure I don't know what you're talking about," I say. Then, with a mild but respectful bow, I depart.

If Esther suspects Hat is still in the city, surely there are others on the council who feel the same. I stop off in a few rooms for ten minutes at a time to make sure no one is following me.

I enter Med Ward and find Hat where I left her. In the oversized Legal dress, she's smaller and paler than I remember.

"How are you doing, Hat?" I say as I crouch beside her.

"I'm all right," she says with a trembling voice and a breathy cough.

For a moment I'm worried that she's caught an actual illness.

But as she grasps my hand, her whole demeanor shifts. She speaks in a clear, quiet voice. "As it turns out, I am a fabulous actor. They really should hire me for the stage plays. I should be getting paid for this."

I sigh in relief, pulling her hand up against my forehead for a moment. "I could kill you or kiss you."

"If you're going to try to kill me, this is the right place for it." She grins.

"Not funny," I say. "Are you having any trouble? Do you think you can stay for another day or so? I . . . did something."

"What did you do?" She knows me well enough to know that it isn't good news.

"I took a stand against the Royal Council," I say.

"That doesn't *sound* bad," Hat says, "which makes me think that you're leaving something important out?"

I tuck my hair behind my ear. "I took a stand . . . by refusing to turn you over. In front of all of them, I prioritized *you* over the welfare of the entire city. Yeah. I did that." I search Hat for a reaction.

I realize now that being able to sense the auras of the Royals and Legals has made it more difficult to read people. On the streets, I studied faces and body language. I read people the way others read books. But now I'm at a loss without being able to sense her aura.

I examine the slight crease between her eyebrows, trying to decode it. "I'm not sure what you're thinking. I used to be good at this."

Hat readjusts on the soft bed. "I'm conflicted. On the one

hand, that kind of sounds like a bad choice. On the other hand, I really like not being executed."

I laugh. Even now, as she pretends to be on her deathbed, hiding from a city hunting her, she smiles, she laughs, and she jokes.

"Well? What did you tell them?" she asks.

"I told them Devil's lie that you were on a fast ship heading south and that I had absolutely no regrets. And then I commanded them to start a search for the missing Nameless."

"Do you think they're going to do it?" she asks.

"No. I don't," I say. "I think maybe I just asked them to do it so I wouldn't feel so guilty about not knowing what's happening. I can't help but feel like I'm being selfish here."

Hat gives me a puzzled look. "It's not selfish to help other people. You did something that no other sovereign has ever done in Seriden's history. You cared about the Nameless, about us. You're allowed to care about yourself, too."

When she says this, my heart almost breaks. "Isn't that what I've always done? Cared about myself? Survived? No matter the cost. I've always cared about you, Hat, but I've never cared *for* you. All I've been doing is letting you down, over and over again. Isn't it foolish to think I'm doing this for anyone else? The only reason I'm here at all is because you were in prison. I never cared about Seriden, about its Legals and Royals—or even its Nameless."

"So why are you still here now?" she asks. "If you really only cared about yourself or about me, why aren't we on that ship? You're acting like it's selfish to survive, but it's not. And

177

now you're fighting for the Nameless and you're fighting for the city. That doesn't sound selfish at all."

I consider her words for a long time, wondering when it was that she grew up, and when it was that she became—of all the things she could have become—kind and wise.

"I'll be delivering a speech out in the city tomorrow night to quell the chaotic masses," I say, "and I'm hoping you can lie low until then. Apparently, interrupting an execution doesn't go unnoticed."

"Makes sense," Hat says. "I think I'll be good for another day or so. They think my name is Shirley, and that I'm a Legal girl who sneaked out of her house in her sister's dress to go to a play, but then I got sick."

"Nicely grifted," I say, patting her shoulder. "You did great. Did you give them a—"

"Last name? Nope," she says. "But if they get suspicious, where should I go?"

I don't want to send her to the city alone or, worse, to Marcher. Instead I tell her about a walk-in closet six doors down the corridor with ample hiding places.

"I'll be back as soon as the speeches are over, tomorrow evening, okay?"

Hat pats my shoulder this time. "Don't get shot. I'll be okay."

"I should hope so," I say as I rise to my feet. "I've gone to a lot of trouble to keep you alive. Do your best to stay that way, yeah?"

She looks worried for me, maybe even scared. I wonder

how much of her vulnerability is a con and how much of it is because of what she went through in prison.

"Stay here, and be ready," I add. "And be safe. Promise me you'll be safe."

Hat lifts an eyebrow. We don't make promises like that. Ever. It's cruel to promise impossible things. We only ever promise to do our best and try to survive. She taps her fist gently against her heart—a signal we've used in countless cons to tell each other that we're strong and we're ready.

"I promise."

CHAPTER 13

I join Esther at the palace library, which is much smaller than the public library out in the city. Of course, beyond the leather bindings, metal hinges, and illuminated drawings, books don't mean much to me. They're good for propping doors and throwing at people, and paper's a great insulator. Last winter, I spent many of my nights in Seriden's library. I would lock myself in a small room and stack books in front of the windows to keep the cold out. Here, the books are more like ornaments, delicately arranged. A small man with gray hair slowly makes his way up and down the aisles. He has a soft white cloth in his gloved hands, and he's wiping dust from the tops of the books.

"Is there a reason we're meeting here?" I ask. "As opposed to a place with more paper and fewer books?" I scrutinize the bookshelves suspiciously.

"Books are made of paper," Esther corrects. "It's a library. Where else are we going to write a speech? Besides, there are a few books here of speeches from old queens and kings of Seriden. They'll make good study material. Then we can get to writing yours in a couple of hours."

I purse my lips.

Esther crosses her arms impatiently. "What's wrong? Can't muster enough focus for a couple of hours?"

"Can't you just tell me about the speeches?" I ask.

"Of course not," she says. "I can't simply summarize old speeches for you. That defeats the purpose. The spirit of a speech isn't in what is said, but *how* it's said. With the right words and the right passion, you can move a city to peace or war."

I shift my weight from one foot to another as if trying to convince my legs not to run.

"What's the matter with you?" Esther asks. "You're acting stranger than usual."

"Remember, I can't read," I say. "How am I supposed to study old speeches?"

A sad smile threatens to overtake Esther's lips, and I hold up a cautionary hand. "I want your advice, not your pity. Neither of us gets to control what we bring to this table. You bring refinement and leadership skills and entitlement. I bring impatience and illiteracy and cleverness. Maybe you don't want the things I bring, but you have me either way."

Her sad smile turns kind. "I was planning to read the speeches aloud to you."

My cheeks flare with heat, and I sit at the table. "That's what I thought."

We spend the rest of the day, all night, and the following day in the library, breaking only for a few hours to sleep. On the first day, Esther reads speeches aloud to me, and I talk through my main speaking points. Esther helps me refine it, and she writes it all down. On the second day, she helps me memorize it.

"How do you think it will go?" I ask after I've managed to recite the speech a couple of times without any mistakes.

"We are making some bold statements," Esther says. "But we will not apologize for being bold."

"Do you think the council will approve it, though?"

"They already have. I delivered it to them this morning," Esther says. "But don't worry. I didn't give them *this* speech."

I grin and tease her. "Have you done something *dishonest*?"

Her hands flutter in her lap. "My father always told me that honesty is a privilege. In every moment we can, we must seek it out. But there are moments that require dishonesty to spare a life or spare pain. I think this falls into both of those categories, don't you?"

"Your father sounds like a nice guy," I say. "Except for giving me a death-sentence tattoo."

Esther shifts in her seat, and I bet she's repressing the urge to chastise me again for not being grateful.

"It is beautiful, though," I say as a way of softening my words.

She stares at the tattoo on my arm, pensive. "Beauty doesn't mean much without context. It's beautiful, maybe. Powerful, definitely. But the history of magic is long and complicated." She scoffs. "Gaiza, it's *short* and complicated too."

I tilt my head. "Did the former heir apparent befoul her tongue with dark words?" I gasp in mock offense, and Esther laughs. For a moment, it's strange, but we're almost getting along.

"We don't have much time left," Esther says. "How are you feeling about the speech?"

I jump from foot to foot energetically. "I'm ready."

"You seem . . . nervous," Esther objects gently.

"Yes. I'm scared. But ready doesn't mean not scared. Ready means ready, despite everything. I'm ready."

"Well, aren't we a pair," Esther says. "The former heir apparent and the impossible queen. I think, under the right circumstances, we could tear the world to pieces."

"Do you see the way the Royals and Legals look at me?" I say. "I think we already have."

"So you're ready, then," she says, standing up tall.

I've gotten very little sleep, but I mirror her posture and take a deep breath. "Ready."

By the time we get to the North Residences, the sky is dark. Belrosa insisted that nighttime would be best for the speech, and I'm still not sure why. She said it was to discourage rioting, that people could go to bed after the speech instead of having an entire day to simmer and stew. I'm not convinced. The riots I escaped were at night, not in broad daylight. But I couldn't explain that without also explaining that I was *at* the first riots.

As people gather along the street in front of the Legal residences, it's difficult if not impossible to see the Nameless. Maybe this is what she wanted: for me to speak to my city but not to my people. The Nameless wear dark clothing, typically scavenged from the Legal's trash. They are like shadows at the edge of the crowd, invisible in the night.

I wear a bright yellow long-sleeved shirt with an armored vest over it. Esther said it makes me look strong, and I agreed because it'll protect me if someone gets too close with a blade.

Two Legal servants set up a podium, and the Legals in the crowd shift uncomfortably.

This, of course, is another calculation by Belrosa. Not only am I a Nameless out of my station and rank, but the Legals are serving me and the Royal Guard is protecting me. I am a misplaced puzzle piece. Worse, I'm a puzzle piece glued to the center of an otherwise beautiful painting. And the painting is on fire.

I am the thing that doesn't make sense.

Faint insults are shouted from somewhere, and I don't even try to find the source. I move forward to help adjust the podium, and one of the Legals is startled by my motion and flinches. The whole podium angles dangerously to the side, and I immediately withdraw, trying to look apologetic as the audience's grumbling increases. I adopt a somber expression and speak out of the corner of my mouth to Esther.

"What's the likelihood someone assassinates me right here?" I ask.

Esther's aura flares in alarm, and she checks the nearest rooftop and alley.

"Relax," I tell her, putting a hand on her elbow. "I'm joking."

"Except you really aren't, though," she says.

I toyed with the idea of telling her earlier that someone might take a shot at me, but I didn't want her to worry, and I needed her to focus. I thought about not telling her at all, but if something goes wrong, she should be prepared.

She twists a thin black ring on her finger nervously, and I wonder if I've made a mistake as an unfamiliar grip of paranoia wraps around her, smothering her aura.

We've practiced this dozens of times throughout the day. I've done everything she has said: *tilt your head here, allow for a moment of silence there, let your eyes roam the crowd here, be firm and strong and unwavering.* I move to the podium, and the crowd is as quiet as they are restless. They're a sea of shifting limbs and dagger glares. I spot Belrosa among them.

I glance to Esther to see if she's noticed her. Esther encourages me forward anyway, and I have a brief fear that Esther and Belrosa are conspiring together. What would be better than having me give a speech in front of everyone where I start raving about unity and laws and putting a stop to all executions? If Belrosa interrupts me before I can finish the speech, it could make things worse instead of better.

I clear my throat and begin.

"We can be stronger," I say. "Together. The city is as strong as its most unified force, but it is as weak as it's disjointed. We just need something to pull us all together." At this point in the speech, I'm supposed to make a grand claim about being able to put the city back together, to resolve hundreds of years of disputes. But something feels wrong about saying that. The crowd, mostly Legals with a few Royals scattered throughout, draws closer to listen to me.

I try to think of what would comfort them but also be honest. A crowd this large, they're already expecting me to give them nothing but empty comfort and reassurances. I've listened to my share of speeches. I know what I'd want to hear.

"I don't know if that is me," I say, feeling a tingling expectation rise through the collective auras of the audience. "I don't know if it can be. . . . But *we*, we can be . . ."

A warm glow sets on the crowd. At first, it's like the return of a brilliant dusk—steady and orange. Then it flickers at the edges as though everyone's auras have combined.

Then I hear the screaming.

Then I see the fire.

The people amassed around me surge toward a set of houses inside the North Residences. The guards abandon me, shouting for the people to fetch water from the nearest firehouse. It's only one street east—a summer spent filching water from the stone-basin reservoirs taught me that. Glenquartz stays by my side with another guard. Two, now three houses on fire.

A crash of glass and a sound like faint thunder. Four houses. Another scream. I pull at the waist of my armored vest, cinching it tighter as I move forward. Glenquartz puts a hand on my arm to stop me, and I don't have time to convince him. I throw an open hand against his chest, and he stumbles, startled but unharmed. I run toward the flames.

Auras all over the street rage with fear. The first two houses are already empty. The third house—there are two auras, like bright embers screaming in the fire. I charge in through the front door. The fire is raging in the sitting room: bright fabric upholstery turning black. I feel a silvery aura come up behind me, like steel and crystal, as Glenquartz joins me. There's nothing restrictive in his aura; it pushes us onward. It gives me strength.

I always thought smoke would be heavy, but it's as light as air and tastes like ash, burning my throat. It isn't too dense, but the burn of it makes it hard to see. A cry for help cuts through me like a sharp flame.

"In the . . . ?" Glenquartz starts to move toward the stairs, and this time I'm the one to put a halting hand on his arm. I pull him toward the sitting room. The fire has spread along the upholstery, up the curtains, curling the wallpaper into ash. The whole ceiling is black with soot and shifts with a denser collection of smoke.

The auras shine with fear. I feel it stronger than the fire. It's so sharp, it's like a dagger in my throat. I can barely breathe. In the room are two men, their auras tangled with each other. One man is obviously immobile, legs emaciated and weak but strong arms, a cushioned chair toppled. The other man doesn't want to move even though he could. I crouch and put my face in front of his.

"I need you to lead us out of here," I tell him.

Dazed, the man focuses on me, his eyes filled with tears.

I grab his shoulder. "Can you do that?"

If he says no, he's getting a cast-iron pot to his head and Glenquartz can drag him to safety. The man nods and staggers to his feet, coughing in the smoke, and goes toward the door. I put an arm around the immobilized man's back and motion for Glenquartz to help. He takes the other side, and together we lift him. He's lighter than I expected.

A creak and crackle rip through the ceiling, and it's all I can do to keep my grip on the man in my arms. I adjust my grip, and my arm touches the man's neck. As soon as our skin touches, his thoughts blaze through me.

Out of the house, out of the house—run!

The man's fear overtakes me, and I double our pace, nearly carrying him by myself. The other man is at the end of the hall, holding the door anxiously.

Run—run!

A heavy splinter of wood from above, a creaking groan, and part of the ceiling collapses. The man at the door staggers outside just as fire blazes in our path.

Glenquartz looks helplessly at me, and I spin to assess the rest of the house. The stairs are engulfed, there are no other doors, and the only window is behind the flaming wreckage of the upper floor. But the flames blocking our path flicker in the air currents, and every few seconds, they almost clear up. We can run. We can make it.

"We have to move fast!" I shout to Glenquartz.

He hesitates, and so does the man in our arms, but we don't have time for fear. I stare at the fire again. I tell myself they can't see it. I imagine the hall without fire and smoke—a startlingly normal scene with clean paint and the light of a mirrored lantern. I check Glenquartz and the man in our arms, and their eyes shine with sudden clarity as they stare at the corridor ahead.

Don't see the flames. Don't even feel the heat. I imagine a cool breeze against their skin. The sensation of water.

I turn my own gaze to the corridor, and a burst of flames rages before us with a gust of hot air that nearly singes the man's feet. But I cling to the image of the safe, clean corridor. They can't see the fire anymore, but I can.

No time for fear. I urge us forward, taking nearly all of the man's weight in my arms.

Six steps to the door, and adrenaline surges through me. Fire blazes to my left, and I feel a searing pain on my arm as I stumble against the burning railing of the stairs.

Four steps, and my lungs are made from smoke, my vision blurring with burning tears.

Two steps, and the house around us groans and cracks. The fire rages.

Then we're out. Gasps of fresh air as I finally let go of the illusion. Together, Glenquartz and I stagger to the edge of the road, and relief overtakes me. The three of us collapse there, and all I want is to be in the arms of the other man, to hold him close and—I let go of the man we've been carrying and the sensation disappears. The other man rushes to us, and the two of them hold each other, each crying in relief. I hear murmurs of "thank you, thank you," but I'm already moving away from them and toward the next fire.

Three glowing auras inside the house, terrified and bright.

Esther rushes past me, a flurry of color and determination, trailing two guards. She's pointing to the same house, ordering the guards forward. "There! Up on the second floor!"

I start after them, and I see Marcher running down the street. He runs after two Nameless clad in black, and I can't see enough of his face to tell whether he is scared or not.

I return my attention to the house. The door is already engulfed in flames, and there's a large window farther along that's shattered. I sense Glenquartz at my side and we join Esther's squad of guards—five of us now. Of the three auras, one is so radiant and sharp, I know it belongs to a child.

As we move forward, another window shatters. Somewhere, the entire house cracks and groans, and the roof shifts—barely at first, but then all at once. There's a heavy, rending crash as the house folds inward and collapses. I head toward the building, but Glenquartz stops me.

The emptiness.

All three auras. Gone. Extinguished.

I almost feel their names on the tip of my tongue, but all I can do is scream at the burning rubble. Then I'm on the ground, elbows on my knees, throat aching from the smoke.

The world around me burns, and I am an ember at its core, white hot and slowly disintegrating. I am raw heat and pain.

Two other houses collapse, but I'm far enough away that I can't sense if anyone is in them. There are other fires in other houses. There are other auras all around me. People are gathered in the streets, carrying pails of water, gawking at the destruction, comforting and carrying each other.

I get up and help. I move with them, numb, doing what I can, carrying water. Glenquartz is never too far away. I'm glad to have him nearby, a familiar aura. At the same time, his pain and fear are like poison to me. The whole world is poison, filled with auras of ash and fear and heartbreak.

Glenquartz checks on me at some point. He's saying something about an injury, and I barely remember falling against the burning railing as we escaped the house. All I want is to take a quiet path to the palace or an even quieter path to Devil's alley. But there is work to be done. I finally find my voice past the hoarse burn in my throat.

"Clear the two houses at the end of the street," I order. "There's two people upstairs in the first house, then one in the back." Glenquartz is hesitant to leave me, but he does. I return to the line of people transporting water for the fires. I know the water is heavy, but my arms are numb.

Still—always—there is work to be done.

I'm not sure how long we are out here, breathing smoke-heated air, but I'm certain that those windows were shattered inward. The fires were not accidental. They were started when someone threw something through the windows.

I realize General Belrosa has been here all along, giving orders and guidance. I'm one of the many following her lead, transporting water and going where I'm needed. I don't want to be grateful, but I am.

I find the doctor from Med Ward near the man I helped carry from his house. She tends to the injured, doling out orders and commands just like General Belrosa. Both of them are in their element, natural leaders.

And I'm a natural follower, I suppose.

As the doctor tends to the man, checking his soot-covered skin for any sign of injury, the second man approaches me.

"Sedgewick," he says, stammering, pointing to his chest. "My name is Sedgewick. I . . . you . . ." He takes a moment for a rasping cough, and I can't help but feel an itch in my throat. "Thank you for saving my husband. Simon. His name. Simon." It's as if the name itself is precious to him, and their auras are tethered to each other.

The itch in my throat burns, and I don't trust my voice to speak, so I nod.

"Thank you, Lady Sovereign," Sedgewick says to me, and he rejoins the doctor at Simon's side.

I stare at the wreckage of the houses that have collapsed. Three people, dead. I sit as close to the sizzling scorched debris as possible, straining with every ounce of strength to sense the faintest glimmer of an aura. But there's nothing. Empty holes in my chest and nothing, nothing.

The fires are out and several houses on both sides of the street are charred and empty; the streets are still filled with people. Belrosa has set up barricades at both ends of the street and recruited some Legals to help transport the injured. Before long, we're in a large, slow procession to the Royal Court.

At first I expect us to stop at one of the medic stations in the court, but we go straight to the palace.

As we walk, Belrosa patrols the line, making sure that no one falls behind. I don't know how to reconcile the Belrosa who was willing to let Hat be executed with the woman before me, tending to the injured with nothing but concern and bravery in her aura. She slows and points at me, and with a hatred that seeps from her like acid, she says, "This is *your* fault. *Yours.*"

I don't have the time or energy to respond before she moves to tend to a stumbling Legal whose clothes are so marred with ash and burns that he looks like one of the Nameless.

Med Ward isn't big enough to hold everyone at once, so the line stretches down the corridor. There's blood on my sleeve, reminding me of my injury, but I don't feel it yet. I sit outside Med Ward, in line with everyone else. It's comforting to be part of the crowd.

Eventually, Glenquartz returns to me. He's coated in soot and ash like me—like all of us—but his aura doesn't pinch with pain anymore. He is as tired as I am. He puts a hand on my bare arm, letting me know he's here. I flinch away out of reflex, not wanting to see his memories or fears. But the soothing energy of his aura spreads from his touch, and I let the feeling overwhelm me and fill me up. Then, somewhere between fear and exhaustion, I fall asleep.

CHAPTER 14

When I wake, someone is holding my arm. For a moment, I'm afraid they're about to slice it off to steal the tattoo—though I've been assured by Glenquartz time and again that that's impossible.

But when I blink away the blurriness, I see that it's Hat. She has propped my arm on her knee, and she's rewrapping my burn with delicate fingers.

"You didn't wake up when I cleaned your burn," Hat says, "which is for the best, because it would have been *very* unpleasant, and I definitely would have had to do it anyway. If you're upset that you missed out on the fun, don't worry. It'll have to be cleaned again before you go to sleep tonight." She uses a pin to fasten the bandage, and she gently moves my arm to my lap. The burned skin underneath stretches, and the sear of it is almost as hot as the fire was.

"What time is it?" I ask when the pain clears up. There are fewer people here than when I fell asleep, and a glow of sunlight peers out from under nearby doors.

"It's morning," Hat explains as she puts a few metal tools in a bag. "I'm sorry it took so long to get to you, but there were a lot of people with a lot of injuries, and I didn't realize you were hurt at first."

"What are you doing?" I ask, taking proper stock of the bandage on my arm and the medical bag in her hands. I realize she's wearing a white jacket that bears the blue crescent symbol for doctors and nurses overtop her loosely fitting Legal dress.

She shrugs slowly, and the smile on her face touches her eyes.

"I'm volunteering," she says. "Helping out. Dr. Rhana says that normally you have to go to a school in Lindragore or Devra to become a doctor. Unless you start young, like me, and take on an apprenticeship."

I scrunch up my face, and I can feel the grime of ash and sweat in the creases of my frown.

"But aren't you worried Rhana will find out you're . . . ," I start, and stop myself.

Hat folds her arms. "She already knows. She wanted to send me home escorted by a guard, and I was going to run. But when the injured started showing up, I asked to stay, and I told her the truth. It turns out, in a tragedy, no one cares who you are. They care if you can help. And if you stay on the throne, I get to stay here, don't I." And she says it like a statement, not a question, as if the mere act of me claiming the throne will change everything. As if she's not asking me to take the throne, but commanding me to.

I can't believe she'd take a risk like telling Dr. Rhana that she's really Nameless. But I'm too tired to argue, and also, I hope that Dr. Rhana is as good and kind as Hat seems to think she is. I hope Hat can stay.

"So much for making a speech to soothe the masses," I say as I test the soreness of my body.

Hat frowns sympathetically. "I think we're far past speeches now. Anyway, I'm glad you're awake." Before she walks away, she points at my arm and recites what sounds like a memorized line: "Burns. Don't touch it for the rest of the day. Scrub it clean when you take a shower tonight. Then come get a new bandage. It'll hurt like spetz, but Dr. Rhana says that it's really important to keep it clean. Could get infected otherwise."

The corridor is still filled, but instead of a sea of gray ashen faces, there are stark white bandages all over the place. There must be a hundred of us at least, here and inside Med Ward. The auras here are like knives pressing against me from every direction. I venture into Med Ward to find Dr. Rhana, and hopefully get some bandages so I won't have to come back later.

As I approach Dr. Rhana, however, something else catches my attention. Someone ducks in and out among the cots, searching for someone. Marcher, dressed in Royal blue colors, ash-free and clean, and searching.

"What the hell are you doing here?" I approach him. There are two syringes on a nearby tray. Either of them could be in my hand one second and in Marcher's throat the next.

"I heard about that," he says, ignoring my demand and instead pointing at the bandage around my arm. "How our fearless queen raced into a fire to save her subjects. Did one of them owe you money?" He chuckles.

I pick up one of the syringes and turn it over between my fingers.

"Answer my question," I say, "or I'll have you arrested."

He tries not to roll his eyes again. "Have you given any more thought to my proposal? The offer still stands."

I open my mouth to call for a guard, and he holds up a hand to stop me.

"I'm looking for someone," he says. "That's all."

"Who?"

He has to think about it for a second, which is how I know he's about to lie to me. "Enough. Enough of this. Guard?" I summon a guard standing not three paces away as I grab Marcher by the elbow.

The guard hurries over to us, and I make sure my bandaged arm with the crown tattoo is facing him.

"This Royal was trying to steal some of the medicine," I say.

Marcher puts a hand against his chest as if he's deeply offended by the accusation.

"I saw him put something in his pocket," I say, pushing Marcher's elbow toward the Guard.

Marcher throws me the quickest of glances, and there's a hint of a repressed smirk.

The guard reaches into Marcher's pocket and fishes out a syringe.

Marcher murmurs to me, "Sleight of hand *and* a reverse pickpocket. Here I was, thinking you'd lost your edge." He tips an imaginary hat in approval.

It makes me angry, but not angry enough to overwhelm the

pride I feel from outsmarting him. Here I am, ever the competitor, just the way he made me.

"A night in the holding cells should do him good," I say.

"Yes, Your Highness," the guard answers.

"Regardless of your terrible mistreatment of me," Marcher says, "the offer still stands. Time is not on your side. Secrets and time—always at war with each other. And the real secret? Time wins every time. Secrets don't stay buried forever. You can hide them away in the darkness, but they'll eventually claw their way to the surface."

The guard gives a small salute before escorting Marcher away.

I realize my whole body is tense, and I try to relax, turning to a Legal woman in a nearby cot.

She has a wound on her head that's been patched with white cloth, but it's in dire need of sutures.

On closer inspection, I realize that her clothes aren't just dirtied from the fire—they're dark and drab from months of wear and stains. The woman isn't a Legal. She's Nameless. Panic wells through me, and I move closer to her as if I can hide her from everyone in the room.

"If you'll give my patient some room," Dr. Rhana says as she edges past me to check on the woman.

"But, I—she . . ." I bite my tongue.

Dr. Rhana rolls one of her shoulders in annoyance. "If you have a problem with any of my patients, I can call the Royal Guard to come explain to you that . . ." Her eyes catch on the tattoo peeking out from under my bandages.

"Oh," she says in a small voice. Then, with more strength: "Oh. It's you. You're you."

"When I'm not being someone else, yeah," I say. "I was worried when I saw she was . . ." I point at the dark, moth-eaten cloth of the woman's sleeve. "Is she going to be all right?"

"She'll be fine. She was in a lot of pain, so she's sleeping now. I heard what you did during the fires, saving that family and helping put out the blazes. Thank you. I'm Dr. Andris. Rhana Andris. Just Rhana, really."

Rhana is maybe in her thirties, and she's vastly outpaced anything I've ever accomplished. There's an awkward moment as she realizes I don't have a name to offer in return.

"I call myself Coin," I say.

She touches her hand to her opposite shoulder and gives a polite bow.

"Will you send word to me when she wakes?" I ask. "I want to make sure she gets out of here safely."

Rhana nods knowingly. "I'll notify you when she is healthy enough to go home."

Rhana returns to her patients, and she doesn't even know the mistake she made. This woman doesn't have a home. Not really. None of the Nameless do.

I turn around, searching for Hat again, but instead I see Esther standing at the bedside of a man three cots away.

I think about the fires. Esther was strong and brave— rushing toward the house before it collapsed. But there's something I can't quite put my finger on as she goes from cot to cot, comforting people. I approach her.

"You knew there were people in that house before it collapsed," I say. It's possible she saw them through a window or heard them, but as I study her face, she hardly reacts. She's about to lie to me.

"Were there?" Esther says. "I guess we won't know until they get through the wreckage." She shakes her head clear of the gruesome thoughts, and her aura is like damp soot and ash.

"I considered at first that you staged the fires," I say, "that maybe you wanted to be the hero who saved people, and the city would push for you to get the crown. I considered the same about Belrosa. But you knew there were people in that house. How did you know? It doesn't make sense. And what have you been doing to the patients here? I've been watching you put people to sleep. Tell me what's going on."

Esther leans in close as if she's about to share a secret. "I don't know what you're talking about. I'm administering a sedative, obviously." She picks up a syringe from the metal tray.

"Then go ahead and do it," I say.

She holds it uncertainly.

"You're a good liar," I say, "but not a good grifter. You didn't guess there were people in that house. You *knew* there were, didn't you? And if you're not administering a sedative, you're doing something else to make these people fall asleep. Something *magical*." Before I can stop myself, I grab on to her left arm just below her shoulder. She winces and withdraws, but I keep my grip.

I level a dead-set glare at her. "Are you going to pretend

that's a bruise from the fires, or am I going to have to reveal your tattoo here for everyone to see?"

I sense the defeat and frustration in her aura, and I can't tell whether she's angry or angrily impressed. I'm right. She has a tattoo like mine.

"I know you're doing something," I say. "What is it?"

Esther pulls me aside, although in a room filled with injured people and clutter, there's not a lot of privacy. She absently picks up a gray jacket from the chair and folds it. "We can talk about it, or I can show you now, and we can save some people from terrible pain today." Her voice is low and forceful. "Do you have a preference?"

I didn't expect her retort to be so biting, and I let go of her arm. I have a million questions screaming in my head. She has a tattoo. She has abilities, like me. How? Why? Is she the queen of another city?

Esther whispers, "You know that you can make other people hallucinate, right?"

"Yes." Is her tattoo a fake? Or is mine? Maybe I'm just a cheap forgery.

"Well," she says, "it started off small for you. You could make people see things that weren't there or not see things that were there. At the execution, you demonstrated that you could cause auditory hallucinations too. You can make people hear things. Then, at the fires, how did you get those people out of the house?"

I take a moment to center myself. My immediate thought is that the tattoo on my arm is meant for Esther and that it fractured onto me. But I don't even understand how that would happen or if it's possible. All I know is that I am, myself, impossible—so any explanation is possible.

I reply, "I made it so they couldn't see the fire or smoke. Then I made it so they couldn't feel the heat. It's what got us out of there."

She nods. "The hallucinations are much more than just visual. You can make people see things, feel things, and hear things. Or you can take it all away. That's part of what I'm doing here. All these people who are hurt and the ones who are dying, I'm trying to take away their pain, to make it easier for them. Sometimes that's all you can do."

I take stock of the Legal man on the bed. His broken leg has been splinted and wrapped in bandages. She places her hand on his arm. He's sleeping fitfully, but as soon as Esther touches his skin, he calms down.

"How did you do that?" I ask.

"I found one of his happy memories, and I guided him there. Now he's asleep. It helps that the entire time, I was sharing soothing feelings. It's like being sung to sleep by a lullaby."

My jaw stiffens, and I study the bandage on the man's leg.

"Oh," she says in a small voice. "You probably never had . . . ?"

"I didn't," I cut in sharply, but then I continue in a softer voice: "I learned one once, though. Heard it through an open window near the South Residences. And for a while, when I was on my own, I sang it to myself. I know that sounds . . . incredibly sad." I force a laugh.

"No, no," Esther says. "I'm sorry." She sounds more than sympathetic—almost guilty.

I wipe my palms on my pants, feeling uncomfortable and vulnerable.

"Tell me how this is possible?" I ask. "Tell me how any of this is possible." My eyes fall to her arm, where—somehow, impossibly—she has a tattoo hiding beneath her sleeve.

Esther bows her head. "Of course."

She leads me to King Fallow's sleeping quarters. A black silk curtain covers the door as a sign of mourning. Esther pulls it aside, opens the door, and enters the room in one swift movement, holding the curtain for me.

This is where King Fallow died, where he spoke my name. The crown faded from his skin and appeared on mine. This room holds the moment when I became queen. The emptiness of the room waits to swallow me.

The wooden floors are rich mahogany, and the walls are alternate panels of the same dark wood and green wallpaper. A row of wardrobes ends at a vanity table and mirror, and the bed is covered by a black sheet. There are a few bookshelves and a writing desk.

Esther sits on the edge of the bed, but I find it difficult to approach.

I know he died here. That's not the problem. I've lived in alleys where men and women gasped through illness and died where they fell. Death doesn't bother me.

It's difficult because this place doesn't belong to me, not in the way it belonged to him. I don't have a hoard of clothes to pile into the wardrobes, or the ability to read the books on the shelves, or the patience to stare at myself in a mirror without seeing a stiff frown contort my features.

When I finally sit on the edge of the bed, Esther removes her ash-stained jacket and brushes away the charcoal smudges on her skin. A black, sharp-angled crown encircles her upper arm—identical to mine in every way.

I reach out a finger and trace the pattern. As soon as I touch her skin, a memory pushes its way into my thoughts. I see a flash of green and feel the cold touch of metal before I pull away.

Esther gives a me a sympathetic pout. "I know. It's difficult." She slips off her blue-heeled shoes and walks up to the head of the bed. The silk sheet crumples with her weight. She points to a framed piece of old paper on the wall.

"This is the treaty," Esther says, placing a hand on the edge of the gilded frame. "Have you seen it before?"

"There's one on the wall of the guest sleeping quarters," I say. The columns of text and scribbled signatures are familiar and yet still foreign to me.

"That's a copy," Esther says. "This is one of the originals."

"If there are multiple originals," I say, "doesn't that make them all copies?"

"No. When the treaties were drawn up over two hundred years ago, they wrote out the whole thing fourteen times. One original for each city."

"That sounds incredibly boring," I say. "Can you please

explain how that connects to the fact that you and I *both* have the crown tattoo? Because I'm not seeing the connection, and I'd really like to."

"Do you know about the old history of magic?" Esther asks.

"I know about the broken five-pin tumbler lock on the baker's rear entrance," I counter.

She glares, and I huff.

"Did you know that magic existed before these tattoos did?" She points to her arm and then mine.

"Hasn't magic always been a weird crown tattoo on your arm?" I ask. "Isn't that why sovereigns wear crowns on their heads?"

"Nice thought," she says, "but the history of magic is older than the idea of the crown. Maybe this is a better question: What *is* magic?"

"If I wanted to get asked questions I don't know the answer to," I say, "I'd wait until my next etiquette lesson."

"It's a rhetorical question that I'm about to answer," Esther says impatiently.

"If it's rhetorical, *can* you answer it?" I muse.

Esther's nostrils flare. "You're being difficult, and it's making this conversation harder."

I hold up a hand to indicate that I'll try to show some restraint.

"Magic is what lets us read people's memories, sense their auras, and make them see and feel things."

"The tattoo, right?" I say.

"That's what we like people to believe," she says. "But magic is much more complicated than that. A long time ago, magic was an object, or really it was a substance. It had this very hard-to-pronounce name, with a silent *k*, I think? Kvaight? I don't know. Putting aside the particulars, magic *was* this substance. The abilities of the sovereigns in the fourteen cities are different, but all of them come from the same thing: that magical substance. Magic used to be wild. It wasn't tied to any place or person like it is now. It was dangerous, and it was the cause of most wars in the previous thousand years."

"What happened?" I ask. "Just because people were using it doesn't mean it was bad, right?"

She gives me a knowing look. "That's exactly what the sovereigns said. There were a number of different territories, and when they finally sat down to do something about the problem of magic, there were fourteen of them. They decided magic was too dangerous to let it run wild. They wanted to contain it and protect people."

"And make it so they were the only ones with magic?" I say.

"Yes," Esther says, "unfortunately. But binding all of magic was complicated and intricate. It literally shaped the world we live in. I don't know how they figured it out, but you notice how all of the cities have the same shape? Maybe you've noticed their arrangement across the continent. It wasn't by accident." She points to a map framed beside the vanity mirror.

"Someone really liked hexagons?" I offer.

"Yes, in fact," Esther says. "When magic was bound, it came with very specific rules. They bound magic to black ink. With it, they wrote the fourteen treaties and created these ink tattoos. So the magic lives in these crowns on our arms, but it also lives in all fourteen treaties across the cities. It's what binds magic to the cities and to the sovereigns! They spelled out the rules in the treaties, which is why we haven't had a war since. And . . . it answers one of the biggest questions." She trails off, unsure she wants to continue. Her aura is still, like a heavy window curtain.

"What biggest question?" I ask, but even as I speak, I realize what it is.

"Why magic doesn't affect the Nameless," Esther says.

I stare at the treaty. I don't understand a single scratch of the ink, but I recognize the difference between the lines of neat text in the center and the fourteen signatures that surround it.

I run a finger along the edge of one of the names.

"I don't think it was their intention to create a divide," Esther says, "but when they signed their names, they bound the magic tattoos to them as sovereigns, and they also bound it to every named citizen of the city. That's why our abilities only affect named citizens. It's why magic has to be passed on by the speaking of a name. It's why when someone is exiled or born Nameless, they aren't part of the city's magic anymore."

I stare at every unrecognizable curve of the signatures. This treaty is the reason for everything I've never understood about the city and magic. Maybe even about myself. It's why people like Belrosa would rather see us dead than in power.

"But why do you and I both have the tattoo?" I ask. "And how can I have one if I don't have a name? I don't understand."

She bobs her head. "I can show you a memory I have of

my father. Rather, you'll be able to see it because of your abilities, and I think it'll answer some of those questions. But it may also create some more." She looks afraid. Ashamed, maybe. Almost sad.

"I have the strangest feeling," I say as I study the downward pinch of her lips, "that you're about to break my heart."

She smiles sadly. "I hope that's not true. But maybe." She sits down on top of the pillows and puts out her hand, palm up. It makes me feel like a child, taking her hand like this, and I sink down to my knees beside her.

"Are you sure?" I ask, my hand hovering above hers. I feel the heat radiating from it. "Whatever this is, I don't want it to . . . hurt you? I guess? I'm worried it might, from the way you're acting."

She offers a faint shrug. "Don't worry. I'll be fine."

I place my hand over hers, and like lightning being drawn to metal, I am pulled sharply into her memory.

It's like a dull pressure against every inch of my body, and then I open my eyes and I'm sitting in a green fabric chair with the cool touch of fabric armrests against my skin. Or, Esther is. I am.

I see the memory from her perspective as she squirms in the chair. She pushes a curvy wave of hair out of her face, and her hands are small and smooth. She's young.

Fallow sits on the edge of his bed, rolls up his sleeve, and shows Esther his crown tattoo.

"You know this tattoo, miya?" Fallow says, and he pats his arm.

Esther nods.

"I want to tell you the story about what happened to this tattoo one generation ago," he says. "My mother was a great queen, and she saw a future for Scriden that was grander than anything we'd seen before. When my brother and I were born—you know Uncle Charlie, right—we were twins. And my mother was clever. She gave us both the same name, and then when she died a few months later, she spoke our shared name. The crown tattoo was given to both of us. We both have the same name, Parson Rejoriak Fallow, but he went by Charles Hamish Fallow."

Esther nods again, but confusion and intrigue swirl through her like gusts of wind.

"My parents were foolish," Fallow says. "They wanted Charlie and me to be twin kings! But as we grew, Charlie didn't want the throne and wasn't suited for it. He wanted nothing more than to continue living a charmed life. When Charlie grew sick last year, we fought. I told him how disappointed I was that he hadn't embraced his abilities and power. I called him a derelict for not wanting the throne."

Fallow's eyes turn weary and sad. "I was angry we didn't get to spend our lives ruling side by side. But having two crowns in one city is in violation of the treaties. We are weaker individually than the other sovereigns, but still stronger when combined. It's an unnatural imbalance. If word got out, it would have caused war between us and the other cities."

Esther raises her hand to her father's shoulder. "Why are you telling me this now?"

"Your uncle," Fallow starts. "Uncle Charlie."

"His real name is Uncle Parson," Esther corrects.

"Yes, dear," Fallow says. "We think he's going to pass to-night."

"Is he giving the tattoo to you?" Esther asks. "To make it whole again?"

Fallow grimaces. "I wish it were that simple. He and I aren't close. He spoke a name this morning, and he has sworn not to speak another before he dies."

"Whose name?" Esther asks.

"I yelled and told him that he was spoiled and irrespon-sible," Fallow says, troubled, "but he said that growing up with the burden of power would do the same damage to anyone else." Fallow takes his daughter's hand in his own. "He has spo-ken your name, Ezzie. He's giving you the crown tattoo."

"Is that what's going to happen to me?" Esther asks, on the verge of tears. "Am I going to become angry like Uncle Charlie?"

Fallow rubs a thumb across Esther's cheek to smooth away a tear. "No, dearest. That's not what it means. You get to be whatever type of person you want to be, as long as you pay at-tention to who you're becoming and make decisions carefully. You know that a sovereign's first priority is their city, right?"

Esther nods.

"You're suited for this life," Fallow says. "I always thought that you would . . . that I would . . ." He pats his arm. "Maybe one generation of the tattoo being split is enough to prove that we shouldn't tamper with magic so frivolously. There are deeper veins of conflict running through this city, more so than the rift between two brothers. I haven't done much as king. Kept us afloat and at peace. Maybe that's enough for my time. But I swear to you that we will not tamper with magic for much longer. The tattoo and this city will be mended in the next generation—your generation."

He holds Esther's face. She feels the warmth of his skin grow hotter. Then something more arid. She pulls away, and the dry sensation vanishes. She glances down at her arm and sees a small black crown tattoo encircling it.

The king's brother is dead.

Esther withdraws her hand from mine, and the memory vanishes. She rubs her palms against her pants, offering a weak smile.

"I thought he meant that he would give me the tattoo when he died," Esther says. "But he didn't. He meant that he would give it to *you*, and that then between us, we'd mend the city. Or you would. The conflict he was talking about wasn't magic: it was the Nameless. He must have known what he wanted of me . . . of us."

"This is where it happened," I say, gesturing at the king's sleeping quarters. While the fabrics and colors have changed, this is the room that holds the memory of her father. This is his room, where he lived, and it must also be where he died. This is where, if I survive long enough to become queen, I'll die too.

"Being here helps me remember," Esther says, "but memories can be influenced by where we are and how we feel. We can even change them. So you can't always trust them."

My heart aches. Memories can hurt us. Sometimes they're more like wounds than scars.

The room smells like books and vanilla, fabric and dust. I don't think I'll ever forget it.

"I wanted to show you this," she says, beckoning me to join her at the headboard again. "This is our ancestor. Maybe I'm the only one who notices, and maybe it isn't even true, but if you look closely, the ink shimmers differently."

I join her, peering at the signature, and I almost see it.

"When I learned you were truly Nameless, I didn't believe it at first," she says. "I thought that if you were Nameless and had the crown, it would break the treaty. That everything we have would fall apart. And I'm still not sure. I think that because I have a tattoo as well, maybe it's my name holding us together. I don't know." She bites her lip.

I sink down against the headboard, wordlessly.

"And there's something else that the council never told you about the Assassins' Festival," she adds.

I raise an eyebrow. Great.

"Between now and the festival, your abilities will keep getting stronger," Esther says. "The day of the festival is the first day that you will be at full strength. But the Council failed to mention that it's also when you'll be at your most vulnerable."

"That's the day I can give away the tattoo," I say, recalling my first meeting with the Royal Council.

"Yes," Esther says, "but it can also be *taken*."

Alarm pings through my chest. "Excuse me?"

Esther grimaces. "If someone kills you during the duels,

they'll take the tattoo from you. Traditionally, if a sovereign is bested in combat, they give the tattoo away peacefully so that no one has to die. But historically . . . it ended in bloodshed."

I run a hand across my forehead. "That explains why they call it the Assassins' Festival, at least. If anyone kills me in the duels or from a distance, they get the tattoo. Perfect."

Esther fidgets guiltily. "The council didn't tell you, because they wanted to make sure you'd attend the festival and not run, and I agreed with them at the time. But the more I've thought about things, the more I've thought about *everything* . . . I know you won't run. I understand something now, and I want to tell you the truth."

"What truth?" I say.

"I really have to *show* you. Let's go somewhere first."

"Why? Why not show me here?" I ask.

She shakes her head. "Perspective is important."

CHAPTER 15

Esther leads me to the five towers that rise from the center of the palace. She explains that the towers are named after prominent Royal families, the ones who most frequently have had the crown tattoo over the generations. Fallow, Demure, Vesania . . . She relates it like a history lesson, impassive. I reach out to sense her aura, but it's smooth like the pale surface of a shell.

Oil lights perch at equal intervals around the first floor of the Fallow tower. In the center is a spiral staircase. The stairs are stone, with a smooth wooden railing that curls up alongside, absorbing the warm lamplight. Carved flowers peek out from the rail every few steps. The rest of the room is a common area, filled with a collection of chairs and sofas, and I reach out into the now-familiar void of space until I sense the texture of auras.

Five of them dot the room like watery paint. That means there are four Royals here besides Esther. Amid the furniture I spot three fancy hats and a head of stylized hair. Esther leads me to the staircase.

"Were you close to your father?" I ask after a while. An ache grinds between my ribs as I sense the pain and loss in her aura.

"Yes and no," Esther says. "I was his daughter, and he taught me how to use my abilities discreetly. Yet, as I grew older, he kept me at arm's length. In the end, we were nearly strangers."

"You seem . . ." I don't know how to finish. I don't know how to have this conversation. I've never lost a parent. I've never even had one to lose.

Her aura pulses like a heartbeat. "Angry. Of course I am. You can love a person, lose them, and still be angry with them."

"Do you know why he kept you at arm's length?"

Esther stops on the stairs and turns to face me. "You tell me." She puts out her hand, palm up, as if asking for coins on the street.

I hesitate, fingers curling at my side.

"Tell me what I'm afraid of," Esther clarifies.

Cautiously, I uncurl my fingers and touch her hand. The rush and silk of sadness and resentment slips over me, and then her fear makes its way through my skin. It pulls at the bones of my hand as if to dismantle me.

"You're afraid of disappointing him," I say slowly, as images of Fallow's downcast, disappointed eyes flash through my mind. "Of failing Seriden and never living up to his expectations." Her fear clings to my bones like metal cobwebs.

She withdraws her hand, and the stiff cobwebs rust and fall away.

"My fear: failing as a ruler, and failing my father," Esther says. "My father saw that every time he touched me. And after a while, I sensed that same fear in him. Then he passed the crown to you. *You* tell me what I'm supposed to feel."

We share a silence that slowly soothes her aura.

"One of my fears?" I offer quietly, like a truce. "I'm afraid the city will never care. And worse, I'm afraid that at some point *I'll* stop caring."

Esther tilts her head in question.

I explain what Hat saw at the prison, how a Nameless boy was taken from his cell and wasn't executed, but just disappeared. I explain what it means to vanish from a place that doesn't even recognize you to begin with. I tell her about Nameless families and Marcher's crew and rumors of forced labor in other cities, about the Nameless who have been going missing more frequently in the past months, about the Nameless who showed up dead just before Fallow died. I tell her about the slaughter Belrosa showed me during the first council meeting.

We reach a small landing the width of three steps, and Esther yanks aside a blue curtain. Behind it, I find that this entire level of the tower is a single room, and it stretches as high as twenty feet. We are near the top of the tower. On the outer wall, there's a heavy stone door.

I examine the room. There's a bed, several identical wardrobes lined along the curving wall, and two low tables scattered with maps.

"Where are we, exactly?" I ask.

"This is where I live," Esther says. "This is where I come to escape the auras."

I don't know how high we are, but I can no longer sense the auras of the Royals in the common area on the first floor of the tower.

"Sometimes I can ignore the auras, and sometimes they

overwhelm me," she explains. "I go days at a time without making any skin contact with people so that their memories or thoughts don't have a chance to force their way into my mind. In fact, it's dangerous for me to do that. If things go properly, I shake their hand and I'm glimpsing their thoughts or memories. If I make a mistake, though, then suddenly I'm showing them *my* memories."

"What?" I say, taken aback. "You can show *your* thoughts to others? Instead of just seeing theirs?"

"Yes," she says. "I can witness their thoughts without them knowing it. But if they see my memories, that's impossible to explain."

"Did anyone ever find out about your tattoo?" I ask.

"I don't think so," she says. "You can never be sure, of course. When I was learning as a child—and still making mistakes—my father was always with me. It was easy enough for them to assume it was him. Then, as I got older, we drifted apart. I learned enough on my own, but it was never easy. And that's why I live up here in the Fallow tower, high above the city and out of its reach."

A draft of cold air rushes into the small room as Esther heaves the door open. She's so close, I feel her aura like a halo of humidity.

The door is smooth peach-colored stone, the same as the outside of the towers. It opens to a bright blue sky, clean and clear. There's a small ledge outside but nothing else. No railing or balcony, nothing but empty space all the way down to the roof of the palace.

I step out onto the ledge. We're nearly at the top of the center tower, and Seriden opens up before me. Far below are the eastern and northern quadrants. East Market crumbles into the harbor, which in turn disintegrates into the ocean. From so far away, the ocean is slow and calm. Whitecaps crest near the coast, and the surface crinkles with waves farther than I've ever seen before.

I lean outward. Wind rushes past me as if to pull me out into the open space. A laugh bubbles in my chest.

Esther comes up behind me, and I realize I've put myself in quite a bad position if she wants to push me. But I don't sense anything cold from her aura, only alarm, like the taste of lemons—sudden and sharp.

She eases herself down into a sitting position, letting her legs dangle out in the open air.

"I have one more memory to show you," she says. "And before I do, I want you to know that any time you want to escape the auras of the city, to have a few precious moments alone, you can come here. You're always welcome."

Her offer reminds me of when Hat and I were in Glenquartz's house and he said that we'd always have a home there. When she extends her hand to me once again, I take it, and her memory rushes into me like air.

It starts with a lullaby. The notes are distant and slow and beautiful. A woman hums a careful melody. It fills my entire body and resonates inside my chest.

The room is blurry, as though Esther's memories are melting

at the edges. She's still quite young, and I feel the presence of the tattoo on her arm.

Then the lullaby stops abruptly, replaced by the discordant sound of two voices arguing. Esther peers around a door, and we're staring into the king's quarters again, except this time, he isn't alone.

A woman is arguing but I can't see her face. Her hair falls in dark brown ringlets to her shoulders, just like Esther's. I see the broad slope of a nose, and the rounded curve of a lip. Esther stands on her toes to get a better view of them, and I finally see the woman's hand resting on her rounded belly.

Esther moves to another memory, and this one is crisp and fresh. She sits at her father's bedside. He's sick—that much is obvious. His skin is dry and his expression reveals an underlying pain.

"I need to tell you something," Fallow says. His voice is uncertain and scratchy. "And I need you to remember it."

"Of course," Esther says, scooting closer, but neither of them reaches out to touch the other. There's a stiff formality between them—a far cry from Esther's childhood.

"You are my daughter," Fallow says. "I know we don't know each other as well as I would have liked . . . but that's the truth. You have the crown tattoo now. I know you'll have a lot of questions, that you may not understand why you have been put in this position."

"I've had it for years now, Father," Esther says. "I understand it well enough."

Fallow continues as if she hasn't spoken. "Two tattoos—it's a dangerous mistake that needs to be rectified. But there is no greater danger to address within Seriden than the plight of the Nameless. No one should be without a name, legal rights, a family, or a home. You should understand that more than anyone."

Fallow clears his throat. "Please understand, dear daughter, that everything that has been done is in service to Seriden. A sovereign's first responsibility is to . . ." Fallow breaks into a fit of coughing.

Esther nudges his glass of water toward him, and she finishes, "A sovereign's first responsibility is to their city. I remember. I understand. I'm ready."

Fallow smiles sorrowfully. "You're not. But you will be. You *both* will be."

Confusion edges in on Esther's thoughts, and she tilts her head.

I let go of Esther's hand this time, pulling us out of the memory.

"What exactly are you trying to show me?" I demand, and already my mind is wheeling and racing. The first memory she shared with me was of the former queen—Fallow's wife, and Esther's mother. The second memory was from the last weeks of Fallow's life.

"My mother . . . ," Esther starts, her voice tight with pain. "She died in childbirth soon after the first memory, and I never saw her again. I always thought . . . everyone thought . . . that the baby died too."

Esther looks at me, really looks. Her eyes roam over my hair and my face, the curve of my nose, the angle of my chin. "My mother died nearly eighteen years ago." *Don't say it, Esther. Don't think it. Don't ask.* "How old are you, Coin?"

My head swims, and I suddenly can't remember how words are supposed to work. "I . . . I don't know. I never knew. Marcher looked after me for as long as I can remember."

"Father wasn't talking to *me*," Esther insists. "When he said those things, he knew we'd be here, sharing this moment. That wasn't him telling me to mend the divide between Seriden's classes. It was him talking to *you*, apologizing for letting you grow up as one of the Nameless when you had a name all along. It was him talking to the *daughter* who never knew him."

I shake my head, stunned.

"It explains why Father knew your name," Esther continues. "How you ended up with Marcher when you were so young, and how you had a name but didn't know it. It explains why he told me that the crown would be reunited in the *next generation*. My generation. *Our* generation. Coin—you're my *sister*." Esther clasps her hands in her lap to stop herself from touching me.

For once, I don't say anything. I stare out at Seriden and beyond to the ocean.

Everything Esther is saying makes sense. It answers every question I've ever had about what happened to my family and how I could have been named queen.

Fallow was my father. I am a king's daughter. *I have a family.* Had. I *had* a family. Fallow is dead.

But Esther. Esther Merelda Fallow, the girl sitting beside me on the edge of a tower, is my sister. I have no father or mother, but I have her. A sister. A family, however small and broken it may be.

"You're the one who told me that memories and fears can lie," I say carefully. "Belrosa showed me her thoughts of the future. Maybe that's all this is. Maybe you're lying to me." But despite everything, I believe her. I *want* to believe her, and that's what makes believing so dangerous.

"I'm so sorry," Esther says. "It could have just as easily been me who ended up on the streets instead of you. I've been so angry because I've been an orphan for two weeks, but you've been alone your entire life. When my father died, I couldn't sense a difference in my tattoo, and I knew he'd given it to someone else. When you came forward, I didn't believe it at first. It took me a while to put it together, but I finally understand."

My head is spinning. I believe everything she believes, because it makes sense.

I rise to my feet and backpedal into her room. She said this place is her sanctuary—her escape from the auras of Seriden's citizens. But all I can sense is her guilt, frustration, and fear—they leach into me like the cold winds of winter.

I don't want to feel *her* pain or *her* guilt. I don't want to see her memories of the family that could have been mine. I can't be here for another second.

Under her watchful, fearful gaze, I do the only thing I can think of.

I do what comes naturally.

I run.

＋

I run down the entire spiral staircase, my mind and heart racing. It's all I can do not to trip over my own feet. I sense Esther's aura as she follows me, but I quickly outpace her. I run out of the tower and down the palace corridors. I cover almost the entire north wing before I make my way to my sleeping quarters. I find Glenquartz there, waiting for me.

"What's going on?" Glenquartz asks as he takes in my breathless, haggard appearance.

"I . . . understand how I became queen." As I walk past him to pace the length of the room, I pickpocket the decorative blade that hangs at his hip.

"Oh?" Glenquartz says, trying to sound politely intrigued instead of intensely curious.

"I was given a name when I was born," I say, throwing the heavy blade in a half rotation so it lands in the soft wood of the wardrobe. "I grew up my entire life as one of the Nameless, thinking I was Nameless, but I had a name the whole time! And now that I'm queen, in a position of power, I *don't* have a name. It died with him."

"Are you sure?" Glenquartz asks, eyeing the wardrobe with concern.

"Esther has a tattoo," I say as I wrench the blade from the wood. "Just like mine. I'm sure."

Glenquartz freezes, his aura coming to rest like a dying wind. "What? How?"

"Because a generation of idiots thought it was a great idea to tamper with magic," I continue, angrily. "And—surprise—they made a mistake. Not only am I a target for basically everyone in the city because of who and what I am, but if any of the other cities found out there was a second tattoo, Seriden would be Royally screwed."

"But why would King Fallow give you the tattoo? How would he have known your name if you don't know it yourself?"

"Esther told me," I say. "Showed me, using her magic. And I believe her. *Them,* I guess. She showed me a memory of her father. She . . . she's my sister, Glen."

"Esther's your sister?" Glenquartz says slowly, as if saying it will make it make sense.

"Yes," I say in disbelief. "I don't even know what it's supposed to mean. We didn't grow up together. We're basically strangers. And what? Everything that I went through was just character building to make me strong? Well, it did more than that. It made me angry. It made me selfish. My entire life is just a single sentence in someone else's story. I'm the daughter of a king raised as an orphan for no other reason than he thought it would make me a good queen."

"That doesn't sound fair," Glenquartz says.

"It's more than unfair," I say, slapping the flat edge of the blade against my hand. "It's unkind. For him to make a decision about my entire life like that? Like he has ownership over me! I've lived my whole life defying ownership from others." I shake my head with frustration. "I don't know what I'm supposed to feel about this."

"I don't think there's a 'supposed to.' I think whatever you're feeling . . . you just *feel* it."

I throw the blade against the wardrobe again, and it thuds with a splintering crack.

"I'm angry," I say as I wrest the blade from the gnarled wood and turn to Glenquartz. "Why would he do this to me? How is this better? How am *I* better?" The shine of steel, heat rushing through my head, and I suddenly realize I'm holding a knife on Glenquartz and he's staring down the edge of the blade. He takes a guarded step backward.

I drop my hand, letting out a sharp exhale.

"I don't know," Glenquartz says, and I don't miss the sliver of fear in his aura.

"And Esther! She's my . . ." I trail off and pointedly set the blade down on the bedside table. "Do you have any siblings?"

He shakes his head. "Not by blood, but I had sisters and brothers in training to become a Royal guard. Some of them have passed, and some of them have drifted away from me over the years."

"How do you have siblings who aren't related to you?" I ask.

"Some friends become best friends, and some best friends become family." He retrieves his blade and secures it in its sheath. I pick idly at the splinters of wood in the wardrobe, silently wishing I could tear the world to pieces.

"How do I know if they're 'like family' if I have nothing to compare it to?" I ask. "Or if I don't have any friends at all?"

Glenquartz doesn't answer for a while. With each passing moment, I feel more and more like a strange rock that's been abandoned on the side of the street.

Glenquartz speaks carefully. "I've heard people say that you can't choose your family but you *can* choose your friends. But, really, you can choose both. You can't change your blood. Who you're related to by birth is something outside your control. But who your family is? You get to choose that. *You* get to pick the people you let into your life and who you keep in your life. Who you choose to love and care about is up to you, not anyone else. You've just found out that Esther is part of your blood family. What you do with that is entirely up to you. It's up to both of you, really. What did she say about what she wanted or expected?"

I try to remember. I was so surprised, I didn't pay much attention to her.

"She said she was sorry for me," I say. "That when she realized we were sisters, she felt guilty about my life as a Nameless. That I had to live my life without a father. And now I'm mad. I'm *angry*. Not at her, but at *him*." I don't realize how strongly I feel it until the words are in my mouth and the rage is in my chest.

I continue, "I'm mad, not only because of the life he sentenced me to and the life he deprived me of. I'm mad because I hate him for it, and that's not fair because I never got the chance to love him. He wanted me to be Nameless when I became queen, but why did that mean I had to grow up alone?"

There are tears rimming Glenquartz's eyes, and seeing them

almost makes me break down too. He shakes his head and extends his arm toward me. It takes me a second to realize he's offering me a hug. The only person I've ever hugged is Hat.

Glenquartz's arm wavers as though he's made a mistake in offering, but I relax and let myself be held.

"Do you trust Esther?" Glenquartz asks.

"I . . . I've seen her help people," I say, pulling out of the embrace. "I *want* to trust her."

"Then do. Trust." Glenquartz shrugs as if it's that simple.

I groan and run a hand over my forehead. "Gaiza. I have to go tell Esther that I told you."

Glenquartz squints, puzzled.

"What if she secretly hates you?" I ask. "And I literally told her biggest secret to the first person I saw. Regardless of whether she's right about us being family, her tattoo is real."

"You think she secretly hates me?" Glenquartz says skeptically. "I don't want to brag, but not a lot of people hate me."

I glare at him. "Lucky you." I drag Glenquartz toward the door, but I stop short of opening it. "If Esther isn't at the Fallow tower, where would I find her?"

Glenquartz pinches his chin. "She spends most of her time in the sparring room. I can take you there tomorrow morning, if you like. Or, judging from your angry eyebrows, I can take you now. Now is great."

"Good choice."

Yet as soon as we open the door, we find Esther standing there. Everything about her posture is apologetic, and I chastise myself for not sensing her aura as she approached.

"I told Glenquartz," I say immediately. "About your . . . arm."

Esther checks an imaginary watch. "That didn't take long. Did you tell anyone else?"

I shake my head no, but I pause. "But I'll probably tell Hat, too."

"Would you like to tell the Royal Council as well?" she suggests impatiently.

"No. That about sums up the people who don't want me dead."

Esther lets out a controlled sigh and steps into the room, closing the door gently behind her. "I've given some thought as to where we go from here. I think we should keep our . . . alliance, for lack of a better term, off the Royal Council's radar. We can still present a united front publicly, though, offering consolation to the victims of the fire."

"If Fallow wanted the crowns reunited in our generation, then it makes my decision easy," I say. "On the morning of the Assassins' Festival, I'll give the crown tattoo to you, Esther. I don't care what the Royal Council wants. Why delay the inevitable?"

Esther shakes her head. "That wasn't the reason I told you those things. I watched you use your abilities and charge into a burning building to rescue someone! Our father wanted you to be queen so that *you* could mend the divide between the classes. I think that when you gain your full abilities on the day of the festival, you might be able to do something no one else ever has—make the Nameless into citizens."

Now it's my turn to shake my head. "How can I defend my

position here in the palace when there are citizens of Seriden who are so against my rule that they murdered at least three people?" I throw my hands into the air. "I can't protect the Legals or the Nameless. Everything I've tried to do since I've gotten here has failed. Everything. I sent food out to the Nameless, and it got poisoned. I tried to find out what's been happening to the disappearing Nameless, and I got nothing but rumors and dead bodies. I tried to have Hat released from prison, and the Royal Guard denied my request. Then, when I saved her life, it led to riots, fires, and deaths. Tell me, how would I make a good queen? Tell me how this city doesn't burn itself alive the moment I try to sit on that throne."

Esther thinks that her—our—father wanted me to be crowned queen. I think she's wrong. I think that on the day of the Assassins' Festival, I'm meant to give my crown to her. There's no other way to reunite the two crowns, unless Fallow was hoping I'd die at the festival. Maybe Esther is supposed to kill me.

She studies the floorboards.

"Then I have four weeks to change your mind," she says at length. "Eldritch's etiquette lessons have helped you learn how to act the part, but that's not what you need anymore. Instead, let Glenquartz train you how to fight so if you decide to duel for your crown, you'll be ready. And let me teach you how to use your magic. There's a reason you stayed at Med Ward with me. I can show you how to use your abilities to defend yourself at the festival. Let me help you. Give me a chance to change your mind."

CHAPTER 16

Throughout the rest of the day, Belrosa is all too eager to flaunt her story of taking command and organizing the brigade that doused the flames. No one talks about the speech I was supposed to give. And honestly, I wouldn't want to try again—not when smoke still hangs in the air and the scent of blood still lingers in Med Ward.

Every time I hear someone say "only three people died" in the fires, I want to rip off their necklaces and pocket watches and shout that there's no *only* about it. The final numbers came in late last night from Rhana. Eight people died. Not three Legals and five Nameless. Eight *people*.

So when one of the Legal servants brings me an extra hot roll and a small cup of wine at dinner, I make a quiet toast to remember the five Nameless who won't be mourned for their loss or celebrated for their heroism.

I meet Esther after breakfast at Med Ward. There are still a lot of injured people from the fires, and Rhana says they're running low on anesthetics.

"What exactly is it that . . . I can do?" I ask.

"You can make people see hallucinations," Esther explains.

"That is only one aspect of your abilities. You can sense the auras and locations of your subjects from a distance, but the closer you are to someone, the more vulnerable you are. Yet it also lets you be more powerful. When you touch one of your subjects, you gain access to their mind. You can push emotional states and images on people. Hallucinations inside their heads. Or you can let them guide you, as we did when I showed you the memories of our . . . King Fallow."

I cough awkwardly. Our father.

"Or," she hurries to continue, "you can make me experience or feel something. You can observe my memories or thoughts. Or you can show me yours. It's like . . . guiding an air current. You can't necessarily tell it what direction to go, but you can control its path. I want you to try again. When you first met Belrosa, you saw flashes of memory or thoughts when you shook her hand in the meeting, right? That's the push of the air current. You can guide that force in a different direction. Take this man's hand. Lead him into a calming memory. He may resist. His memories and fears could overwhelm you. They may be strong, but you can be stronger."

I steady my nerves, reach out, and place my hand on his.

In an instant, my body curls and coils, and sharp pain embeds itself in my leg. I know with absolute certainty that I'll never walk again. I try to move forward and imagine something else, but fire springs to life all around me. Walls rise to enclose me. I pound my fists against the burning wall again and again, and splinters of wood dig into my hands. Smoke and ash fill my eyes, my throat, and my lungs. All I can hear is a high-pitched scream that trembles through my entire body, and my leg—*my leg, I'll never walk again.*

I fall to my knees, and suddenly I'm once again in Med Ward, collapsed beside the bed, gasping lungfuls of fresh air. It tastes of antiseptic.

I breathe heavily. "That was horrible." I can hear the heart-rending pain in my own voice. I can't shake the loss that carves itself inside my chest. My body is fine. There's no fire beneath my fists, no wounds to my legs.

Esther sits on the floor right beside me. "It's okay to feel it." She's gripping the hems of her sleeves, and I can sense that she wants nothing more than to move closer to me, to put a hand on my shoulder.

"I don't understand," I say, shaking my head. "I shouldn't be feeling this."

"I know, I know," she says. "It's his. You're feeling what he felt. The loss and anger, the pain. Most importantly: the fear. That's what we're trying to save him from."

I shake my head again. "But it isn't mine." I say it as though to comfort myself.

"You're right," she says, "but that doesn't make it any less real. Whatever he's feeling, you're feeling. You can let yourself feel it. Then you can let it pass."

Esther rises to a crouch and offers me her hand. A warm soothing energy fills me, along with the image of sunlit sails in the harbor, shifting slowly in the ocean wind. I let the sensation fill me up from my fingertips to my toes, and for the first time

I can see how beautiful the harbor really is. When she lets go, the vision fades and I feel like myself again, with my familiar distaste for the ocean restored.

Then she takes the man's hand, and he soothes instantly, his body relaxing.

"If it helps, approach this like . . . like it's a con," Esther says. "Like you're tricking him into experiencing something that isn't his. Be in control. Try again, now that he's calmer. Focus on your own thoughts. Guide him. You're using both aspects of your powers at once: experiencing his thoughts and memories, and then showing him an illusion and controlling what he sees, but in his mind."

It takes a minute for me to prepare myself. Once I do, I place my hand upon his. I focus on a memory as though it's a trinket in my hand, shaping its details with my mind.

At first, everything is black, calm and cool. Then pinpricks of stars open up overhead, and a warm summer breeze rushes over our skin. I'm sitting on top of the library in the Inner Ring. I've had a good week stealing from the markets, and I have enough extra food to make a special evening for myself. I'm eating a cold fruit pastry, sitting above a thousand books that I'll never be able to read. The stars are as brilliant as they've ever been.

Then I'm remembering the first time I saw the stars at the harbor—the way the ocean crumpled the image of the sky and made it sparkle a thousand times brighter. Then an uncommonly clear sky in winter: starlight seen through the icy window of the baker's shop, a rare flash of light right after dusk, patches of black clouds obscuring constellations—all of it beautiful and precious and everywhere at once.

When I leave the memory, it's like letting go. In those last moments, I feel the man's decision to stay there, staring up at the black sky, which now holds more constellations than I ever thought possible.

I release the Legal's arm, and he's quiet now, resting peacefully on the cot. I try not to look too astounded or confused.

"What did you show him?" Esther asks.

"I showed him the sky," I say. "A hundred different times, but all at once."

"Good. Very good." She nods. "When you leave them like that, they use those images and memories as launching points for their own dreams. He probably won't remember your original memory when he wakes."

"How did you learn all of this?" I ask. "If you're a secret, when did you ever get any practice?"

I check if anyone's close enough to eavesdrop, but no one is. Rhana is having a discussion with her apprentices about how to make sure people take their medicine. And while Rhana herself is facing us, the small group of apprentices is facing away.

"My father taught me a lot, brought me here a couple times. Until he wouldn't anymore. And when I knew enough to know I could help, I came here on my own."

"That's so . . . good and responsible of you," I say. I half expect her to shrug or play it off as no big deal.

"Yes," Esther agrees. "It is. It's part of the job, part of the life. Being responsible and doing good . . . You're in the enviable position of having power. There's so much you can do with it. When most people have an idea of being sovereign or ruling the city, their idea of power is wrapped up in a single goal. A person wants to be powerful because they think it's their right, or they want to prove they can do it, or they want to fix a specific problem. But being a sovereign is about being the type of person who deserves that power and who makes good decisions with it."

"You make it sound so noble," I say, doing a half curtsy.

"It is," she says wholeheartedly. "And it should be. But. You really just have to know what you want to do with that power and what it means to you. More importantly, you have to know what kind of person you want to be, because power won't change you. Power only allows you to change yourself."

I cycle through the sarcastic quips I want to respond with: that my idea of power involves power napping, that I want to be the kind of person who doesn't get distracted by jingling pockets, or that the only change I want to see in myself is a nice haircut.

Instead, I remain quiet and observe the room. I catch sight of Hat as she tends to a patient. She wears a white training cap, and her hair is pulled back sharply. She looks nothing like the girl I saved from the gallows. She looks everything like the woman she could become. She is changing as much as I am. Only, while Hat is taking charge of her new responsibilities, I'm trying to give mine away to Esther. And not only does Esther refuse to accept that I am ill-equipped for power, but she's also waiting patiently for me to embrace it. It's almost annoying.

For the first time in my life, someone expects *goodness* from me. And, for the first time, I want to try.

✦

Each day for two weeks, I meet with Esther at Med Ward to practice my magic, and then I train with Glenquartz in a sparring room in the southern part of the palace. Really it used to be an assembly room, but there's a one-inch soft mat across a large section of the floor and a table that currently holds four different types of swords.

I hold one of the swords lazily, with the blade resting gently against the floor.

"You're the one who said you wanted to train for the duels," Glenquartz says. "You've got to focus if you want to be prepared. You don't know who's going to challenge you or how many people you're going to have to fight. It could be a hundred people. And between now and then, sure—the Royal Council has agreed to wait until the Assassins' Festival for you to pass the tattoo peacefully, but it's possible that there are people who are more willing to risk destroying magic if it means they get a chance at the tattoo."

"You think they're going to come at me with swords?" I observe the sharp steel skeptically and return it to the table.

"Probably not," he says impatiently. "That's why we'll also train in hand-to-hand."

I cross my arms and brace my right foot behind me.

The briefest grin passes over Glenquartz's face, and he

reaches for me to put me in a restriction hold or tackle me, but in two seconds flat, he's on the floor.

"Did you just punch me in the sternum?" he asks between gasps.

"My reflex is to go for the throat," I explain. "But that seemed kind of rude."

He reassesses me. "Thank you, I guess?"

"You think I never got in a fight before?" I say. "Though I could do with some proper sparring tips. All my moves are to incapacitate and flee. Stomp on a foot, punch a throat, and escape into the night with a solid gold harp." I stare through the window wistfully.

Glenquartz's eyes bug out. "That was *you*?"

I shrug. "I don't know what you're talking about."

"No," Glenquartz says. "I know it was you, because that was *me*."

I stare down my nose at him where he still sits on the floor.

"I was guarding a shipment as it was being unloaded at the docks," he says. "We were accepting a Royal gift from Lady Sovereign Olefar, and I was transporting it personally when some Nameless bandits attacked us."

"Nameless *bandits*?" I say as if I'm unfamiliar with the word. I study him for a moment, trying to stay serious.

Then we both burst with laughter.

"No more distractions," I say, smiling. "Show me how to fight."

I enjoy fighting far more than I should. Striking fists is an outlet for every anger that has made a home in my chest, every anxious fear in my head. What it does best, however, is clear my mind before I join Esther at Med Ward.

I'm baffled by why Hat would want to spend her time here. But she's happily buzzing between cots, checking on injuries, changing medications, and learning words like "aspirate" and "suture."

When Esther and I take a break, I join her where she's sitting on an empty cot in the corner of the room. I've since caught her up on the whole "Esther and I both have magical tattoos" secret, and she helps distract Dr. Rhana when Esther and I visit Med Ward to practice my abilities.

"I kind of feel like I'm cheating, coming to this place," I say to Hat.

She cocks her head to the side. "What do you mean?"

"You're helping people. I'm practicing my magical hallucination-inducing abilities." When I say it out loud, it sounds silly.

Hat's chin lifts. "I'm here for selfish reasons too. I'm no longer on the streets or in prison. Rhana is looking after me, and I'm helping people. And I'm learning a lot."

I remember rescuing Hat from execution. No shame in truth, I told her.

"I think it's time I take a page from your book," I say.

Hat nods approvingly. "I'm about to impart some sage wisdom, okay?" She holds my shoulder as if to comfort me.

I hide a humored smile.

"You could be doing whatever you want with your magic,"

Hat says. "Stealing from annoying Royals like we used to, or burning down the palace from the inside. But you're not. We're not. That's good, isn't it?"

Hat pulls me to the cot of a patient whose arms are tied to the bed frame with cloth.

"Is this one of the rioters?" I ask, gesturing at the restraints. I can sense the man's aura, sharp and pained.

Hat shakes her head. "He has burns on his arms, his wrists, his hands, and his chest. And he keeps scratching, which is bad for the burns, which is why he's restrained. If you could calm him down, I can put some ointment on his wrists."

She holds a dark glass jar filled with cream and a small wooden applicator.

I let out a small breath. I haven't done this without Esther yet.

The man is clearly agitated, restless and unaware of my presence. I place my hand beneath his ear, at his jawline.

His skin is hot, and I pull my hand away, as if touched by fire.

"He has a fever," Hat says. "It's one of the reasons he really needs the medicine."

I again place my hand on his neck. At first, it's a sharp tug of fear in my gut. Then I see a wall of fire so close it sears my skin.

I try to pull away, but the sensation is too strong.

The man stumbles away from the fire. His body isn't yet burned. This is his house. For a moment, he wants to go in, but a flash of movement steals his attention. A man in gray clothing flees the fire.

Suspicion and anger flare through the man's chest. He follows after the man in gray, who seems to be carrying fire in his hands. That can't be right.

He pursues as the gray man slinks toward the next house. He's holding a torch. From a bag, he pulls out a book. He fans the pages and touches them to the torch, then hurls it through the window. There's a shatter of glass, and then a low glow emanates from within. More screams from inside. The man heads toward the screams and toward the heat.

Pain sears my arms in the memory, and I turn us away from the terrible sight. I take us to West Market—my familiar hunting grounds. I imagine the scent of freshly seared chicken and spiced peppers. I share the feeling of sweat against my chilled skin and warm gloves on my hands.

As I withdraw, the man calms down. He takes the memory from me, and suddenly he's sitting on the rooftop with a small child—his son.

I remove my hand, and I'm standing beside Hat again next to the cot. She has finished applying the medicine, and she bows her head in thanks.

"I saw part of his memory from the fire," I say, shaking my head as I try to recapture the image in my mind.

"That must have been hard," Hat says.

Esther joins us, an eyebrow arched skeptically. "Did you do it without me?" she says, trying to be surreptitious around Hat.

I don't answer her. "Hat, what did you say about the people who took that Nameless boy from the prison?"

Esther's aura perks up, and I realize she hasn't met Hat yet and probably didn't know she was Nameless. "Hat? Are you . . . the girl from the execution?"

Hat tilts her head. "And you're the king's daughter?"

I wave my hand as if to brush away their conversation and the sensation of Esther's curious aura—like the prickling of mosquito legs on my arms. "Hat. The people from the prison. What did they look like?"

"Right. Yes. It was dark and I never saw their faces, but I thought they were maybe wearing uniforms."

"Is it possible the uniforms were gray?" I ask.

Hat shrugs.

"What are you talking about?" Esther asks.

I tell her about the memory I witnessed: a gray-uniformed man setting fires. "Is it possible he's a soldier from another city?"

"It's unlikely," Esther says. "None of the other cities have gray as the color for their Royal guards."

In the pause that follows, Hat says, "Dr. Rhana told me this morning that the Nameless woman you've been checking on is ready to leave."

"Can we escort her home?" Esther asks me.

"She probably lives on the streets or in the alleys," I say.

Esther's shoulders stiffen. "All the more reason for us to give her an escort. We should make sure she gets someplace safe."

The Nameless woman calls herself Spell. She says she has a daughter, but she doesn't know if she survived the fire. I don't tell her that five Nameless bodies were pulled from the wreckage.

I bring Spell a bright blue coat for her to wear so that people will assume she's a Royal when we move through the city. Spell still has a bit of a rasp in her voice from the smoke, but she's well enough to whisper directions once we get out of the palace.

Glenquartz accompanies me and Esther with another three Royal guards in case my mere presence sets off another riot.

As we move through the Inner Ring and to the South Residences, I can tell that some people recognize me. They do a double take and hurry out of the way.

We come upon the road with the six burned-down houses, and Spell stumbles when she sees the extent of the blackened wreckage.

The sight makes my heart seize. Four of the houses each have a dark black curtain hanging over the doorway. For the house that collapsed, the black curtain is strung up crooked between two fractured support beams. The curtains are heavy enough to hang straight, but light enough to shift like black frames of water in the gentle winds. It's beautiful and horrifying. I hold Spell's elbow to keep her steady, but she pushes away my hands and keeps onward, staring at a house with a partially collapsed roof at the far end of the street.

"Wasn't that rude?" Esther whispers to me as Spell walks faster and farther ahead.

I shake my head. "No. She told me she's searching for her daughter. She wants to be strong."

Glenquartz's shoulders tighten, and his aura pulls inward. "Is the daughter . . . ?"

"We don't know," I say. I feel like an insensitive cur. I brought Glenquartz out here so we could find out if this woman's daughter had survived the fires, and it didn't occur to me that it would be difficult for him since he lost little Flannery. He followed me here on faith and obligation.

When we reach the house, it's badly damaged, but it's still standing. The door is open, and there's movement somewhere beyond the black curtain. Spell would be running, no doubt, if she wasn't clearly still in pain from her injuries.

Without pause, Spell bursts into the home, and Glenquartz, Esther, and I are on her heels. I make a motion for the other Royal guards to stay outside.

"Excuse me?" a Legal woman says. She stands, thin and tall like an elegant bird, beside a long table. All sorts of recovered keepsakes sit upon it: cracked dishes, a tangle of jewelry, a collection of burned toys. This woman has children. I sense two small shining auras upstairs, just out of sight.

Spell presses a hand to her heart, and she opens her mouth but doesn't speak.

I move forward. "We're here to inquire about the fire. Were there any . . . any deaths in this house?"

The woman glances behind us at the mourning veil, and she almost crumbles. "My husband."

Spell finally finds the strength to speak. "My daughter. Is she here?"

The Legal woman freezes in place. She stares at Spell as if seeing her for the first time.

"It's you." She moves forward suddenly and extends her hand to Spell. "My name is Agatha. I live here with my sons." She turns toward the stairs urgently. "Remi! Lin!"

A patter of hesitant footsteps tiptoe down the stairs. But it's three children that come down. There are two boys with sandy brown hair like Agatha's, and there's a small girl with a halo of dark hair.

"Nani!" Spell shouts, and the little girl runs to her mother.

"You tried to save my husband in the fire," Agatha says. "I . . . I saw you run in."

"I came for my daughter," Spell says, her voice cracking. "I was looking for Nani when I found him. I tried to pull him out . . . but I didn't make it. And then the ceiling was on fire. I don't remember much after that. I'm . . ." She removes the bright blue Royal's coat to show that her clothes are tattered and streaked with black dye. "I was living in your cellar with my daughter. We're very quiet during the day. We've never stolen much more than the food you've thrown away."

"I knew," Agatha says suddenly. "I knew you were there. At first I was scared. I didn't know why you were here. But then I learned our children had befriended each other, and I still didn't want to acknowledge your presence, because I would have been breaking the law by housing you here. I wouldn't be sent to prison, not really, but you and your family . . ." She trails off.

"The house is big enough," says one of Agatha's boys. "I don't see the problem."

Agatha turns to us, taking in our Royal clothing. "I'm hoping you won't say anything to anyone?" The curious, questioning tone in her voice almost makes me laugh with relief. Her gaze moves between the crown on my arm and Glenquartz's holstered pistol. When she recognizes Esther on sight, her lips part in shock.

"Of course I won't," I say. I didn't know it could be like this. I imagine Hat sitting with these children. She'd fit right in.

"Why do you call yourself Spell?" Agatha asks.

"Oh, you shouldn't ask that," I say, holding up a cautionary hand. "The Nameless pick their own names, but the reason why is personal and sometimes painful."

Spell nods slowly.

"Thank you for trying to save my husband, Spell," Agatha says.

Spell inclines her head. "Thank you for looking after my daughter, Agatha."

Agatha wipes the tears from her cheeks and speaks to Glenquartz. "Have you found out who was responsible for starting the fires? The only thing I remember was that someone threw a book of some kind through the glass, and then the flames! They were everywhere."

Glenquartz straightens, always the loyal guard. His voice has a slight waver to it when he speaks. "I haven't heard of any progress in the inquiry." He gives a small bow of apology.

"It's some kind of group, isn't it?" Agatha says. "I saw some of them. They were all in gray, like a uniform. Some of them had these long guns. But I didn't recognize any of them."

I feel Esther staring at me, and I wish she wouldn't.

"We will look into this," I say, realizing immediately that I sound like a political grandstander, like a speaker announcing a new tax law from the gazebo at West Market. I advance and loosen my shoulders, actively repressing every lesson I've ever had from Eldritch about posture and politics. I put a hand on each of their shoulders, feeling the fears seep into me from Agatha and feeling nothing but warm skin from Spell.

"I will find out who did this," I say. "I'll find out why, and I'll make sure they suffer for it."

We pass through the mourning curtain on our way out, and I'm chased by the image of three children and two mothers huddled together in a half-burned house. Glenquartz is doing his best to hide how shaken he is, so I slip my arm into his, letting him hold on to me as we walk toward the Royal Court. I take care to keep my sleeves pulled down so I don't accidentally touch his arm and allow his memories to seep into me.

What we just saw—four weeks ago, I would have thought it was impossible. If two mothers can care for each other's families, then why can't the city take note? Why can't Seriden work the same way?

When we round the last corner, nearly a hundred Nameless men and women stand in complete silence in front of the gates. The guards behind me all draw their rifles, except for Glenquartz, who puts his hand on my shoulder. I immediately stretch out an arm in front of their weapons, but they don't make a move to lower them.

"If you don't put down your weapons," I say to the guards, "I'll put *you* down."

Slowly, they obey. I am their queen, after all. The Nameless nearest to us ease up a bit, but none of them move. I've never seen anything like this. The Nameless don't work together. They don't gather in groups. They don't . . . read. They're all holding books. Some hold them like torches; others clutch them to their chests like shields. As we begin walking, many turn toward the gates and gently hold the books toward me.

"Our names, our names," they murmur as we pass.

"Please, our names. Please."

I've seen these books before, stacked and organized at the library. I've seen newer copies in the hands of commerce keepers who march door-to-door every month. They are the population records used to tally the named citizens. The Nameless before us hold in their hands the names of strangers.

Walking past them is like moving through a garden of sculptures, cold and empty. I can't sense their auras.

"You can do this," an older woman says to me. "You, our queen. You can do this. Give us names."

Their voices flow around me, almost like the tide of an aura.

"My queen . . . Our names . . . Please."

Their words haunt every piece of my heart.

CHAPTER 17

There has been so much violence, I'm startled to find people who are willing to stand in peaceful protest. They just want to be heard. And I want to listen.

There is a group of people hunting the Nameless, a group of guards who refused to release Hat from prison despite a pardon from the sovereign herself, and a group who set deadly fires during my speech. There could be three distinct groups doing three separate terrible things. Or there's just one. Who would be more organized and surreptitious than a rogue sect of Royal guards? And I know who will have answers.

I find Belrosa at the archery range. She's training the newer Royal Guard recruits. Even though Seriden hasn't fought a war in over two centuries, long-range weaponry is still a required lesson.

My first impression on entering the range is that it's smaller than I expected. I thought there would be rows and rows of targets and maybe even moving targets. Instead it's a relatively narrow building where everyone is shooting from the middle of the room down two long lanes, where hay bales are stacked with painted targets.

Belrosa is critiquing someone's form, lowering their elbow and talking about an anchor point. I don't know what she's saying, but I did learn how to shoot two years ago for a con Hat and I pulled on a group of visiting diplomats.

"What do you think of the new guards, my lady?" Belrosa asks, putting her hands on her hips. Her aura ripples with pride.

"I have a question for you," I say. "You won't like it." I glance pointedly at the other guards.

Belrosa squints, and her aura flashes with disdain. Nonetheless, she takes the hint and dismisses them, watching them disappear around the corner before she turns to me.

"Gotten anyone else killed since the fires?" Belrosa asks.

I tell myself not to lose my nerve or my patience.

"What do you know about the missing Nameless?" I ask.

Belrosa's snide smile freezes. "I'm not sure what you're asking."

I pause. There's something off about her aura, a creeping chill lingering like the first bite of an ocean storm. It's like cold, gritty sand between my teeth.

"Have any of your guards been acting suspicious lately?" I ask. I move to one of the standing quivers and run my fingers along the brown fletching of an arrow. "When I visited the victims of the fire today, some of them mentioned seeing soldiers dressed in gray."

Belrosa scoffs. "Gray is not the color of the Royal Guard. We wear red. It's bold and easy to find. Strong. Gray is less than common. It's barely the status of Legals."

"Which would suit them nicely if their activities are . . . less than legal."

Belrosa's brow furrows into a mask of concern. "Some of

them *have* been acting strangely lately. I will definitely look into it."

Liar. I don't believe her for a second. When the fires happened, I thought maybe Marcher had done it. I even considered that Esther had orchestrated it to convince the public that she was deserving of the throne. But Belrosa is the one who tried to get Hat executed. I need proof.

One touch. That's all I need. One touch.

"That would be splendid," I say with a polite curtsy. I slip past her, placing a hand on her arm as I go. I feel a few bursts of aggression and confidence like a gust of hot air from a stove. But then the fear. Trapped deep beneath the surface, buried beneath layers of rock.

She's afraid.

I feel it. I know it.

In the brief moment that my hand is on her arm, her fear grows. She is afraid that I *know*. I get flashes of color, gray and black cloth, cold stone, the taste of metal, and something slick between my fingers. Water drips down a dark stone wall. Sounds echo through the narrow halls. A damp sensation crawls over my skin, and a hundred feet stomp in unison.

As I break contact, it all vanishes.

She has secrets. That much is clear. And she's afraid of something. In the strange bursts, I saw—no, I *felt*—the presence of a large crowd. She knows more about the gray-clad fire starters than she admits. She's the one training them.

If I touch her arm and ask her directly, I'll know for sure. She won't be able to hide her reaction from me. But if I confront her, what happens next? I should have brought Glenquartz. He, at least, would have a weapon. I swallow hard.

"I will begin the inquiry with my guards tomorrow morning." She smiles to reassure me, but it prickles my senses as false.

I suppress a shudder and turn it into a solemn nod. "Of course. Thank you."

She departs, and I can't help but hang on the fact that she said "my guards." A group of militants like the one that set the fires would have to take orders from someone. From her.

I leave the range and return to the palace, mind racing.

I think about it well into the night, and slowly—ever so slowly—a few pieces start fitting together.

At Agatha's house, Spell said that she and her daughter had lived in the cellar. And at Med Ward after the fires, Marcher said that secrets don't stay buried for long.

If I had a legion of Royal guards training and planning to set fires, where could they go where no one would stumble upon them?

I remember my very first night here in the palace, when I spent the night in the dungeon. I thought I could sense the breathing of the city, like a heartbeat. But what if that wasn't a sensation from my new magical abilities? What if it was real— the real sounds of a group of Royal guards hiding out and planning underneath the palace?

If Belrosa buried the truth, maybe that's where I'll find it.

The dungeon is as dark and unpleasant as I remember, and I even pay a special curtsy to my old cell as I pass by. As I explore the dark tunnels, I rub my eyes, blinking away blurry shadows. It only takes a half hour before the cold and fatigue are creeping through my bones. As I round a corner, I hear footsteps: a single person, impatient, walking quickly. Then I see the light.

I move quickly, slipping inside an empty cell. The light bobs closer, rounding the curve. The wall is cold against my neck, and I fight the shiver crawling up my spine. I crouch down.

The light grows brighter and brighter. Then it flares. A pulse of energy: the man's aura as he passes. It's rigid and stern. He's definitely a guard. I reenter the tunnel. His uniform is red, not gray.

I put a gentle hand over my tattoo. Two choices: con my way into getting his key, or take it. A struggle could alert other guards in the area.

"You there, Guard!" I do my best to sound regal.

He spins around, startled. His heels click together to stand at attention.

I suppress a grin with a stern frown. "Do you know who I am?"

He is young, and he reminds me of a softer, younger version of Glenquartz. I remember seeing him during one of my tours of the palace. We were introduced. Kael Rajesh.

Kael's hand quivers at his side, as he decides whether or not to go for the single shot pistol at his hip or the musket from his shoulder.

I turn my shoulder toward him to show him the crown tattoo. "I am the Nameless queen." Saying it sends heat through my bones, energizes me. Strong.

Kael's fear bridges the gap between us like a static shock. I try to sense more of his aura, but when his hand twitches near the sheathed bayonet, that's enough.

I walk toward him slowly, talking to distract him.

"I've gotten myself lost," I say. "I figured the stairs would bring me to a food cellar."

Kael tenses as I halve the distance between us. Now I'm three steps away.

"You're not supposed to be down here." Kael's aura spikes with fear like crystallizing ice.

"I'm not? But I'm queen. Can't I go anywhere?" My fingers grow cold.

He focuses on my actions, his aura slowing down, like motes of dust suspended in sunlight. The sensation of frost crawls over my skin as his aura cools with suspicion. His hand grips the bayonet handle. He opens his mouth to speak. *Now.*

I close the gap, striking his throat so he can't call for help. The heat of his skin is like embers. He chokes and drops his lantern. I crouch and catch it an inch above the ground as he sputters for breath.

Kael twists forward, slamming his knee into my body, and there goes the lantern. With a crack of glass, oil spills onto the floor and flames jump to life on the stones. The fire is barely at our ankles, but I scramble away from the heat, striking at Kael's knee.

I hit his other knee, bringing him down to my level. He throws a wide punch, and I raise my arm to block it. As soon as I feel the hit, I trap his hand under my arm. *Got you.*

I twist his body away from me and grab his shoulder. Gaining leverage, I slam him into the wall. He meets the stones face-first and crumples to the ground. I pull him away from the steady flames as the lantern oil burns.

There's an unpleasant dark red outline of rock on Kael's forehead. I check for a pulse. Still alive, but unconscious.

I flip open his jacket and find the small key fitted through the cloth loop. I rip the key free. I don't know when he'll wake, but I don't want him running off and telling anyone.

And, down the tunnel: a perfectly good cell waiting for an occupant.

Five minutes later, Kael lies on the floor of the cell. Before closing the door, I take Kael's coat. I can't hide my hair this time, but from a distance I might pass as a Royal guard.

Oil settles into the cracks between stones, and the last traces of fire lick up in a grid pattern. With a sidelong glance at the broken lantern, I rip off part of Kael's shirtsleeve. I use it to soak up what remains of the lantern's oil from the cracked glass well. I stow the foul-smelling cloth in my boot.

I envision my map. Most of the dungeon's tunnels interlock like a maze, and I've covered a lot of area so far.

I walk carefully. A low rushing sound fills the air, like the steady roll of a drum. At first, I think it's the drainage pipes.

Soon enough, I recognize it as the sound of heavy feet. As I round a curve, a door comes into view. A thin smudge of light stretches from beneath it, and I hear another pulse of voices.

This is where General Belrosa's militant guards are training.

The door is twelve steps ahead. My boots grind the grime and dirt. The hairs on my arms rise.

Six steps, and I can hear the voices behind the door. Synchronized shouts and stomping feet.

Two steps.

One.

I stand outside the door, placing my hand on it. I could bring reinforcements, go to the few allies I have: The Legal servant who transported food to the Nameless; the doctor who tended my wounds and cared for my friends; Devil, who gave me shelter even if it was for a price. Glenquartz. Hat. Esther, even. But I'm already here. The room beyond the door feels empty. It's a gray blank spot on the map in my head. The door is wooden, rotted along the edges, heavy.

I can't see the hinges, which means it opens inward. The doorknob is metal, rusted slightly, so I can assume the hinges are the same. I'll have to open it carefully, pressing it tight to keep it quiet.

I take a deep breath: slow, steady, and calm. I use Kael's key, turn the lock silently, twist the doorknob, and push.

My shoulders and knees ache as I crouch in the doorway. A bar of light sneaks into the hall, broadening as the door opens. It casts a cold glare onto the wet stones.

I peer inside. Five steps from the doorway is a railing, and the room opens up beyond that. There's movement and the flicker of firelight, but I can't tell how many people there are. Hundreds, at least. I stay close to the door, peering along the inside edge of the room.

A dark sea of movement shifts beyond the rail.

I slip through the door, keeping the doorknob turned until I close the door behind me. There's no one on the walkway in either direction, so I move toward the railing, crouching. The center of the room is a pit.

Together, a group of nearly three hundred people moves in unison. They step forward and bring the guns up to aim. Pivot to the side, aim, lower their weapons, pivot again.

I've seen little of the military aside from the Royal guards who patrol Seriden. Yet I know without a doubt that this is organized training.

This is not a small group of rogue militants.

This is an army.

In the firelight, General Belrosa emerges from the sea of soldiers. They freeze and stand at attention. She walks up the far staircase.

Gaiza. She wasn't supposed to be here.

"It took you long enough to find your way to my training grounds." Her voice echoes, distorting off the walls. She turns at the top of the stairs and begins the long trek around the walkway, fixing her gaze on me.

"I knew you sensed something from me at the archery range," Belrosa says. "But you caught me unprepared. That won't happen again."

She strides toward me, and I want to stay strong and brave, but I back away. I caught her by surprise at the archery range, but I've only practiced my abilities on injured patients at Med Ward. I doubt I'd stand strong against her.

She observes me, coming to a stop a few paces away. "It's tough, isn't it? Being connected to your subjects and seeing their fears and thoughts. People think that being sovereign is all about power and strength. But with that crown, you're more a slave to them. To me."

I remind myself of my power: to create illusions and to read memories and thoughts. What can I show her to make her afraid?

But I can barely focus on her movements as she approaches me, let alone focus well enough to make a hallucination.

"I'm here to make a deal with you," I say.

She snarls. "A deal?" Her aura pulses, dark red with disgust.

"You have secrets. You are vulnerable." I motion to the army of men and women. "You've seen what I can do. At the gallows. At the fires. I am not powerless."

Belrosa laughs. It scrunches her eyes and shows her straight teeth. A second later, her laugh disappears and her eyes are a slow burn of ice. "I'll spare you the details of how the Royal Council won't believe you, and instead I'll tell you how they'll kill you."

A shudder snakes down my arms.

Belrosa's face flickers in the firelight. "The council will finally realize that you are unfit to continue as the heir. The riots, the execution, the fire! All under your watch, because you are

Nameless. Seriden is on the brink of civil war! What the city needs is a firm, militaristic rule. No longer will a two-hundred-year-old, antiquated treaty dictate our actions. We need an army to control the madness of this city. The city needs a familiar face in power. And whose name will they force from your lips when they finally agree? Who, of all of the Royals, is fit to take your place?"

I grind my teeth.

"I know what you're thinking," Belrosa says coldly. "You won't speak my name. Oh, but consider what happens if you don't. I will track down your little Nameless friend who escaped the gallows. She will suffer in ways you never dreamed a person could suffer."

The fire in my chest flares. I can't feel the cold hatred of her aura, because my own anger crawls along my skin like beads of molten metal.

"Or," she says, "in two weeks, at the Assassins' Festival, you simply pass the tattoo to me peacefully. No need for violence. No need for suffering."

"No." I set my jaw.

"No?" Belrosa's mouth twitches.

"No," I say more firmly. "I'm not here to take your threats. I'm here to make a deal."

"Are you?" Belrosa grins. "I was under the impression that you weren't making any more deals." Her gaze shifts to something behind me.

I take a cautious step, sure to keep the firelight between us. Another figure walks along the curving walkway.

"What's this I hear about a deal to be made?" Marcher says.

I feel as if the blood's been drained from my body. "This is why you keep coming in and out of the palace. But I don't understand. Why work with her?"

Usually, I never admit when I don't understand something. But I know Marcher. He'll seize the opportunity to undermine me. As expected, a slimy smile appears on his face.

"Our lives," Marcher says, "the lives of the Nameless, they aren't so black and white, legal and illegal. Sure, we can't hold a job or own a house. But since when has a system ever abided by its own rules? Why do *you* think I'm here?"

His taunting smirk rolls up his cheeks like spreading mold.

"To get me here," I say. "To the palace. To the dungeon."

Now I can see why Marcher is so pleased. To them, I am a dancing marionette: strings pulled, limbs flailing.

"To get you to the palace?" Marcher says. "No, that was inevitable once you found the tattoo."

"So, what, then?" I demand. "You're here to join a secret army?"

He frowns in disappointment. "You've got it all wrong."

"So all of this?" I gesture at the army. "It's not a secret?"

"I didn't say *that*," Marcher says.

"You mean you don't know?" Condescension drips from Belrosa's tongue.

I grind my teeth.

"Well, you are in a stressful spot right now, I suppose," Belrosa says. "And I guess it's hard to sense something that isn't there." Belrosa beams with smug pride. I try again to think of a hallucination that would get me out of this, but nothing I do would fool Marcher.

"You're too focused on me," Belrosa says, dropping her voice to a whisper. "You're not paying attention. Let me ask you. How many auras do you sense in this room?"

I answer out of reflex, like breathing. "One."

A twinge runs through me, and I turn my gaze out at the hundreds of people in the pit.

I know I'm wrong. I know what I said can't be true. It's like sand on my tongue. Belrosa is the only person with an aura in this room. The dark pit is filled with people and yet somehow empty.

"They're . . ." I stare at the hundreds of women and men, teens, adults.

"Yes," Belrosa says. "They're Nameless. My Nameless army."

CHAPTER 18

"Why?" I stare at the Nameless faces, all stern and unflinching.

"Why are they Nameless?" Marcher suggests.

Belrosa adds, "Or why are we training?"

I glare at them. "Both."

"It's the same answer, really," Marcher says, deferring to Belrosa.

She strides to the railing, surveying her soldiers, and I move to keep them both in my sight.

"Seriden is struggling," Belrosa says. "The Royal Council blames the Nameless, calls them the criminal scourge dragging us down. They're wrong. Seriden's problem is that a Nameless teenager is poised to take the throne and magic has historically been shunted between lackluster Royals who have no vision for the future."

"This is your answer? Build an illegal army in the shadows to overthrow Seriden?" The Royal Council will never support it. When I take proof of Belrosa's misdeeds to the council, they'll have to arrest her.

Marcher walks calmly past me. "The Nameless have no identity, no loyalty, and no allegiance. Yes, it's illegal to build an army. But none of those laws apply to the Nameless. In fact, every Nameless you thought I sent off to their death, every Nameless that's gone missing, has come here for food, shelter, and a soldier's training."

"With minor exceptions for those few Nameless who refused." Belrosa shrugs. "I am better equipped to help Seriden thrive than you ever could be."

It makes sense. That's why there would be no trace of the Nameless who disappeared. They weren't taken by force. They were recruited. Except for those who refused. I think of Anchor, the Nameless boy who showed up dead two weeks before I was named queen. He must've turned down the offer to become a soldier, and so Belrosa had him killed.

In Belrosa's aura, a strong fire burns. She's not like the Legals I con in the markets or the deckhands who tilt with whisky. She has seen me lying, and she has seen me honest. I need to throw her off long enough to gain a new advantage.

Honesty it is, then.

I scoff, unimpressed. "Just because Nameless soldiers rise from the streets doesn't mean it's a mystery who's pulling the strings. You expect to take over Seriden and avoid suspicion by blaming the Nameless? It won't work."

"Care to enlighten me?" Belrosa's arms are angled sharply on her hips as she moves to the center of the walkway, just beyond the flickering torch.

I've been clocking Marcher and Belrosa, tracking their movements. But it's now, as Marcher takes a firm stance in the middle of the walkway behind and Belrosa moves into place ahead, that I realize they've blocked both my exits.

I'm trapped.

I thought I was being clever. That was my first mistake.

I scrutinize Belrosa. If I'm quick enough, I can push my way past her, but if she's ready for me, one touch could break me. I've gotten some practice working with the patients at Med Ward, but none of them were ever trying to actively push dark thoughts or memories at me. And I've never been able to get past Marcher before. The only time I came close was the time I tried to kill him, and then I had surprise on my side. And it didn't work. Plus, he's Nameless, and my magic won't even affect him.

I pretend to survey the Nameless army, but I'm really scoping out the rest of the room. I could run down the unguarded side of the walkway. But given the curvature of the path, the soldiers would rush up the stairs and block my exit to the other door. I wouldn't make it in time.

I recognize a few faces among the Nameless soldiers, a couple I would have even called "friends" once. But they all have the same stern expression. I wonder if, by some unspoken Nameless bond, they would show me mercy. I doubt it.

I crouch down, gripping the railing bars like a prison door. "You've changed everything."

"I have," Belrosa says proudly. "And I will *take* everything."

Now we're just testing each other. Who moves first? Who takes the first step? The first lunge, the first strike? I can sense her eagerness to spring forward, to match me in a duel like the ones planned for the festival.

"Leave it to a mad general to recruit the unwanted for an

army," I say. "If I wasn't so outmatched, I might be impressed."
I fiddle with my boot, pulling out the oil-soaked cloth.

"I give them a home, be it in the dark underbelly of the beast," Belrosa says, projecting her voice for the army's benefit. "I see to their needs, and I give them structure, order, training, a soldier's bond. They will win our war, and finally hold a place in the world."

So that's how she got their loyalty. She promised them a future beyond the battle. But she will usurp the throne, and there will be no place for them then.

I test Belrosa's aura. It's firm and unwavering.

"You may have their loyalty," I say loudly, "but do they have *yours*? Don't forget, Belrosa, I can sense your aura. You may guard it, and you may project confidence . . ." I walk up to her so that only shadows dance in the space between us.

". . . but you're afraid," I add, speaking even louder so the soldiers will hear us. "Afraid that they'll learn your deceitful plans for them. You promise them names and position, but you don't have the power to give that to them. When your battles are done, once you've finished exploiting them, whoever survives is as good as dead."

My voice carries through the room, and I hear the faint rustling of feet. Belrosa doesn't react. She knows I'm not telling the truth.

I grin and whisper, "But it sounded like the truth, didn't it?"

She growls and advances toward me.

I make my move. I whip the oily cloth through the flames of the nearby torch. It catches fire, and I throw it at her face.

It lands on her left shoulder, setting part of her uniform on fire. I use my ability to make her think the fire is stronger, spreading faster, hotter.

Marcher charges from behind me, but he won't get to me in time. He grabs for my jacket, but he loses his grip as I heave myself over the railing and down into the pit of soldiers.

I don't have unrealistic expectations.

I don't expect the Nameless army to welcome me with open arms.

I don't expect them to suddenly betray the people who trained them, taught them, and gave them the only possessions they have.

The only thing I expect is for them to hesitate.

When I launch myself over the railing, fall twelve feet through the air, and absorb the impact with a forward roll, no one moves.

I'm four feet from the sewer drain, and it's the perfect size.

I dive to the ground, digging my fingers into the slats of the heavy grate. I wrench it upward and throw it to the side. A body hurtles through the air at me.

A sweep of brown hair and lean, strong dark arms, and—slam—I'm sideways on the floor.

I roll an extra length away and search wildly for my opponent. Her short hair hangs shy of her fierce eyes. Dare. She disappeared from the streets at least a year ago. Marcher has been building this army for a very long time.

Before I can square off to face her, I feel the heat of a body behind me. I crouch and throw my body weight backward with my elbow. I catch the Nameless soldier in the gut, and he doubles over.

Dare raises her fists as if we're about to have a street tussle. I don't know what kind of training they've learned. But my instinct isn't to fight, and it isn't to kill.

My instinct is to survive.

As Dare lunges at me, I curl in toward her and bring my arm down onto the crook of her elbow. Her arm folds inward, and she tries to pull away. As she does, I spin and come at her fast. I throw a hit at her neck with the side of my fist. Off balance, she staggers.

A couple of soldiers advance on me. Up on the walkway, Belrosa, now free of the illusion, grips the railing, her whole body tense with fury. Marcher stands beside her, looking amused.

I give them a quick two-finger salute and jump down into the tunnel. I pull my arms tight against my body and fall into darkness.

I fall for less than a second, but the tunnel is curved, and my right ankle takes a twist as I land in an unpleasant pool of water and filth. The sewer. Not an ideal escape plan, but effective.

As thudding boots descend the ladder, I break into a run. I don't know how familiar the Nameless soldiers are with the tunnels, but I know nothing about this area. If Marcher had anything to do with teaching them, they might know every twist, turn, and dead end.

My ankle flares with each step, but I press onward. In my head, I already have a map of the palace and the dungeon. The network of drainage tunnels likely lines up with the rooms of the palace.

In the pitch black, my run is more of a staggering jog. One hand follows the curved wall while the other feels the empty space ahead. The tunnel wall curves sharply, and my hand falls to open air. The tunnel curves in two directions. Left and right. The chorus of wet footsteps crashes down the tunnels behind me, getting closer each second.

I realize I'm not far from the east stairs of the dungeon and there should be a drainage cover nearby. I backtrack and head down the right tunnel. I take a few running steps, stop, and press myself against the wall.

The clattering footsteps draw to a stop, and a pale gold light shimmers off the slimy walls.

"Which way?" a soldier asks. I don't recognize his voice.

I hold my breath. I have a fifty-fifty chance. If they go left, I can wait until they're out of earshot. Even if they split up, I have a better shot.

"Go right," Darc says.

Gaiza.

I start running again.

A victorious shout, and they pursue me. They'll catch up soon. There are three of them, their footsteps getting louder. I struggle to pick out shapes in the darkness, but there are only occasional drains overhead that let in sludgy blurs of light.

I've only got a small window to do something clever and escape. I could probably take them one at a time, but I can't fight off three trained soldiers at once. Not for long, anyway.

My right hand gives way as another smaller tunnel branches out, and I slip lithely in through the empty space. Enough running. I slide down until I'm sitting on my heels, leaning against the wall. As the quick slap of boots turns the corner, I stick out a leg.

One of the runners catches my leg hard, rocketing face-first to the ground. He doesn't get up. The runner behind him trips as well, stumbling and falling, but with less force. My hip jars with the impact, but I push myself into a crouch.

The third person was farther along and pulls to a stop before reaching me. I snatch up the musket that dropped from the first runner's grasp. The standing soldier pulls the musket from his shoulder.

I doubt his is loaded, just as I doubt mine is. As he aims his musket toward me, I pull mine upward into the bottom of his chin. His whole body stiffens, rising an inch, before he collapses downward, unconscious.

The second runner has recovered, and she throws a punch. I'm not fast enough to dodge it, so I take the hit. I collapse downward and put my weight on my arms. Muck and water cling to my skin, cold and slimy.

I kick, striking her knee. There's a terrible crunch. Her knee fractures and dislocates.

She twists to the side, taking the weight off her leg, and she falls against the wall.

"You vittin prens," Dare says through gritted teeth.

A twinge of guilt pinches in my chest at her injuries, but

not enough for me to stick around. I grab the lantern the first soldier dropped. It's cracked and leaking but unbroken.

"Thanks." I lift the lantern. "And sorry."

Dare holds her leg and pops it into place, and she throws me a withering glare.

With light to guide me, I sprint down the tunnels, leaving the three soldiers far behind.

CHAPTER 19

I know I should go to Med Ward, but I'm not sure how I'd explain the state of my clothes to Hat without having to explain Belrosa and Marcher, and I don't want to do that yet.

Instead I head to my sleeping quarters, which are empty and quiet. I take a shower, sending the filth from my skin back down to the sewer. After a half hour of staring at the sooty lantern shell, I hear a knock at the door. I bolt upright.

I find my voice, aiming for soothing honey. "Yes?"

Belrosa's low voice answers. "We should talk."

I don't have a weapon.

I could hide. Bar the door. Open the skylight and escape along the roof. But she's not barging in. She's not firing her musket through the door. She wants to talk. I snatch my old coat from under the bed, digging for my knife. I hold it pressed up against my arm so it's not visible.

I open the door, and Belrosa steps inside.

Part of me wants her to laugh and explain that it's all a hoax, that she was testing my loyalties or something. The other part of me wants her to rage through the doorway, bring up her musket, and confront me head-on.

Instead she surveys the room with stony eyes. I feel her aura like a brick wall: cold and unbreachable.

"What do you want?" I ask casually, as if I don't know why she's here.

"To discuss our predicament." Belrosa scans the room.

Is she making sure I don't have an escape route? Making sure there are no witnesses? I flip the knife to face forward so she knows I have it.

"That," Belrosa says, pointing at the knife, "is not the right choice."

"Oh, and you know the best choice?" I gesture angrily with the blade.

"Sure," Belrosa says. "The best choice is to listen to the deal I'm offering. You simply need to turn over the crown tattoo at the Assassins' Festival. It's in two weeks. We can even have a duel if you like so you can return to the streets with some good stories about fighting the big bad general of the Royal Guard."

"Why would I do that?" I ask.

"If you try to reveal the existence of the Nameless army," Belrosa says, "the Royal Council won't believe you. They'll laugh in your face. Now, if you refuse to meet my duel challenge—if you don't give me the crown—you'll see the true danger of an underprivileged class who has been taught to fight. You thought the riots we arranged in the streets were bad? You thought the fires Marcher helped me orchestrate were tragic? Just wait until the Nameless army rises up and starts slaughtering the attendants of the Assassins' Festival. And who takes the blame for the Nameless scourge killing hundreds of innocent people?"

Belrosa rolls her stiff shoulders, one of which is scorched, and I sense a pulse of fear from her. As soon as I sense it, it's gone.

Belrosa observes me. "Felt that, did you? Yes, I'm familiar with your . . . abilities. More than you are, I'd wager. The late King Fallow and I had a unique relationship. Rifles and military equipment don't come easy. I had years to practice on him. In fact"—she steps toward me and puts out her hand—"I know *your* weaknesses."

I stare at her hand. I want to grab it and crush it, feel the pop of bones, watch her features curl in pain. If Belrosa thinks she can use the same trick on me twice, I'm out to prove her wrong. I can do this.

I take her hand in mine. I try to push her into one of my memories from the streets.

"Are you trying to push my thoughts?" Belrosa chuckles. "It's a great burden to sense the auras and memories of your subjects, you know. To have all that exposed, raw emotion coursing through you, gliding past. Well, I've had a lot of practice. I can make it *stick*." With that, she grasps my hand tightly.

A surge of energy courses through her, up my arm, and into my body. The tattoo on my left arm sears, burning like ice.

Then a hundred terrible, horrible memories and thoughts splinter through me. Burning fear like fire, every piece of me scorching.

It cripples me.

I feel the pain of loss, the heat of uncontrollable anger—its poison seeping through my skin and down to my bones. The dark, gnawing acid of hate. Fear so inconsolably rigid that it digs to my heart and hollows it out. Before I know it, I'm on my knees.

Belrosa stands over me, gripping my hand with iron strength. Cold tears fall down my cheeks. Bones burn as I realize I've lost every single thing in the world that I ever loved. I am alone.

Belrosa twists my hand, putting a popping strain on my wrist, and my body spasms, my legs curling to my chest.

With a slow and controlled sigh, Belrosa kneels down. "This is what power brings to the powerless." Her words reach me like the hiss of smoke from a fire. "Pain. And now you have mine. Every moment when fear ruled over me and every pain I've ever experienced. Every struggle, every ache, all rushing together at once. And it *burns* you."

I try to pull my hand from her grasp, but I don't have the strength. Every effort goes toward stopping the outbursts of terror that surge through me. I grit my teeth. My jaw aches.

Belrosa leans down as if she's about to kiss my cheek. She lets go of my hand but draws a finger up my arm to the tattoo. It's like a flame tearing its way up my skin. She presses gently against the ink crown, and a sharp physical pain shoots through me. Shattering terror pierces me. I am empty. I am broken. Everything I am pours out of me, replaced by pain.

She whispers in my ear, "This crown will be mine, one way or another."

Once again, her fears flood me with the slam of metal and touch of cold stone. Then she lets go.

Belrosa marches to the door. "Have a lovely evening, Your *Highness*." She gives a courteous bow. The door slams shut behind her.

My connection to Belrosa is gone, but I can't stop gasping for air, and I can't forget the searing pain racing through my entire body.

I am alone. I have ice burning my skin and fire searing my chest, and I have no one.

I can't stay here.

As I slowly regain my body, I push up from the floor. I will not stay where she left me, curled on the floor in pain and defeat. I will not suffer this way. I grab a coat, tighten the laces of my boots, and turn down the flickering lantern flame. I leave the sleeping quarters, abandoning the bed my body wants to collapse in.

I hurry down the long empty corridors, which take every small sound and amplify it. I hear the faint squelch of my leather boots, the uneasy, uneven gusts of breath in my chest, and every creak in the floors.

I go to the last place I'd expect. I go to the king's quarters, to the solid, polished oak door covered by a black curtain. I slip inside, and it's just as Esther and I left it. The faint layer of dust is still undisturbed, and the bed is so smooth, it's as if it's never been touched.

If I survive long enough, I could die here of old age, but if someone from Belrosa's army finds me here tonight, death may come sooner.

With a sigh, I realize that I wish Esther was here. I wish Hat and Glenquartz were here too. I even wish Devil was here.

I stand tentatively at the side of the bed, and I think about pulling the blankets down onto the floor as I did on my first night in the guest sleeping quarters.

Instead I crawl into the bed. There's a faint smell of body oil and perfume, and I feel my eyes burn as I realize that this is what my father smelled like. This was the man who sentenced me to a life on the streets, but also the man who spoke my name in the moments before his death. I never learned what his laugh sounded like or had the chance to memorize his smile.

I never met my father, but somehow—impossibly—I miss him.

+

Someone opens the door. In an instant, I've rolled off the opposite side of the bed, shifted my knife to an offensive grip, and gotten a lock on the person coming inside. When I see the dark ringlets of hair and tan skin, I relax.

Esther's startled gaze fixes on the blade in my hand, and I quickly slide it into my pocket.

"Glenquartz said you were missing," Esther says. "We've been searching for you all morning. We didn't know if someone killed you, or took you, or if you ran off. In any case, it's only us that know. We didn't want to alarm the council. Is everything . . . Are you okay?"

I rise to my feet, and I summon the blade to my fingertips at a moment's notice again as heat and anger flood me. I slam the blade sideways, burying an inch of steel into the canopy bedpost.

Esther gasps, and I know on some level that I've damaged something I shouldn't have. I wrench the blade free and stalk past her toward the door.

"I'm not talking about it," I say angrily. Then, a second later, as I reach the door, I turn around and say, just as angrily, "Fine. I'll talk about it. But bring Glenquartz. I'm not going through it more than once."

When she leaves to fetch him, I pace the room.

The fear and hurt I felt last night have morphed entirely into anger. What would I do if I was already queen? I wonder if I would have Belrosa executed on the spot, or if I'd have her arrested and taken before the judiciary. I might even go to the Royal Council for support.

I grip the handle of my knife tighter and tighter. None of that would help me, because I'm Nameless. It doesn't matter that I have a crown tattoo. I don't have rights.

"I could do this alone," I say quietly to the empty room, testing the lie to see how it feels. I could find Devil, leave Seriden. All it would take is for me to walk through that door, past the black curtain, and out of the palace.

But for the first time, I don't want to be alone. I don't want to face every pain the world has offered me by myself. So I sit on the edge of the bed, and I wait.

Esther returns fifteen minutes later, and she has both Glenquartz and Hat.

"I couldn't convince her to stay behind," Glenquartz says apologetically. "Has . . . something happened?"

Hat pushes past Glenquartz and stands in front of me. She studies my face for a minute, and I feel my cheeks burn red. I take a deep breath and tilt my head down, running through what I want to say.

Hat puts a hand on my shoulder, and I flinch. She bends down to meet my downcast gaze.

"Eyes up," she says consolingly. "Remember?"

I try to take a stand before them, but I have too much energy, and I begin pacing.

"I was alone," I start. "For a very long time. I grew up in a crew of as many as twenty children underneath the leadership of a Nameless man called Marcher."

Hat cringes and sits on the bed, pulling a pillow to her stomach.

"It wasn't like this for everyone," I say, "but there were no friendships for me. There were no companions or mentors. There was just Marcher and the insane, competitive, challenging, impossible world he raised me in. And then I did make a friend. Another kid in our group called Echo. And Marcher got her killed. I was so angry that I . . . ." I pause to roll my shoulders and get my head on straight. "I tried to kill Marcher, and I failed. I failed because you showed up." I gesture at Hat, and her eyes are shining.

"I almost did it," I say. "But I didn't. And it occurred to me in that moment that even if Marcher got someone else killed, he was looking after the rest of the kids in a way that no one else could, and in a way that the city never would. So I compromised, and I just left. Over the next few years, I struck out alone and made a name for myself. I became a grifter and a survivor, no matter what else that meant."

Glenquartz eases down into a chair by the wardrobe, and Esther remains standing.

"Every time I saw you, Hat," I say, "I knew there were more like you. And I couldn't look after all of them or *any* of them. Somehow, that meant I couldn't look after just you. I don't know if I was wrong to think like that, but I'm sorry for everything it meant for you. And . . . this is the first time in my entire life that I haven't felt like I have to do everything alone." A weak smile flickers on my face.

"Something happened," I confirm. "Something is *happening*. And I don't want to deal with it alone. I want to tell you what happened, and then I want to ask for your help."

All three of them stand firm. All of them are ready.

I tell them about the army. About Marcher. About Belrosa's visit, how fears I'd never imagined and angers I'd never considered burned through my body like ice. I tell Esther that Belrosa implied that she'd practiced her abilities on Fallow, subjecting him to her cruel thoughts and fears the same way she did me.

Esther's eyes shift from troubled and pained to something darker. Her shoulders tighten, and her lip twitches in disgust. Her expression grows fierce and desperate as her fists curl tightly, her arms trembling.

I recognize what she's thinking. Her aura is cold yet distant, like the freezing of ice behind a sheet of glass.

I step closer. "Don't," I say, gentle but firm.

"Don't what," Esther says, but she doesn't even say it like a question. She grits her teeth. Her eyes flit to the knife in my hand.

"I know that look," I say. "I know what it means." She wants to kill Belrosa.

"Do you?" Esther challenges, her hands balled into fists. "Because I just realized my father probably spent my entire life suffering at the hand of the person who was supposed to protect him. No wonder he kept me at a distance! He was protecting me from her. Tell me: What Belrosa did to you, was it the worst pain you'd ever felt?"

I consider briefly whether I should lie, but at this point, she'd know.

"Yes."

Esther's resolution wavers. Her aura shifts from the fear of ice to the splintering of glass.

"This isn't about whether or not Belrosa deserves it," I say. "It's not about her. It's about you, and whether or not you can live with yourself."

Esther stares at me hard.

"You knew our father better than anyone," I say. "Would he want you to become a killer?"

I don't need an answer to sense the softening of her aura, the anger melting and falling away, the heavy grief crawling to replace it. She relaxes and falls silent.

Hat stands now, as though it's her turn for outrage. "We should confront her. As a group. She can't do what she did to me or to Glenquartz."

I shake my head. "No. You don't understand. You're trying to help, but you don't understand. I shouldn't have even told you."

"Not tell me?" She glowers.

"I want to protect you from things like this and from people like that!" I say.

"You can't do that, Coin," she says. "You can't protect me from everything."

"Why the hell not?" I demand. "I grew up in fear and anger! That was my whole life, and it was all I knew. Then I was alone until . . . until you came to me and asked me to teach you how to be brave. I don't want this for you, Hat."

"You turned out fine," Hat says.

"No, I didn't," I say. "I'm broken. And yes, I may have found a way to be happy sometimes, but I'm not a happy person. Not like you are."

Hat narrows her eyes, annoyed. "I'm not just happy by nature. You know that, right?"

I stare at her. "Of course you are. You have this inherent optimism that I don't have."

Hat nearly scoffs. "Then you don't understand me at all! You think I was happy to live out on the streets and spend every night in that house full of kids who are so competitive with each other that none of us have any real friends? You think it's easy for me to spend every day with you, knowing that you can only bear to have me around for half the day before you send me back to Marcher? No. All of that hurts. The whole world hurts. I can't stop it or control it. But it's like you said to me after you saved me. You have to let things make you strong instead of damaged. You have to choose how the world shapes you."

I open my mouth to speak, but she keeps going.

"So, yeah, I choose to be happy," she says. "I make an effort to wake up each morning in the best mood I can, because I know it will go downhill if I let it. I don't want to end up like those Nameless who sit on the corners of stoops, staring at nothing and starving to death because the world doesn't care about them and they've forgotten how to care for themselves. I want *friends*. I want a *family*. I want to learn how to take care of myself and be as badass as you are. So don't think anything is easy, because nothing is. Stop acting like happiness is something you can't have." Hat huffs in frustration, and she stalks away from me. She stands at the far end of the room, staring out the window.

"The Assassins' Festival is in thirteen days," I say gently "We only have twelve days to prepare. I've spent . . . most of my life on my own. Even when I probably shouldn't have." I glance guiltily at Hat, and even though she's picking at some dried wax on the writing desk, she's listening.

I continue, "I'm asking for your help. For all of your help. Belrosa has manipulated me twice with a single touch. She tried to kill Hat in front of hundreds of spectators. She arranged the riots and the fires, all to undermine me and prepare the city to accept military rule. People have died. I don't want more people to die, and I don't want to face this alone. Belrosa is expecting me to duel her and lose, and the lives of innocent people hang in the balance. Please help me."

"Of course," Glenquartz says, bowing his head.

"Absolutely," Esther says.

Hat walks over and puts an arm tentatively around me, until she has slipped into a hug. "Yes."

CHAPTER 20

We spend the rest of the day coming up with the plan for the festival. Then, over the next week, it's nonstop drills of hand-to-hand combat with Glenquartz and practicing magic with Esther; then we start combining the two. All the while, the Royal Council thinks I'm attending etiquette lessons with Eldritch Weathers, and everyone—including Belrosa— still thinks Esther and I hate each other. The council is content if I decide to keep my head down until the festival, and Belrosa probably thinks I'm scared of her. Good. Let them be wrong.

"You know," I say to Esther, "if you'd asked me a month ago to fight you, I would've gladly accepted." I test my footing on the matted floor.

"You weren't my biggest supporter," she says. "But for good reason. I wasn't supportive of you, either. Our relationship was precarious at best, volatile at worst."

"If you can just keep channeling your inner pretentious Royal, that'll make this a lot easier." I crack my knuckles.

"What do you mean, 'pretentious'?" Esther says. "I am simply—"

I cut her off, holding up a finger. "Starting a sentence with 'I am simply' is pretty much all the evidence I need."

She lets out a low growl.

I continue, "Glenquartz has been teaching me how to spar for weeks now, so why do we need to do this? I want you to keep teaching me magic. Besides, I don't think the former princess of Seriden is qualified to—"

The next breath is blown from my chest. I don't even see it happen. All I know is I'm on the floor.

"Did you just . . . ?" I say as I try to breathe.

"Sternum punch?" Esther says cheerily. "Glenquartz said that was payback. I grew up thinking I was going to be queen one day, and you've only known it for about five weeks. I've been training my entire life to win duels." She cocks her head patiently to the side, not offering to help me up.

I consider whether a well-placed kick to her leg would bring her down to my level, but instead she skips away.

"Are you sure you can't read my thoughts?" I ask as I prop myself up on my knees.

"Very sure," she says. "Reading thoughts only works with physical contact, and you're Nameless, so I can't sense anything from you. Which gives you an advantage, actually." She extends a gloved hand to help me up.

"You know what sort of advantage I'd like? The napping kind." I fold my arms under my head and stretch out.

She nudges me with a toe impatiently, and I curl in toward her and bring her down to the floor. She gasps, somewhere between pleasantly surprised and angry, and I smile.

"All right," I say. "We can fight fairly now."

She glares at me through a few misplaced strands of dark hair. "You're very competitive, you know that?" she says with a huff.

I smirk. "More competitive than you, I bet."

She shakes her head, holding up a hand to stop me. "As I was saying, between you and me you have the advantage. I can't sense you, which means I'm going to be like every other dueler you face. You can sense me, and I can't sense you. Right?"

I pull myself to my feet. "Yeah, except my abilities don't work the same way as yours. When you make someone see an illusion, you see it too, right?"

She nods.

"My illusions don't work like that," I say. "I can't see what I make other people see, which is very funny to watch, but also not very useful to me. How do I know if what I'm making you see is really there?"

"I think it's even more useful," Esther says. "At the execution, you made everyone hear loud bells and you made their vision go dark. That didn't affect you, so you were able to run through the crowd unharmed. That's an advantage I've never had, and that's how you were able to save your friend."

"That's me! I'm that friend!" Hat shouts from outside the door. She skids into the room. "I ran here all the way from Med Ward." She pulls off her apron and hat and stuffs them into a shoulder bag.

"What are you doing here?" I ask.

"Glenquartz told me you're sparring," Hat says. "That means

I'll get to see one or both of you get beaten up by the other. I can't think of a better way to spend an afternoon." She sits at the edge of the mat and leans forward on her knees.

I point at her. "You are a menace."

Esther objects. "It's good that she stays. You'll have observers at the festival, so you'll have to be able to focus when you're the center of attention. Hat will be a good audience." Esther winks at Hat.

"I love being the center of attention," I say sarcastically.

"You watch Coin," Esther says to Hat. "If we do this right, you'll be able to see her actions and I won't. If she makes any mistakes, you let me know, okay?"

Hat jumps to her feet eagerly.

"Now," Esther says, "I want us to work on three things. One: I want you to make it so I can't see you. Two: make me see you somewhere else. Three: control a secondary illusion while you fight, like snakes or storm clouds or lightning. The things you want to practice most are not letting the magic distract you from the fight and not letting the fight distract you from the magic."

I groan. "I'm not good at multitasking. I'm good at focusing. One thing, over and over until I'm an expert."

"In duels," Esther explains, "there is going to be very little physical contact. Mostly swords and padded clothing. If you do get ahold of someone, though, you can put them to sleep or use something in their memories against them. If you can find out what they fear, you can find a way to control them. If I was afraid of snakes or spiders, for example, you could use those against me."

"Or snake-spiders," I say.

Esther smiles. "You may remember that visual hallucinations are the easiest, but if you want to make people hear or feel things, it's more difficult. It all gets easier with physical contact, because that's what gives you direct access into their mind."

"So why can't I just look at a challenger and make them feel pain?" I say, knowing I sound a bit like a monster.

"It's dicey," Esther says. "It's not as effective as you think. As soon as you stop, it fades pretty fast, since it wasn't real to begin with. You could stop someone in the middle of a fight and make them stumble, but it would be unlikely to convince them to stop dueling you. What was the first thing you did with your abilities?"

I sigh, trying to remember. "I saw the memory of a Royal and got my first glimpse of King Fallow on his deathbed. Then, in the market, when Hat was in danger, this idiot cadet was about to use his secondary weapon to execute her for an unconfirmed class-one offense! I shouted to quiet down the marketplace, and I think I used my ability to make sure everyone heard me. I didn't quite understand my abilities yet, but that's what happened."

Esther appraises me. "I'd like to point out that the first time you used your abilities was to help someone. The first time I used mine was to steal sweets from the kitchen. But . . . the way you talk about your life is . . . It's a series of insane events, and you talk about them so casually."

"It's my normal," I say with a shrug. "Or it was."

Esther gestures at the pair of us, practicing magic and sparring in preparation for the Assassins' Festival. "I think it's still your normal."

"And you give speeches," I say, "and live your life as a stage actor. That must seem normal to you. Do you wonder if King Fallow, when he talked about the crowns being reunited, which of us he meant? I mean, obviously he thought something was supposed to happen since I'm Nameless. But I don't know what that is."

"I think he meant for it to be you," Esther says. "He didn't choose to give me the crown. His brother did. He picked *you*. He didn't pick me."

She stares distractedly up at the ceiling.

"I guess we're both in the dark," I say.

"I don't know exactly what he thought would happen or what he was afraid would happen," Esther says. "All I know is that I'm going to help you stay alive."

"Sounds like a plan to me."

"Okay, then. I want you to create the illusion of rain," she says, "and I want you to maintain it when I come at you." She wipes at her skin, brushing off invisible flecks of rainwater.

Hat giggles at the absurdity of it. Neither of us can see what Esther sees.

Esther lashes out and, after a few jabs, stops.

"The illusion slipped," she says.

I groan in frustration and punch the wall with my gloved fist.

"I think I might know why it's so difficult for you," Esther says. "You've already seen your disadvantage, what Belrosa can do to you. You're letting it get in your head and distract you."

I imagine a bolt of lightning at Esther's feet, and she yelps as it strikes. Then she growls at me.

"Lashing out won't make you better at this," she says.

"What *will*?" I shout. "We only have one week left. I can't do it."

"Come after me," she encourages. "You keep fighting defensively. You need to be offensive! You need to take control."

"When I run a con," I say, "I don't plan for everything to go perfectly. I plan for things to fall apart. In every scenario, I know how to escape. I live my life on the defensive. But what you're asking me to do—face Belrosa in a duel in front of everyone at the Assassins' Festival—is the *opposite* of an escape plan."

"So what do you have planned for *this* moment?" Esther says, picking up a sword from the long table.

I know she's trying to bait me. It's working. Glenquartz's training runs through my head: get a comparable weapon, take up a stance at a safe distance, and prepare to fight. But the only sword is the one in Esther's hand.

"Even the playing field," Esther commands. "Open a chasm between us. Surround me with walls. But know that even though I can see the illusion, I'll know it isn't real. Level the playing field." She advances more quickly, and I skirt around the edge of the table to keep the distance between us.

"I'm older and stronger than you," Esther adds. "I have an army at my command. You need to find a way to stop me."

"Level the playing field," I agree. "But how do you expect to fight me with no weapon?" I point at the sword in her hand, except I'm using every speck of energy I have to compel her to forget the sword. Just like the pillows in the dungeon, I imagine nothing but air.

Shock passes over her features as she flexes her fingers, and I have to remember to also compel her hand not to feel anything. As if on command, her hand goes slack, and the sword clatters to the floor. The sound of it startles her, and I take two long strides, picking it up as I go, and place an arm against her throat and rest the flat of the blade on her shoulder.

"Why pick an even playing field when I can have the advantage?" I say. I release my illusion on the sword, and she can suddenly feel the cold of the blade against her skin.

"That was great!" she says. "I wouldn't have thought of that! I thought you'd make me see another sword or weapon. You did great!"

I glow with pride.

"Now all you have to do is learn how to create and sustain an illusion," Esther says.

"You make it sound easy," I say. "But I can barely do it at all. I can't see what I'm creating."

She nods, trying to understand. "I suppose that if I were to put my hand out and tell you that I'm holding a small bird, anyone else in the room would see it. I would see it. Once I see it, I can shape it and improve it. I can keep it around for a very long time." She moves her hand as if petting a small animal. "In fact, I did. As a child, I made a violet bird and kept it as an imaginary pet. I named her Ray-la." She smiles a wistful smile and then closes her fist. "But I suppose you can't have that, and it makes it more difficult to maintain an illusion. We'll start more slowly, then. We'll practice making illusions and then maintaining them, and then maintaining them while you fight. I'll join you for your sparring lessons with Glenquartz, and you can train for both at once. Don't worry. We still have about a week. More than enough time."

"Six days," I correct, "if we're being exact. That doesn't feel like a very long time."

"The hallucinations you create can look and feel very real," Esther explains. "It's important to remember they're not real. But anything that distracts your dueler puts you at an advantage. Just keep in mind that anyone from the Nameless army in the audience won't see the illusions. You need to get better at this. It's not going to come easily."

"What about what I did during the fires, making Glen hallucinate that the fire wasn't there?" I say defensively.

"That was instinct. This is skill." She claps her hands. "Focus."

"So, the advantage is that I can create these distractions and not be distracted by them myself?"

"Yes."

"But if I can't see them, how do I know they're working?" I ask. "I have no concept of what these hallucinations are like, so how can I effectively sustain them?"

Hat is watching us, and she's snacking on a bowl of salted treats. "I have an idea." She brushes her hands off on her pants. "The problem is that Coin's making these fancy hallucinations or illusions or whatever, but she and I can't see them, right?"

"Right," Esther says.

"You can see the hallucination, though, yes?" Hat says.

"That's the whole point," Esther says, "but *she* can't."

Hat joins us on the mat, bouncing excitedly from foot to foot. "But here's the thing. Coin can read your memories, right? See what you see? Including the hallucination?" She points between the two of us. "Imagine something cool. Something super cool. Like fire and electric sparks! With . . . red-and-black smoke!"

I place my hand up in the air, facing upward. I imagine a flame, then a small ball of fire. I tell it to have golden flames with white-blue sparks. Then the smoke: I imagine it rotating upward slowly as a dense black spiral with flares of red.

Esther is alight with interest, and I close my hand and drop it to my side.

If this is going to be the first time I see one of my own hallucinations, I want it to be good. Or at least as good as I can make it so I know how much I have to improve.

Esther holds out her hand. "Well? I'm definitely thinking about what I just saw, so whenever you're ready to read my thoughts . . ."

I hesitate. I've never quite been able to understand what it is I do.

"What if it's really, really bad?" I wring my hands together for a moment before laying a hand on top of Esther's.

I see myself for the first time from someone else's perspective. I'm a little taller than Esther, but I'm standing casually, haphazardly holding a blade in one hand with the other hand facing upward.

In my palm, a single spark of flame crackles to life. The flame flickers with blue electricity, and then smoke begins to coil upward. The smoke rises. It's textured like cloth and spins with bands of red and black. It's amazing.

I let go of Esther's hand, and the images, the memories, vanish.

"You can see the hallucinations you create, right?" I ask. "Then show me what you can do."

Esther puts out her hand. I can tell she's watching something happen. It lasts five or six seconds.

"That should be more than enough," she says, and she puts out her hand once again.

I take it, and every detail of her memory blossoms in my mind. There's a small violet bird in her palm. It teeters to its feet, stretches its wings, and launches into the air with a screeching squawk, trailing behind its wings a storm of black clouds, which blanket the entire room, as if my vision has gone dark.

I feel the damp against her skin and the humidity in her lungs.

Then she lets go of my hand, and the memory vanishes. I search the wide room, expecting the bird to fly out of a dark corner.

"I'm guessing that was Ray-la?" I say, pointing at where the imaginary bird disappeared.

"Yes," Esther says.

"You didn't tell me your pet was a scary creature of darkness." I chuckle, and Esther grins. Then Esther withdraws a circle of metal from the bag she brought with her. It's a patterned, stylized circlet.

"Is that a crown?" I ask.

"It is," she says. "This was going to be the crown I wore when I stepped forward as queen. It's simple, but strong. You should wear it tomorrow at the festival. It will remind people of your position."

I shake my head. "I don't think so. That's yours. And we're not even sure I'll be walking out of that arena alive, let alone with the tattoo."

Esther runs a finger along the metal circlet. "I want you to wear it."

I keep forgetting how convinced she is that I'm meant to be queen. I take the circlet and inspect the braided metal. It's beautiful, in its own way, but it's cold in my hand. I feel her aura poised like a frog about to leap. She waits for me to try it on.

"I'll just . . . put this someplace safe, shall I?" I offer. Before she can object, I escape the sparring room and take the circlet to my sleeping quarters. All the while, it slowly warms against my skin. By the time I stow it in the wardrobe, it almost feels comfortable in my grasp.

When I get back to the sparring room, I stop outside the door when I overhear Esther and Hat talking to each other.

"I can tell that you look up to her," Esther says.

I lean up against the door, listening in.

"We're . . ." Hat struggles to continue. "Sometimes I can't tell if she's scared of caring about me or scared of losing me. But I'm not asking her to be my mother or anything. I want to be her friend. We can have each other's backs, but she doesn't get that yet. She still thinks I'm a kid."

"You guys seem really close," Esther says.

"I don't know. Maybe."

"What would you call it?" Esther asks.

"Well," Hat says, "I'm not sure what you call it when you care about someone and they're afraid to care about you because they already care about you too much. We're not quite friends. I don't know what we are. But we're something. I mean, you don't rush out to the gallows to save just anyone from execution, right? What we are . . . I guess it's Nameless." And pride fills her voice.

"Isn't that difficult?" Esther asks. "Don't you want to define it or understand it?"

"Gaiza," Hat says. "Every time I try to understand Coin, I take twenty steps in the wrong direction. But some of the best things are Nameless, I think. Like . . . like that feeling you get somewhere between your heart and your stomach when you're about to pickpocket someone. It's a mix of fear and excitement, and you have no idea what's going to happen next. That whole big feeling? There isn't a name for it. It's Nameless."

I hear the smile in Esther's voice when she echoes Hat's words. "And some of the best things are Nameless."

CHAPTER 21

For the rest of the day, I do my best to avoid the Royal Council, and I have my dinner brought straight to the sparring room. The last thing I want to do is run into Belrosa or Marcher in the corridors.

I don't even feel comfortable staying in the guest quarters tonight. Everyone knows that's where I've been sleeping. If anyone feels inclined to murder me in the morning to steal the crown tattoo, it's best they don't know where I am. We consider if I should stay in the king's quarters, but that's not an un-reasonable place for someone to look either.

In the end, the four of us go to the top floor of the Fallow tower to spend the night in Esther's home. The tower is quiet and dark, and the only two auras I sense from this high up are Esther's and Glenquartz's. Esther takes a bright velvet chaise, and the remaining three of us take the oversized bed. Esther douses the lantern. In the darkness, I listen to them breathing. After a while, dark shapes crisp into edges and objects with depth.

I know parts of a lullaby. Some of the tune I picked up over the years, mumbled by mothers to their children. Some of it I heard in Esther's memory of her mother. Tonight I hum the tune gently, more breath than notes. I tap the rhythm against the ribbed decorations on the dagger's sheath.

I sit awake, guarding my friends. Maybe this is what a family is. Not the crew of orphans guided and guarded by Marcher, and not the strings of last names and color-coordinated dresses here in the palace. Maybe it's this: staying awake, listening to them breathe, humming a lullaby.

Without a watch, it's hard to tell how much time passes. Out on the street, I would light a candle and mark off the hours along the wax. When the candle burned past its mark, we'd switch shifts. Now I simply stare out into the dark room, following the curving gray outlines of bodies beneath blankets.

When morning comes, I'm surprised to find I actually fell asleep.

Esther is already up, sitting in the cushioned window seat.

"I was going to wait a bit longer before waking anyone," she says.

Faint light is just starting to brighten the hues of the room, casting a glittery glow from the translucent curtains onto the ceiling. Everything is warm.

"It's beautiful, isn't it?" Esther says, staring at us.

Glenquartz sleeps on his side in full uniform, and Hat is curled up in a ball between us. Her body is still accustomed to curling for warmth on cold nights.

I gently rise from the bed so I don't disturb them. "Precious."

It hurts to think that they'd be just as beautiful if I wasn't here.

"I mean everything about this moment," Esther says. "You. Me. Sisters. One Royal and one Nameless. Glenquartz and Hat, one Legal and one Nameless. Think of everything it took for this moment to happen: the four of us sleeping in one room . . . almost like . . ." Her eyes flutter and she looks away, not finishing her thought. "When people call you the impossible heir, I think this is what they're afraid of. After everything and despite everything, when we're all alone and scared, we come together, no matter what."

If I was any kind of gracious, I would tell her in this moment that *yes*, we are sisters. That *yes*, we are family, we can *be* a family. We can be everything to one another that each of us has always hoped for. We can love one another. But I can't bring myself to say it, because it doesn't seem like *enough*.

I don't have the words for it yet. I don't have them in my heart. This is a language I've only just begun to learn how to speak. I put an arm around her shoulders and tip my head against hers.

She hugs me, and everything we don't know how to say to each other is wrapped inside this moment. *Sister. Family. Friend.*

It's all I can do to hold on to her. Hold on, knowing that at some point I'll have to let go.

✦

The Assassins' Festival is everything I thought it would be.

I'm in the Royal Court arena, perched behind a row of

booths and tables where Legals are shouting about special delicacies and one-of-a-kind culinary treats.

I remind myself why I am here. I don't need to prove to my allies that I'm strong. I need to prove it to my enemies. Today, I'm vulnerable. Anyone walking by could slide a blade between my ribs. Anyone with a clear shot from a long distance could pick me off. Paranoia is not my friend, but it is with me like a shadow today—a shadow grafting to my bones.

The arena fills slowly at first, like a few raindrops falling into a stone basin. Then more quickly, gathering in small pools. Then it's a deep well of bodies and voices, heat and motion. A rush of conversation swirls in the air, and soon the entire arena is an echo chamber filled with a sound like rushing water. There are hundreds of people here. Over a thousand now. Somewhere out in that crowd are the Nameless. I see some of them in their dark clothes, loitering near the waste bins.

Today, I am anything but frivolous. I am lean and prepared. I considered wearing a dress—it would have allowed me to hide the movement of my legs during a duel, but its weight would have been too cumbersome. I settled for a long coat belted at my waist, dark pants, and a bright red blouse, which we had the tailor dye with three diagonal black streaks. It's like the clothes Royals and Legals throw away, when they mar the fabric with dark paint in fear that a Nameless will steal it and try to pass themselves off as a proper citizen. It's bold and unapologetic, like the claw marks of a monster, and I love it. I've braided my hair to keep it close to my scalp and out of my eyes. And to round out the ensemble: boots, of course.

A railing surrounds the arena, keeping the audience at a distance. I reach out toward them, sensing their auras. It's like being in the market. Sounds and people and feelings buzz in the air. Some people have claimed their spots early, draping coats and cowls over sections of railing. I scan the faces for anyone recognizable. Belrosa threatened that the army would be here. I know as well as anyone that with the right colors and cloth, no one looks at you twice.

I scrutinize the crowd, wondering which of them are from Belrosa's and Marcher's Nameless army. The Legal with the wide-brimmed hat who spends too much time staring at the sugar bread but never actually buys it. The Royal wearing a luxurious scarf so big that it covers half his face. Occasionally I send Glenquartz on a scout run to check my blind spots.

There's a sheltered viewing area for the Royal Council that would provide good cover for anyone with a rifle. That's where Esther will be, among my contenders and my enemies. Any of them or all of them could be waiting for the right moment.

The only other structures aside from the viewing booths are the vending stalls that dot the surrounding area. The whole event is more festive and lively than I expected. The entire day of "try to kill the thief-turned-queen" is a novelty to the Legals and Royals. They're selling chains of popcorn shaped like nooses and bread and biscuits shaped like daggers and swords.

The first of the Royal Council arrives—General Belrosa, of course—followed quickly by the others. Hat emerges from behind the seating area, hopping the fence lithely, dressed in Royals' clothes.

"Coin, look!" Hat says as she reaches me. "I have my own med bag. Isn't that great?" She opens it and starts shuffling things around to show me. I only register enough to know that she has a lot of bandages.

"You sure are prepared," I say, and I truly am pleased.

"Yep," she says with a big smile. "I mean, don't die or anything today, but if you *do*, I'll be very ready to help save your life." Her grin is infectious. "Although . . . Rhana says that I have to help *anyone* who gets injured."

Suddenly I want to do nothing else but throw my arms around her and wrap her tight. While she's as calm and confident as I want to be, all I can think is that at least she'll be okay. Everything about who I am and what I'm doing today could get me killed. But at least she'll be okay.

Glenquartz joins us, and he lights up when he sees Hat with her med bag.

He puts a hand on my shoulder, and his fear springs to life inside my chest. It's both unnerving and comforting to know that he has imagined as many terrible outcomes as I have. I put my hand over his, trying to hide the shortness of breath I feel every time someone's thoughts shock through my body.

"Don't worry," I tell him. "I'm coursing with pure adrenaline right now. Not even the wind could sneak up on me." I make a faint chopping and punching motion as if I'm going to fight the eastern breeze.

Glenquartz smiles and withdraws his hand apologetically. "I'll be with you in thought. Make me a promise?"

I raise an eyebrow.

"While you're out there," he says, "you'll act like the thieving queen you are." His excited aura makes laughter bubble in my chest.

"I'll do my best," I say with a faint curtsy. "And you make me a promise too? Keep Hat safe."

"Honest oath." He nods gravely, then adds, "I swear by everything Nameless." Glenquartz guides Hat toward one of the gateways of the arena. I watch them until they disappear.

Esther strides to the center of the arena. She wears a pale blue dress that is light enough to be stirred by the breeze and a dark blue jacket that covers her tattoo. Her hair is done up with a white headband that could be mistaken for a crown from far away. She holds the first page of the duel challenger list that has been posted outside the dining hall for nearly six weeks now. The highest-ranked challenger on the paper is General Belrosa, but we have something better than a plan—we have a con.

When the crowd has gathered, Esther begins to speak. It's obviously a rehearsed speech, written years ago when the Assassins' Festival was still a deadly affair. There's a lot of posturing about tradition and strength and competition being the fuel for success.

She doesn't make eye contact with me during her speech, which is for the best. Everyone here still thinks we're enemies. That's the whole point. I take a deep breath. Esther is going to announce our surprise duel, and then, together, we'll pull a con on the entire crowd. I'm ready for this.

I'm not prepared for what actually happens. As Esther nears the end of her speech and the crowd grows anxious, Belrosa steps out of the audience. Before Esther can even finish her speech, Belrosa strides to the center of the arena to summon me to our duel.

CHAPTER 22

With Belrosa standing beside her, Esther speaks more slowly and carefully.

"And of course," Esther says, stumbling over her rehearsed words, "the Assassins' Festival officially begins with the highest-ranked duel . . . which is between General Belrosa Demure and the sovereign of Seriden herself."

Esther gestures toward me, meeting my gaze with a flash of alarm. I silently plead for her to continue, to say the next lines we planned: *But I, Esther Fallow, supersede that duel with a challenge of my own. I challenge the Nameless queen to duel for her crown.*

But she falters, and Belrosa is already leaving Esther behind and marching toward me. If I were to call Esther out to duel now, it would seem as though I'm afraid of Belrosa.

I steel myself and step into the open arena. Away from the crowd, I feel the steady breeze rush through the knots of my braids, prickling my scalp. I feel the charged energy of 3,628 auras. Too many auras to track individually, but each of them like a pinprick of light. Together, they're a blurring constellation.

Belrosa is dressed in her formal general's uniform, complete with ceremonial sword and an oddly tilted hat. Perfect. Not only do I have to fight Belrosa in front of everyone, but her entire appearance is designed to remind the people watching that she is their protector. She's the beacon of Scriden pride.

Come on, Esther. Say something. Do something.

Belrosa stops four steps shy of the arena's center, and we face each other. She presents her weapon, and I present mine, both of us holding swords.

We bow, ever so slightly, maintaining eye contact. Then, before either of us finishes, the first sharp movement snakes outward.

Steel clangs against steel as we meet blows. Her first swing is strong and high, but I do more than block it. It takes me three quick strikes to put her on the defensive, and then I'm advancing at an angle to move toward her weaker side.

She matches my strides and then counters, jabbing toward my left. As I twist to dodge the strike, I carry through with a kick that catches her hard in the shoulder. She stumbles but doesn't fall. Her eyes flash with fear as she realizes that I'm not as untrained as she thought. My sword has a jeweled, decorative hilt just like hers. I'm using Glenquartz's sword. His thoughts are with me, and so is his most cherished weapon.

Both Belrosa and I are focused enough on the blades and our movements to trade blows but not injure each other. We make real contact in the nonlethal blows from fists and knees and feet.

The fight has stretched on for nearly two minutes—what feels like an eternity. If we were on the streets, I would have picked up one of the rocks on the ground to get a long-distance shot at her. Or I would have pickpocketed a pistol from a spectator. But this is the Royal arena, where a display of treachery would cost me more than what I would gain by winning the fight.

I kick Belrosa's knee, and as she recovers, I glance at Esther. If she's going to salvage our con, she needs to interrupt the duel. It can't be me.

Esther tenses in fear, and then I feel the blow hit my waist. It's a sword, but it feels like a punch to the gut. I duck and roll a few paces away on the ground. When I push myself into a crouch, I grip my side with pain plastered on my face.

Belrosa readies herself to charge me again. Ice sweeps from her aura, and I know that she'll kill me if she gets the chance.

Esther finally steps into the arena. "I challenge the Nameless queen!"

Her shout echoes out into the air, and I wonder if I'm the only one who sees through her indignant anger to the fear beneath it. Belrosa immediately falters, nearly tripping over her own feet.

"My lady?" Belrosa says, her sword hand jittering at her side.

"A higher-ranked challenger can interrupt an ongoing duel, according to the terms of the Assassins' Festival." Esther walks right up to Belrosa. I don't know how she manages to be graceful even now. If we weren't in a hot field of stones surrounded by thousands of Seriden's citizens, I would have thought she was interrupting a wine-serving ceremony. I take the opportunity to rise to my feet, but I keep my hand pressed to my side as though to stanch a wound. Royals and Legals on the inside edge of the audience stretch on their toes, trying to see how badly I've been wounded.

Belrosa is still so wild and tense with the energy of battle that she doesn't even try to steady her hands enough to sheathe her sword. She gives a curt bow and retreats a few steps away, but she doesn't leave the main arena or join the crowd, as if she's not quite willing to step away from the fight.

Murmurs flow through the spectators, who are jostling elbows and pointing fingers.

Esther takes Belrosa's position. She has rehearsed her lines several times over the past day, and her voice hardly wavers as she speaks.

"You are an impossible queen," Esther says. "You are Nameless and reckless, and I would be ignoring the wishes of my people if I did not challenge your right to the throne. I don't believe my father would name someone like you as the next sovereign of Scriden, and I am not convinced you are the true heir. Everything about you could be a lie."

I hide the grin that wants to play on my lips. Instead I rise to a standing position, pretending to wince as I straighten up.

"I am the crowned heir of this city, the first to live in the palace as Nameless. What, I wonder, would convince you?" The crowd is as silent as the Nameless protestors outside the Royal Court gates.

"Nothing," Esther says, and she picks up my sword from the ground and presents it as her duel weapon.

A tremulous whisper rises in the crowd.

I have no weapon. I hold out my arms.

"I am unlike anything that came before me," I say. "I am unlike *everyone* that came before me. The sovereigns of Seriden's past, they may have been able to conjure images of fire."

I hold out my right hand and imagine a column of flame bursting upward from my palm.

"They may have been able to conjure images that seemed to test the very nature of this world."

I hold up my left hand, and imagine lightning striking me from the sky above.

Esther staggers in a show of astonishment. In truth, Esther is helping me. I can't see any of the illusions I create, but she can see all of them. Anywhere my illusions fail, hers can continue.

"But the one thing that's different for me is not just my name," I shout. "It's not just my life. It's my power."

I clap my hands together and imagine ripples of fire and electric energy spiraling outward, rising up into the sky, and forming a halo rotating far above the arena.

Three seconds pass, and then Esther lifts her sword and charges at me, swinging the blade toward me. I let Esther take over the illusions overhead. The heads in the audience are all tilted upward at the spectacle and marvel of it all.

I imagine myself standing before Esther. Then I imagine another version four feet closer, then three feet to the left and three feet to the right.

Esther swings at the open air before me.

I hear the gasps of the crowd as the blade passes through the air. Gasps again as she swings in another direction.

Esther, seemingly frustrated with swiping her blade through nothing but air, throws down the sword. It clatters to the stones.

"Show yourself!" she shouts.

I release the hold I have over the hallucinations around me, letting myself appear to her. Everyone falls quiet, and I will my voice to project over them so that everyone can hear me.

"You think I am a mistake," I say to her. "But I am not. You think I am impossible, but when the impossible stands before you, what do you call it then? What do you call me?"

On cue, Esther releases her control over the images far overhead. There is no more spiraling halo of fire or bursts of lightning.

"I will not rule with fear," I say. "I will not rule through intimidation or a hunger for control. Don't be afraid of what you don't understand. But understand this: I am not impossible. I stand before you. Your father trusted me enough to name me queen. You believed in his leadership. You have faith in his choices. I am one of those choices. So why not have faith in me?"

Esther stares at me. She's trying her best to appear angry and thoughtful. I know what we're saying is for the benefit of the crowd—it's all a con—but at least to her, every single word of it is true.

"You understand the responsibility you're accepting?" Esther shouts. "You understand that the moment this day ends, the only way the tattoo will leave your arm is with your death?"

"If I become unfit to rule," I say, "it is a sacrifice I will readily make."

Esther considers this for a moment, and the crowd waits in near-absolute silence.

"You said you did not believe I was the heir to Seriden's throne," I say. "What do you think now?"

"I think you are strong," Esther says, and I can see the truth of it in her aura. "You are making the decisions you think are best, and if you'll take the council of the Royals into consideration, you could do great things for this city. You clearly have power and control; all you need is the support of the city. You are Seriden's true sovereign."

Esther spreads her arms out. "I yield to you," she announces. "Do all other challengers yield?"

There's no small amount of hands that go up into the air. All the hands mean that they're ready to follow Esther's lead. Glenquartz joins us and gives me a formal salute, showing the audience that at least part of the Royal Guard is on my side.

Esther's gaze falls to General Belrosa Demure, who stands across the arena. Belrosa, at last, under the pressure of the audience, raises her hand as well. She meets Esther's gaze, furious in the face of the shifted alliance. She walks toward us, to where Glenquartz, Esther, and I stand in a row.

"If someone such as you," Belrosa says to Esther as she approaches us, "can find your way to accepting the Nameless queen, then who am I to speak against her?"

I watch the way Belrosa advances. She hasn't bothered to

sheathe her sword, and its long blade catches the light as she moves. I stay on my guard. If Belrosa's coming in for a formal handshake, one thing is clear: she's going to try to kill me.

Her aura is still as cold as ice.

This must be Belrosa's con: cede the duel and get close enough to take the tattoo by force. She starts to the left, going in to shake Glenquartz's hand, and it's smart: it allows her to approach me from the side instead of head-on.

She clasps Glenquartz's hand in her left. "I commend you for your good work, Lieutenant. Your talents far exceed your rank."

To everyone else, it sounds like a compliment. Glenquartz's aura is like steel.

Belrosa shakes Esther's hand next and says, "Bravely fought and bravely spoken."

Then she comes to me, and her aura is like a force that almost pushes me. She extends her left hand, and I see her grip on her sword tighten.

"Your Highness," she says, with a downward tilt of her head. "That display was . . . as inexplicable and impossible as you are. And it certainly *sounded* like the truth." She reaches out to take my hand the same way she did the first time I met her at the Royal Council. This time, however, she won't catch me off guard. I've been practicing with Esther. I can do this.

But then, as I reach out to take her hand, preparing for the onslaught of fear and anger from her touch, everything goes wrong at once.

"If I cannot have your crown . . . ," Belrosa whispers, trailing off. There's a sharp movement, and people start screaming. My heart drops, and I wonder if this is the signal to her army to start slaughtering people. But then I see the shine of her sword as she reaches sideways and doesn't do a single thing to harm me, but instead stabs Esther.

CHAPTER 23

The crowd surges in outrage, and the entire Royal Council is on their feet in alarm.

"Then I will have *your* crown," Belrosa says to Esther.

Simple confusion fills Esther's aura. She pulls her arm to her body as Belrosa withdraws the blade, and then she falls to her knees.

Glenquartz is in front of us in an instant, and I've never seen him with such spitting rage. Belrosa staggers as she parries Glenquartz's forceful swings, and Esther's tattoo has already started to fade from her arm and transfer to Belrosa.

"Esther!" I cry, collapsing to my knees as she falls into my arms.

I hear Hat's voice as she calls my name and races toward us, trying to push her way through but getting caught behind a surge of angry spectators.

I press down hard. It's the only thing I know to do. I pull off her jacket, which is the cleanest cloth I can see, and I bundle it against her wound. Blood seeps through.

Esther's hand goes up to her arm, where I've exposed her crown tattoo.

"It's a bit late for that," I say, my voice heavy and raw. Of course Belrosa knew about Esther's tattoo. She tortured Esther's father for years. He would have told her.

Rising above the yells of the crowd are Glenquartz's and Belrosa's voices as they fight each other.

Glenquartz, all rage and fury: "You are a disgrace to your position! You are a murderer!"

Belrosa shouts something in response, but all I can hear is my heartbeat pounding in my ears.

"Esther, Esther," I say, as she searches the sky somewhere above me. "Come on, Esther."

Esther's tattoo fades to gray on her arm, and I grab her hand. "Stay with me."

She shakes her head. "You need to take it." She brings her hand up to her chest.

"Take what?" I ask.

She shifts to the side, turning her left arm upward to show me the fading ink of the tattoo.

"I need you to have this," she says. She almost laughs. "It didn't even occur to me that I'd be vulnerable today, just like you. But it makes sense, I guess, since our abilities are tied together. I wonder if Father knew when I first got the tattoo. Why didn't he have me give him my tattoo? Or why wouldn't he give me his? But now I see. It's because we need this."

I shake my head. "What we need to do is stop this bleeding."

Esther says weakly, "You can't let Belrosa get this tattoo from me. I'd speak your name if I knew it. Do this peacefully, if I could. But I can't. The only way I can give it to you is if you're the one to kill me."

I shake my head. "Absolutely not."

"If I'm dying anyway," Esther says, "where's the harm? I'm much too spiteful to let Belrosa be the one who kills me. Do me the courtesy of letting it be you, instead? After all, you could use some practice being courteous. You are meant to have this. It has to be you."

"You are not going to die," I command.

"I'll do my best, Your Highness," she says. "I believe in you, Coin. I know that sounds like on-my-deathbed nonsense, but it's true. You're my sister. And I love you. I don't care if you don't have a name. You are worthy of the crown, and you are strong enough to hold its weight."

Hat arrives, and she skids to her knees beside Esther.

"How bad is it?" Hat asks me.

I fumble for words. "It's really bad. But she's talking and moving. That's good, right? She's . . . fading. Tell me you can do something, please."

"I'll do what I can," she says, scanning the crowd. "Where's Dr. Rhana?"

I try to give Hat space, but Esther reaches out and grabs my sleeve.

"Coin, I need you to do me a favor," Esther says. And despite everything—the blood pooling up through Hat's fingers and the colorless wash of her skin—she smiles. "Go kick the general's ass, would you?"

It's as if the tattoo knows its other half. As Esther lets go of me, pain stabs into my shoulder at my tattoo. Ink flows from Esther's arm, down across her fingers, and onto my skin like a

315

snake. The ink flows up my arm to my crisp black crown tattoo, and suddenly the tattoo is darker and burning with heat. The surge of energy courses through me. It is fire at my feet, as though I could scorch the earth with every step. Her tattoo has reunited with mine.

Impossible. Esther didn't speak my name. I didn't kill her. How can this happen?

Esther's hand falls limp against the cold stones. Hat doesn't look at me, but she works more quickly at Esther's wound, and I feel Esther's aura fading, overwhelmed and drowned out—emptied—by the anger of the crowd surrounding us.

I rise slowly to my feet and turn on a heel toward the open arena, where Glenquartz and Belrosa are still fighting.

I walk toward them.

Belrosa seems to have the upper hand over Glenquartz. He's starting to slow down. I pick up the sword that Esther dropped, and its hilt warms quickly in my grasp.

"Glenquartz!" I shout, and I will my voice to reverberate through the air like a clap of thunder. He falters in his fight, and Belrosa herself staggers sideways, searching her arm as if the ink has crawled under her sleeve to hide from her.

In my periphery, I see Hat gesture for Glenquartz to help her. One look between Glenquartz and me, and he rushes past me, heading for Hat. I fix my sight on Belrosa.

Esther's tattoo has fused with mine. I would be surprised or confused, except that everything about me and my life—about this tattoo and magic itself—is impossible. What's one more impossible thing?

"Then it's you," Belrosa says, wielding her sword.

Every fragment of me that has ever felt fragile is like steel now, fiercer and sharper than the tempered blade in my hand.

I haven't felt certainty like this in a long time. The strength of both tattoos fuels me. I thought I knew power before. I thought I knew strength. It was nothing as wild and untamed as what I feel now. Everything is different. I feel it in my bones. I stretch my arms, and the blade is like air, light and quick.

Belrosa advances.

As Glenquartz trained me, I know the stances expected of me now for a proper duel. I know the etiquette. But we are far past etiquette, and we are far past kindness and mercy.

I fight to have a steady voice, though I hear it shake with rage when I speak.

"General Belrosa Demure," I say to her. "I speak as the sovereign of Seriden, queen of this city, commander of all that it rules, and a Nameless wretch in your court. You have broken every faith this city has placed in you, undermined its laws and treaties, and betrayed those who needed your protection most."

Belrosa is stalking toward me now, as though she doesn't want to give me the satisfaction of a long, drawn-out speech. So I meet her in battle.

This fight is nothing like the duel we had before. I swing with every ounce of strength I have.

"If it is you I must kill, so be it," Belrosa says. "You do not deserve that power."

One touch is all I need, or one touch will destroy me.

Occasionally, she reaches for me or takes a swing at my

face. When she sees me flinch, her face lights up. My fear has given her a target, and suddenly I know that if she had a pistol or a rifle with her, this would all be over. A violent parry sends us both reeling backward, and Belrosa takes stock of the crowd as if to remind me that she has an army out there.

My mind is too tangled with anger to make any sense of consequences.

I know the Nameless soldiers won't see any illusion I create, but the crowd is growing restless, and I don't want them to interfere, so I imagine a wall surrounding us made of solid white stone.

Belrosa's eyes dart behind me as my fake wall surrounds us. I swing my sword, and she barely has enough time to dodge it.

She grabs for my arm and gets a brief hold over me. A hollow ache of fear makes its way up to my shoulder before I spin out of her reach. She chuckles maniacally as if finally seizing my weakness. She lunges for me again, arm outstretched.

This time, I let her.

Her cold fingers wrap around my wrist. If I can't do this, then she wins. It's as if a wall of ice builds between us. Both of us press against it, waiting to see which way it will shatter.

It shatters inward.

Belrosa grips my wrist and crushes it, feeling the bones crack. Angry triumph fills her, and she brings her sword forward through a thick layer of armor and then through my body and blood.

"Your power is mine," Belrosa shouts. The smooth black ink of the tattoo materializes on her arm. The wall disintegrates, and the crowd gapes in shock and silence. Then she feels the pain of the tattoo—like needles jabbing into her arm. Auras burst like fireworks around her—a concoction of light and fear. She rises to her feet and violently withdraws her blade from the body of the dead queen, the Nameless wretch.

"She thought she could steal our city!" Belrosa shouts to the crowd. "Rest easy under my leadership. Your Nameless queen is dead!" She raises an arm, and a spear of earth rises up from the ground, taking the form of the towers of Seriden's palace.

"I can make Seriden the conqueror of magic and of all cities," Belrosa says. "Do you stand with me?"

The crowd stirs but remains silent. There is no rallying cry. She does not see obedience or faith. She sees hatred. Soldiers from the Nameless army emerge from the audience into the edge of the arena, their sleek gray uniforms slowly turning to black.

The Royal Council stands together, their horror transmuting into anger

The soldiers, one by one, slowly advance. Then the Royal guards.

"What are you doing?" Belrosa demands in disbelief. "You have to follow me! I will lead you in battle like no sovereign has done for Seriden in two hundred years!"

"How could you!" the redheaded girl screams from where Esther lies dead. Her young face is etched with fury. "You killed them!" With angry tears on her face and Esther's blood on her hands, she races forward. The loyal lieutenant joins her.

Then, the crowd.

Fear fills Belrosa's veins—a deep and abiding pain as she realizes they've turned on her. The city she has done everything to protect is after her blood.

"No!" Belrosa shouts as they advance.

The crowd closes in.

"You don't understand!" Belrosa says. "I'm protecting you! I'm protecting you!"

But she knows in her heart that they don't believe her, that they're coming to tear her limb from limb. The city she killed to protect is killing her. Her own screams echo in her ears as the first hand seizes her from behind.

Everything shatters inward.

I blink, letting go of Belrosa's wrist. We're still standing in the center of the arena. Belrosa thought she overpowered me— she thought she killed me—but instead I went inside her mind and walked her through her greatest fear. And, like turning a key, I've locked the door on my way out.

General Belrosa falls to the ground at my feet, staring blankly at the sky. She's trapped inside her own mind, reliving her worst fear over and over again: gaining power over the city and being rejected and betrayed by those most loyal to her.

The crowd is still firmly rooted outside the arena. Glenquartz and Hat still hover at Esther's side. The Royal Council still perches in their gilded viewing box.

The world is silent around me, and I crouch down to place my hand on Belrosa's forehead, feeling the icy chill of her constant fear.

My whole body is filled with energy, and I feel like I could take on a hundred duelers.

I search the crowd, and as I watch, five, then ten, then twenty Nameless push to the front. I tense. Belrosa's fail-safe: her Nameless army.

No one moves. I hardly breathe.

"I accept you," I say to them tentatively. "No matter what you've done or been made to do. No matter what life you've lived or the person you've become to survive. If you want a life here in Seriden, one not wrapped up in an obligation of fighting and serving someone else, you can stay here. You can stay."

Most of them don't react. But in a few of them I sense a glimmer of hope. Their hope is like spirals of light inside a dense fog; it's like sparks against my skin, electric. It rises and rises, like a fire climbing higher.

Marcher steps forward. For the first time, I see him as he really is. He's wearing all black, comfortable and strong.

He joins me in the arena as the crowd watches my every movement.

"Whatever you're doing with Belrosa," I say, "it's over now. They can all stay. You can stay, even." My throat runs dry, but I hold my stance. If I can't mean it for him, how can I mean it for everyone else?

"Little Coin," he says. "Matching every challenge. Defeating every challenger. How like you. I did well raising you, I think."

I grind my teeth, trying very hard to remain cordial. But it's been forever since I punched him in the face, and it seems like he's due for another. I remind myself of the army behind him, of the city watching us.

Marcher leans in, and I grip the hilt of my sword. "You're right," Marcher says. "Belrosa is gone. But her plans were never *my* plans. And I've promised them more than that." He pats my shoulder twice and disappears into the crowd.

The gray soldiers turn and follow him. But there are a couple—a few, even—who stay behind. They're wavering in their certainty, but they're clinging to hope. I feel alive with it. Pride builds in my chest.

"Coin!" Hat shouts from far behind me, and my pride crumbles in an instant.

Across the arena, Hat is kneeling over Esther, and her voice is hoarse and tight. "She's still alive!"

I rush across the open arena to where Hat and now Dr. Rhana are both frenetically treating Esther's wound. I reach Esther and collapse to my knees beside her. I grab her hand, and a surge of pain doubles through my system. It's all I can do to hold on. Esther's pain is excruciating, her fear mind-numbing.

"The only time I've felt worse," Esther says with a tight, painful smile, "is when I learned you had the tattoo." She winces as Hat presses a clean bandage on her wound.

A heartbroken sob gets trapped in my throat.

In a calm voice, Rhana says, "We need to get her to Med

Ward." She orders a nearby guard to bring a table so they can carry her; then she discusses the injury with Hat in hushed tones.

Rhana crouches beside me and speaks with a hand on my shoulder. "I know you've been practicing your abilities with Esther in Med Ward. Don't look at me like that—Esther's been visiting my ward for years. Of course I knew. The tattoo is yours now, and I don't know what that means, but hopefully you can still help her. We're out of anesthetic since the fires. Her heart is racing, and it's going to pump too much of her blood out of that wound. When we get to Med Ward, I'll need to cut into her to help her. So I need you to keep her calm, because it's going to hurt. I need you to do this for Esther, Coin. Keep her calm. Send her mind someplace else. Let us save her life. Are you ready?"

Her confidence steadies me. "Yes."

"Do it now, okay?" She positions herself behind Esther's shoulder. Glenquartz positions himself at her feet.

My eyes are burning. My lungs. My heart. Everything I am is dissolving into fire. Esther's pain is so great that I don't know how to touch it. I close my eyes, as we grip each other's hands, and I focus on soothing her aura.

"Esther Merelda Fallow," I whisper like a lullaby into her ear. The sound of the arena drops away, and lights dance in my mind until they coalesce into an image. I don't know what to show her at first. I don't know what her happiest place is—the memory of her father, or farther, to the faint memories she has

323

of her mother. I want to show her something beautiful. So I show her Hat, the first time we met.

Then I show her snowfall in the city. The chill is sharp and harsh against my skin.

I show her the snow in the alley I slept in—it glistened, untouched by footprints or cart tracks. It's smooth and frozen and beautiful, and I think hazily that it wouldn't be the worst place to die. I show a winter storm that came early one year, and I had to unbury myself from two crates and a tarp I was sleeping beneath.

I show her every moment of my life where the harsh world was beautiful, where laughter won out over everything. The look on a Legal's face when he opened his door and found his living room empty and bare. Devil's shelf of collected odds and ends, and her voice saying, "Find me something *interesting* from the palace."

When I first called the tattoo beautiful, Esther said that beauty needed context. So I show her the first time I got caught while pickpocketing. The first execution I saw. Every hurt and injury. The ache in my chest when I stole food from a family who needed it, and the all-consuming hunger that filled my body when I didn't. I share with her the moments I almost died, the feeling when Marcher told me my friend was dead. The moment I realized there was a tattoo around my arm and that my life would never be the same.

I show her everything.

Through it all, Esther's hand is in mine.

I show her my most recent memories of Hat, including the moment Esther herself was stabbed and fell, and Hat—of everyone who froze, of everyone who was afraid—pushed her way through the crowd to try to save her. I show her Khana, somehow every bit the fierce leader I wish I could be, smart and kind.

Then I show her what *could* be: Hat accepted as an apprentice of the medical ward, growing and training and becoming a skilled doctor who serves Seriden. I show her the Nameless building houses just outside the city walls and joining the farmhands and shop workers on their treks each morning, wearing clothes that fit. I show her—and my heart breaks—herself. I paint her cheeks delicately with fine lines, aged by years with grace and laughter. We sit together on twin thrones, ruling side by side.

There's only one crown. We've done what our father asked. But why should one crown be the same thing as one queen?

The last thing I show her is the four of us. Her, a Royal in a pristine blue gown with gems in her dark brown hair. Me, the Nameless impossible heir dressed in black with a silver crown. Glenquartz, the first Legal promoted past lieutenant's station, with the general's stripes on his shoulders. And Hat, standing by his side, a white doctor's apron and a beautiful blue-trimmed hat upon her head. All of us: a family together. The ones given to each other by chance and the ones we've chosen to love.

Esther's hand grows weak in my grasp, and I feel my own

grip slipping. I would lock us away forever inside this moment if I knew how. I hold on with every bit of strength I have left. As darkness seeps through my mind, I speak as much to myself as I do to her:

Hold on, hold on.

I don't know which of us is the first to let go.

CHAPTER 24

I wake up the same way I fell asleep: holding Esther's hand, kneeling on the floor of Med Ward, and Nameless. But I am no longer the same.

Esther groans and opens her eyes.

I pull my aching body to my feet. "Esther?"

Her left arm is strapped in a sling to keep her from aggravating her injury, but she's breathing and alive.

"Well, if you're here," Esther says, "then that must mean you're not dead. And I'm not dead. That's good."

"No one's dead," I say with a tremulous smile.

"Belrosa?"

I hold out my hand, and for the first time, when I imagine a violet wren with crystal eyes and a shock of blue feathers along its wings, I see it as it appears. It hops around my hand, surveying the room. I feel its claws pressing against the calluses on my palm.

When it turns toward Esther, it lifts its beak, and the most beautiful birdsong fills the room. It fills me with the feeling of flowing honey and the chime of cymbals. I realize it's the sensation of my own aura, and I giggle with pride.

Esther puts out her hand, and I will the bird to hop over.

She laughs with childlike delight as it tilts its body down and rubs the side of its head against her fingers, getting petted.

"And you . . . ?" Esther asks.

"I can see it, too." I pat the imaginary bird on its head.

"You did it!" Esther says. "If you can see your illusions, does that mean all the Nameless can too? Are all of them citizens?"

"All of them, including me," I say with a giddy laugh. "Except . . . I don't think it was just me who allowed this to happen. It was you, too. You gave me your tattoo, and you never even knew my name. It took both of us accepting the Nameless and accepting each other to fix everything. Our father was right. The tattoo has been reunited. He didn't make me Nameless so that I'd grow up and accept them as citizens. He made me Nameless so that *you* would grow up as a powerful leader and so that *you* would accept me as your sister and as Nameless. He did it so that we would accept each other and ourselves. It was about you all along, Esther."

"It was both of us together," Esther says. "But is Belrosa . . . ?"

"She's alive. I guess."

"Did she escape?" Esther asks. "We can send a Royal guard—I mean, if there are any that aren't still loyal to her." She tries to pull herself up into a seated position, and she winces.

From across the room, I gesture for Rhana to join us.

"I did something maybe worse," I explain as Rhana picks her way through the cots. "I don't even know how I did it, exactly. I trapped Belrosa in her own worst fear. As far as I can tell, she's living it over and over again."

"Belrosa's here," Hat says. She points to a cot in the distant corner, where Belrosa's sleeping form lies motionless. Esther's jaw tightens, and she leans up to catch a glimpse.

"Oh no you don't," Rhana says. She taps the center of Esther's forehead. "That's enough of that, Your Highness. You'll pull out your sutures if you keep that up. Don't make me have your sister put you back to sleep."

Both our eyes widen in alarm. She knows we're sisters?

"Sorry!" Hat says from two cots away. She's obviously been eavesdropping the entire time. She scampers to join us. "That was me! I told her. During the surgery, it looked like Esther might need some transfused blood—which is a new but *very* cool procedure—and she didn't know who would have compatible blood. So I sold you out. But she didn't end up taking any of your blood! Isn't that great?" Hat twists a curly lock of red hair between her fingers.

Rhana pats Esther's shoulder. "I kept your secret for a very long time. I can keep this one too."

"Apparently, you were one of her most difficult surgeries," Hat says with a weird sense of pride.

"And one of my most successful," Rhana says.

"You should have seen it!" Hat gushes. "There was so much blood."

"Hat is learning very quickly," Rhana says. "Your friend will be a great doctor someday."

"She will," Esther says.

A slow smile overtakes me. "But you've got it wrong. She's not my friend."

Hat's eyes fall.

"She's my sister," I say, smiling. "They both are."

I wrap my arm around Esther's shoulders, and Hat leans in and puts an arm around my waist.

"You're my family," I say to Hat, pulling her close and wrapping my arm around her. "I choose you to be in my life. You make it better. And, as terrifying as it is to care about someone, I care about you. There's no way around it."

Glenquartz clears his throat to let me know that, as always, he's standing as a shadow at the edge of the room. He has a few bruises on his face, but his beard is excellent as ever.

I extend my arm to him, and his eyes crinkle with delight as he joins us.

"All right—off, off!" Rhana chastises, shooing us away from the bed. "Let her rest. And you can have this back now." Rhana opens a small drawer in the bedside table and pulls out the metal circlet, but it's badly dented.

"What? Why is that here?" I ask.

Esther frowns at it. "You put it away in your wardrobe, so I stole it back. You're a terrible influence on me, it must be said. I was going to give it to you at the festival—crown you in front of everyone. It was a great image in my head."

"Well, it saved your life," Rhana says. "You had it in the inside pocket of your jacket, and it deflected the sword when you got stabbed."

"I guess it's not good for wearing anymore," Esther says with a sigh. I can tell she's getting tired.

"Actually," I say, "if you're not using it, I'll take that."

"Really? I don't think it'll sit on your head properly," Esther says, gesturing for Rhana to pass it to me.

"I owe Devil something interesting," I say. "And this will fit the bill nicely."

Glenquartz moves to the foot of Esther's bed, leaning forward on the balls of his feet and drumming his fingers on the sheet. He's doing everything short of jumping with his arms waving.

"Oh my goodness, Glen-beard," I say. "Your aura is buzzing like three hundred *thousand* bees. What is it you want to tell me?"

"That is one thing I won't miss about the auras," Esther says, and I realize she can no longer sense auras or use magic. But she doesn't seem sad.

"I have some news to share with you," Glenquartz says.

"Is it *good* news?" I ask, already tired.

"It's not *great* news," he says.

I frown. "What is it?"

"The man you called Marcher?" he says. "You spoke to him in the middle of the duels. From what I can tell, he's gone."

I pinch the sheet between my fingers. "Gone where?"

"During the chaos after the duels, he disappeared," Glenquartz says. "So did most of those Nameless soldiers. A few of them did stay behind, and there's two of them out in the corridor who wish to speak with you."

"Funny thing about being queen," Esther says, suppressing a yawn. "It's not so much a job as it is your life now."

"Oh, sure," I tease. "*Now* you tell me."

"I'll be recovering for weeks," she says, shooing me. "But a crisis cannot wait, Coin."

When she says my name, it flickers through me like a spark of pride. A swish of blue, a lingering warmth, and her aura settles into its place.

Hat touches my elbow to reassure me that she has everything in hand. As she does, I'm filled with a rushing sense of golden light. This must be her happiness, her joy. It overwhelms me, and I could almost laugh and cry at the same time.

I take my leave, shadowed by Glenquartz.

In the corridor, two Royal guards are watching over two Nameless soldiers. They both spring to their feet when I approach, and stand at attention. They remind me of the Royal guards, and I make a note to ask Glenquartz how many guards were loyal to Belrosa and were arrested during the festival.

"Ma'am," the girl soldier says.

The boy soldier says, "Your Highness." He's older than me by a couple of years, and he's familiar, as though I might have met him once.

"I call myself Kit," says the girl. "And this is Goldie."

Their auras rest close to their skin like sweaters or armor.

"I call myself Coin," I say. "And please, do call me Coin. I insist."

"Is it true?" Kit asks. "Do you really think we'll have a home here in Seriden?" Her voice grows heavy, and her eyes brim with tears. The way she holds Goldie's hand—I don't expect she'll ever let go.

I take a moment to keep my own eyes dry. I put out both my

hands and imagine a sterling silver crown forming with sharp angles that mirror the tattoo on my arm. They watch it come to life and build itself.

When it's done, I place the crown upon my head.

"You are citizens of Seriden," I say, "just as I am its queen."

Goldie's breath catches in his throat, and tears fall down his cheeks. He leans his forehead against Kit's hair, his hand trembling on her shoulder. I hear him mutter "home" again and again.

"Can you tell me something?" I ask. "Do you know where Marcher is going? What did he promise you to get all those soldiers to leave with him?"

Goldie sniffs and wipes his nose, trying to speak coherently. "He said he was after . . . He promised us . . ." He laughs as though it's nonsense now.

"What did he promise?" I ask.

Kit shakes her head like she doesn't believe it either. "He promised us a city. A *Nameless* city." She lifts a shoulder in a half shrug. "But that's what you offered us. And *you*, I think I can trust."

"Thank you," I say to both of them. "Truly. How many of you were there?"

"There were at least two hundred of us near the end," Kit says. "Maybe ten of us stayed here in Seriden."

"He said he was taking a ship in the harbor," Goldie says, barely moving as he breathes in the scent of Kit's hair. "We don't know which one, but I'm sure it's gone by now."

I offer my thanks again, and I order the guards to take them to the guest sleeping quarters, where they can safely spend the night. I don't quite know what I'll do tomorrow when the Royal Council asks me what is happening to all the Nameless and what is happening to Seriden itself.

As they go, I shove my hands deep into my pockets, wondering if I should follow them and find a change of clothes. My fingers touch paper. I frown. I didn't put anything in my jacket before the Assassins' Festival. I pull it out. It's a large piece of paper folded in half. I open it and find a handwritten note along with another, smaller piece of folded paper that is yellowed with age. I hand both to Glenquartz.

"Could you read this for me?" I ask.

He takes it, and as soon as he starts skimming it, his arms tense. His aura jumps around like barely boiling water, and he obviously doesn't like what he's reading.

"What is it?" I ask.

He stammers. "We—we don't have to talk about it now," he says. "A day more of rest, I think."

I give him my best *don't you dare* glare.

"It says how eighteen years ago," Glenquartz says, "King Fallow asked him to look after his youngest daughter. You. And he gave him a piece of paper with the daughter's name. The instruction was to give you your name if your life was in danger or after you secured the throne. And Marcher told the king that in exchange for a 'truly astonishing amount of money,' he promised to give you everything that King Fallow left for you, including your name." He stuffs the newer paper into his pocket, but he holds out the folded piece of paper in my direction.

"Wait." I stare at the piece of old paper in his hand. I don't know what to be confused about first: that Marcher had a deal with the king, or that I'm surprised. Marcher always said he had looked after me since the day I was born. How true.

"Yes," Glenquartz says, reading my mind. "It's your name, apparently. Your birth name. I didn't open it—not that it would make much of a difference at this point. After what you did at the festival, the Nameless are citizens now. So you don't *have* to read it if you don't want to."

The paper is folded in half, creased a few times.

How is finding my name this simple? When I came to the palace, I was in chains. When I stayed, it was to protect someone I loved. But a part of the reason I stayed was because this place was the best chance I had to find my name. Yet the person who had my name all along was the oldest part of my life, one of the Nameless. And a spetzing bastard at that.

I don't know what to say, so I say the only thing that feels right. "Thank you."

"It's up to you," he says, and he walks in the direction of Med Ward. He's giving me privacy.

I have the urge to follow him. To return to Med Ward and rejoin the small family that has built itself around me. I don't know if it will last forever, or if "family" is the right word for what we are. But maybe we're something better than that, something Nameless that is, in its own way, perfect.

I take a deep breath, my fingertips tingling, and I open the paper.

Handwritten ink letters stain the page, smudged in a few places. The stark sunlight illuminates every bend of ink, every sloping curve and sharp turn.

On this paper is my name.

This is the legalized life I could have lived. This is the person I would've been if my mother had not died, and if King Fallow had cared more for my life than for the life of his city. This is an innocent name, a version of myself untouched by the streets, which at times were both beautiful and cruel. This is who I could be, the Royal status awaiting me: a life of leadership and fear, and the name for this city's Nameless queen.

There's only one problem.

I can't read.

I laugh, running my finger over the beveled ink. Foreign characters sprawl across the paper, and I have no idea what they say.

I've gone through a lot of names. The Nameless queen. The impossible heir. The sovereign ruler. Alley trash. Coin, the thief and dabbling grifter.

But none of them are me, not in the way I want them to be.

I had this idea of who I was. I thought I was selfish, that I was small and unimportant like a coin on the streets. Then I had this grand vision of who I could be: a queen, a diplomat, and a selfless optimist.

I figured that when I found my name, I would realize that

I hadn't changed at all. I would realize I am the same person I have always been.

But I'm not.

I am a thief. I am queen. I am impossible.

I am a lost child of this city, I am family to the Nameless, and I am Coin.

Gently, I fold the scrap of paper and put it away. I am everything this paper says I am.

And I am more.

ACKNOWLEDGMENTS

Thank you for reading this book. Unless you're *just* reading the acknowledgments and not the book, which is *okay*, I guess. Weird, but okay. So, thanks for reading the acknowledgments, too.

I know this is odd, but I'd also like to thank Past Me. Past Me did all the hard work, while Current Me is sitting in a library with a seasonal coffee. I respect the effort and time I put into this book, and I want to acknowledge it. Okay. Acknowledged. Moving on. The remainder of these acknowledgments are in four parts: People, Things, Apologies, and You're Welcome.

People. Pete Knapp, my terrific agent, who is my ceaseless advocate and champion. It all started with velociraptors. Phoebe Yeh, my diligent editor who worked tirelessly to help me make the book what it is today. *Aside: Allow me to add that it took me over two years to tell my agent and editor that they should call me Becky instead of Rebecca, so—honestly—they are real troupers for making it this far with me.* Melissa, my twin, who read multiple versions, answered every phone call, listened to every rant, transcribed, brainstormed, and all-around tolerated every random swing I went through. My mother, Dawn, who let me send her every chunk of writing as I wrote the very first draft and who kindly and impatiently demanded more. Laura Steven, my mentor and friend who coached me through early big revisions and was always willing to console, cuss, and cheer on my behalf. Brittany, Tiffany, Isabel, Heather, Nina, Grandma, and Travas, and all of my friends and family who read early drafts and gave an approving head nod.

Things. My organizational tools: dot journal, Sharpie pens, sticky tabs, and highlighters. National Novel Writing Month. Word processing programs. The laptop that died, and the laptop that heroically replaced it. Whiteboards, paper, pens, twine, and tape. Half gloves, rice socks, and hair ties. So. Much. Music.

Apologies. To Travas: Sorry I ruined that one song for you by playing it on repeat for three hours. To Melissa: Sorry I called you more than zero times at two a.m. To Mom, Nina, and Brittany: Sorry I cut one of your favorite characters. To everyone not listed here: Thank you.

You're Welcome. Coworker pals: The book has a wolf. You were right all along. To everyone who loved Ren: Have a wren instead. Ariel and Travas: Ren dies. Mom and Nina: Hat doesn't. Mary: The book is published now, so you definitely have to read it. Dad: It's finally here. I told you so. Nerdfighteria: Deadpan.

ABOUT THE AUTHOR

Rebecca McLaughlin is a Michigan nerd who appreciates sweet coffee, kindness, and the scientific method. She got her degree in chemistry and creative writing in 2014. Since that time, she's worked as a technical writer in Michigan. When not working or crafting stories, Rebecca can be found practicing her knife-throwing skills or seeking out the perfect cup of coffee. She wrote *Nameless Queen* because she grew up lower-middle class (which was not ideal), went to a private college (which was weird), and made good friends along the way (which was wonderful). She realized that exploring the social and economic divide is difficult, but magic makes that exploration easier—or at least more entertaining.

mcrebecky.wordpress.com

@McRebecky